The ADVENTURES *of*

CARAWAY KIM

. . . SOUTHPAW

The ADVENTURES *of*

CARAWAY KIM

. . . SOUTHPAW

DON TRUCKEY

thistledown press

Library and Archives Canada Cataloguing in Publication

Truckey, Don, 1955-
The adventures of Caraway Kim... southpaw / Don Truckey.

ISBN 1-894345-90-8

I. Title.

PS8639.R827A63 2005   jC813'.6   C2005-900869-5

Cover artwork by Lynn Harvey
Cover and book design by Jackie Forrie
Printed and bound in Canada on acid-free paper

Thistledown Press Ltd.
633 Main Street
Saskatoon, Saskatchewan, S7H 0J8
www.thistledown.sk.ca

abook4boys.com

 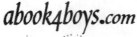

Canadian   Patrimoine
Heritage   canadien

SASKATCHEWAN
ARTS BOARD

Canada Council   Conseil des Arts
for the Arts   du Canada

Thistledown Press gratefully acknowledges the financial assistance of the Canada Council
for the Arts, the Saskatchewan Arts Board, and the Government of Canada through the
Book Publishing Industry Development Program for its publishing program.

To my son, who helped me live these stories all over again.

CONTENTS

9   Barefoot and the Pigs

13   Capture the Flag

32   Kim's Trick Goes Wrong

41   "Got it!"

45   Flashes of Sunlight Through the Trees

48   Caraway

55   The Pig Farm

67   Riot at the Haunted House

83   Arrested!

88   The Kid Who Threw the Rock

94   In the Nick of Time

105   "Three Miles. Let's Get Started."

108   Fresh Ice at Beaches' Pond

115   The Super Cub

121   The Giant

127   The Switcheroo

128   Ninety Below

138   Off Course!

144   The Crusher Versus Moby Joe

155   The Road Back

162   Tommy's Triumph

170   Barefoot and the Pulley

178   How To Put Out a Fire In a Big Hurry

188   Kicked Out!

196   Can Caraway Days Do It Again?

223   "Dear Kim . . . "

226   A Map, the Hard Way

238   Beverly Banana and Caraway Kim

247   The Auction Mart Lead

257   Elvis at the Strand

269   Free!

278   The Draw

283   The Pitching Duel

BAREFOOT AND THE PIGS

*G*ood thing I'm used to the smell of pigs, Kim thought.

He was face down in a pig yard and any kid not *entirely* familiar with the awful, rotten, overpowering smell of pigs would be in big trouble! But Kim was used to pigs and the putrid stench they created, even though he was not a farm kid. He'd been around pigs and he'd been around pig slop too — a mixture of pig poop, pig pee, water, mud, grass and dirt. Pigs lived in it and it was stinky beyond belief!

Kim breathed through his mouth to keep from gagging.

If he could see me, he would have noticed by now, was Kim's next thought as he looked out across the pig yard.

Kim lay flat on the surface of the mud, where it had hardened in the sun and was solid and less smelly. He kept perfectly still. A few tufts of grass sheltered him from the view of Barefoot McGranger who, Kim had learned earlier, was the keeper of these pigs and not a man to be messed with, no, not at all.

"Someone there?" Barefoot called out. "Who's there!"

Barefoot carried a pitchfork and the way he hefted it left absolutely no doubt he could easily stab a kid like Kim through the ribs and flick him into the trees. Barefoot was also, as his name indicated, lacking in the shoe department.

His feet were bare and his pants were ripped off below the knee, revealing white, hairy legs. The rest of him was hairy too, especially his wild wispy beard, which covered his face almost up to his black, piercing eyes.

"Huh, nobody . . . " Barefoot muttered to himself, then added loudly, "Yo boy! Come on!"

Kim cringed. The word "boy" hit him like a brick. Did Barefoot see him? He almost hauled himself upright and stammered an explanation, but he peered across the pig yard and saw that Barefoot had turned away and was talking to a pony.

Kim took a few deep breaths. *This is not the time to panic, Kim!* he screamed inwardly, causing the thought to ricochet around his skull like a rock in a rain barrel. He looked around and forced himself to calm down.

Hmmm. No dog, Kim said to himself, for he had realized just why Barefoot had not found him and why he might, just might, pull off this job without discovery. There were chickens in a separate pen, pecking, squawking and strutting about, and there were goats rooting around on the *roof* of Barefoot's house, because he was a hillbilly and lived, yes, in a hill. His house was built right into it, allowing the goats to ramble on top and rip and chew at the grass. And there was the pony farther off and the pigs everywhere . . . but no dog.

Good thing, Kim thought. *You can't fool a dog.*

He eyeballed his target.

Across the pig yard was a water well. Hanging over it, suspended from a beam, was a pulley with a rope through it. Barefoot used it to draw water for his animals. Kim didn't need water — he needed the rope and the pulley. He ran over his plan in his mind:

All right . . . if I can crawl through the grass at the base of the fence . . . and come up from behind the well where he can't see me . . . and if he doesn't hear me . . . then I have to climb up onto the well and unhook the pulley and haul the rope out of the well . . . and there's probably a pail attached to it that I can't see . . . but then I'll be in plain view . . .

Kim lay still for a moment. The blazing Alberta sun pressed on his back like a hot waffle iron.

Won't work, Kim concluded silently. *He'll see me for sure.*

"Yo boy, get out of the sun," he heard Barefoot say from a distance. The midday heat was getting to him too, and to his animals. He tethered the pony in a shed across the yard.

Then Barefoot did something Kim did not expect.

He ambled back through the yard toward Kim — *Straight at me!* Kim screamed to himself — then suddenly stabbed the pitchfork in the ground and hunkered down against a few posts. There was a bit of shade and Kim could see the edge of an old mattress propped there. Barefoot set a raggedy wide old hat on his head and settled in against the posts.

He's going to take a nap, Kim said to himself. *Great! Right where he can see me!*

Sure enough, Barefoot's shoulders relaxed and he stretched out in the attitude of a man preparing to snooze. But he twitched and writhed quite a bit too. More than once he sighed loudly and snorted like a horse as he tried to get comfortable.

How long would it take Barefoot to nod off? And how deeply would he sleep? Kim certainly had no idea.

Guess I gotta wait, he said to himself, but he knew there was an opportunity here. Barefoot asleep was better than Barefoot awake.

The problem now was figuring out whether he could unhook the pulley without arousing Barefoot.

All in all, Kim didn't think so. He reasoned that a farmer like Barefoot, without a dog, probably had something close to dog's ears himself and that meant that the slightest little sound would disturb him.

Kim looked around for a distraction.

The rest of the animals in the strange little farmyard were dozing off too. Even the chickens were quieter. There were ducks Kim hadn't noticed before, gently preening their feathers in the cool grass. As for the pigs, well, pigs in sun and mud are a recipe for sloth, so the ones that could find shade had already slumped into the shadows and the ones that couldn't were content to roll into the liquid stinky pig slop and fall asleep there.

There were, however, some little piglets nearby and Kim pegged them as his best bet.

Okay, little piggies, he said to himself. *You're going to be my friends, right . . . ?*

There were three of them, panting in the heat, but still alert. Their darting, pink-lined eyes found him now and again. Kim figured it would work, using the piglets, but he had to wait until Barefoot was sound asleep. The hillbilly was still tossing around on the mattress.

The scorching sun seemed to peel the skin right off Kim's neck as he lay there, lay there and wondered . . . *How the heck did I get in this mess anyway?*

CAPTURE THE FLAG

They had been playing a game called Capture the Flag.

"We're on the same team!" Kim's friend Tom exclaimed excitedly when the sides were drawn up, but Kim greeted the news with something more like dread. Tom was his friend, for sure, but as teammates go Tom was never any kid's first pick, or even tenth pick. "Tummy Tom" was a nickname that occurred to Kim sometimes, for Tom certainly had a tummy and he could never quite get his shirt to cover it. Along with glasses and a tendency to squint, and with his shirt absolutely never tucked in, Tom did not strike anyone as an advantage, team-wise.

They were at summer cub camp and the game of Capture the Flag was designed to occupy one entire long hot afternoon.

"Why don't we get any of the big guys?" a voice behind them demanded and Dennis shambled up to join them. Kim's spirits improved, because Dennis was a mudder, a kid you could rely on in a pinch.

They all looked across the camp's playing field at the other team and there was no question about it: those guys were older and bigger. They were tying blue ribbons around their foreheads in the same fashion that Kim and his team had tied red ribbons around theirs.

"Those guys've been hanging around together all week," Kim observed. "You'd think they'd break them up to even out the teams . . . "

"Guess not," Dennis added dryly. "Oh well."

Dennis was a bit of an "oh well" kind of kid, but Kim didn't mind. He was easygoing most of the time, maybe too much so, because once he did a really stupid thing and got hung with a kind of long nickname. Well, it wasn't a nickname at all, but a description of the sort a lot of kids had: Dennis was "the kid who drank the gasoline."

Incredible as it might seem, one day back in Caraway — the town where they all lived — Dennis spotted a bottle of orange Fanta just lying on the concrete outside a garage and since there was only a little "pop" left, wham, he drank it down without sniffing it, testing it, and certainly without thinking about it. It was gasoline!

Boy, did that cause a commotion. Dennis threw up right there and rolled around on the ground, screaming. His whole body was clenched and knotted like a fist. He was rushed to the hospital and the doctors pumped his stomach, which was not a process Kim entirely understood, but he heard it involved a lot of tubes and more action than a wrestling match.

Dennis had a gravelly, raspy voice and it was easy to imagine that the tubes had somehow altered his throat. He also had little specks of foam at the side of his mouth that formed when he talked. Sometimes a tiny bubble would emerge from his nostril and expand to cover it, then pop. All in all, a grimy kid whose dirty blond hair only deepened the impression. Rough and ready, that was Dennis. "The kid who drank the gasoline." That was Dennis in spades. Kim sympathized, for he understood that getting such a "description nickname" was rarely a fair deal. It stuck on you like an ink stain.

He had one too and he'd give anything to get rid of it.

"Where do ya think we should hide our flag?" Dennis said in his growly voice.

"Ssssh!" Tom cautioned. "They'll hear!"

Of course, Tom's attempt at silence was the loudest thing yet. Kim jerked his head sideways to call for a huddle and the group of "Reds" put their heads, and their red ribbons, together.

"You know the clearing behind the baseball diamond?" Kim said. "About a hundred yards behind it? It would be . . . northwest of it." Kim had an unfailing sense of direction.

The group nodded and Kim realized he had suddenly been elected leader, simply for making a decent suggestion. Fair enough. He scanned the group quickly and could see why they were perfectly agreeable to being ordered around. These cubs were mostly nine and ten-year-olds. Kim, Tom and Dennis were all eleven. The Blues across the way — they were laughing and joking loudly now — were at least eleven and most of them were twelve and twelve-going-on-thirteen, as old as a boy could be and stay in cubs. It was a killer age gap and Kim and his friends were on the wrong end of it.

"Are you boys ready?" they heard Baloo call from across the field. All of the adults who ran the cub pack took animal names and Baloo meant "bear," although Kim thought that Baloo didn't resemble a bear at all, since he was a tall and lean man. Kim didn't even know his real name, but he sure liked Baloo because he had spent extra time with the younger group of cubs during their week of cub camp. As so often happened with boys, the forty or so cubs at the camp had cleaved pretty much down the middle into a group of older ones — who now formed the Blue team — and a group of younger ones, Kim and Tom and Dennis's team. Baloo was not exactly their official protector or guide for camp, but sometimes it felt like it and that made Kim and his friends feel a lot better.

"Do you all know the rules?" Baloo asked.

"First we find a place to hide our flag," Tom offered.

"And we should have a captain and assistant captain," one of the young cubs chirped.

"I think Kim's the captain," Dennis said and, as Kim had guessed, it was a fact since no one objected to it.

"Then you be the assistant captain," Kim said to Dennis. As captain, he figured it was his right to do that and, although it seemed a little fishy that they both appointed each other, it was clear the younger cubs needed leadership, so why beat around the bush?

Baloo smiled at the exchange. "What else?"

"We need a strategy!" one of the youngsters blurted out.

"Yes, you do," Baloo said, "and you can work that out among yourselves. What about the rest of the rules?"

Now Kim spoke directly to his troops: "If they get your ribbon, you're dead, right? Same as if you get theirs. Once a kid loses his ribbon, he finds his way back to the field here and reports in that he's dead. Over there."

He pointed to where a table was set up. Akela, the adult who was the head of the pack, was supervising.

"Don't put up too much of a fight, because those big guys'll make you pay for it. They'll probably travel in two's and three's — that's what we're going to do — so if they corner you, it's okay to just give up. If you have an opening, run like crazy to get away.

"But remember, the real object is to capture their flag. The game's not over until one team does that. So we have to find their flag and figure out a way to get through them and grab it."

Two of the young cubs looked at each other and made faces with their mouths open in horror as if to say, *And how are we gonna do that?*

Kim ignored them. "Then you have to bring the flag back here to become the official winner."

The immensity of the challenge ahead of them sank in around the circle of a dozen or so young cubs. Baloo smiled again and chuckled a little.

"Do we have to?" a young cub asked.

"Have to what?" Dennis said.

"Participate."

Kim glanced at Baloo and the cub leader met his look with a shrug. Obviously, it was up to Kim.

"No, you don't," Kim said. "Any kid who wants off the Red team can go now."

The little boy who had asked the question immediately left the group at a quick march, his arms swinging straight out from his shoulders.

"Where you going?" Kim called.

"Crafts."

Baloo smiled again and spoke to the remainder of them. "Listen boys, what Kim said is absolutely correct: nobody is forcing you to do this. It's just a little game of Capture the Flag and the intention is to have fun. Understood?"

They all nodded and they all understood.

"Okay, we'll start in ten minutes," Baloo finished and he walked away with a wave of his hand.

Kim exhaled a deep breath and puffed out his cheeks. *Yeah right*, he thought, *it's all about having fun. Even though we all know if you don't have fair teams, "fun" is the last thing anyone's going to have!*

Kim put the thought aside and spoke to the Red team.

"All right, listen. We're going to have to be extra smart to have a chance in this game, because the other team is older and stronger. Maybe that won't matter if we don't start running around like a bunch of chickens with our heads cut off. The first thing we're going to do is let them leave before we do. I don't want them getting any clue about where we're going."

Across the yard, the Blues were milling around excitedly and sure enough, half a minute later, started out of the camp at a trot. Some of them turned around to run backward and toss a few taunts at the Red team. Kim and the other boys made a show of ignoring them.

"And," Kim added, "it looks to me like they're pretty overconfident. They're probably already bragging to each other how they're going to win. That could help us too."

Cheered by Kim's words, the Red team began to amble toward the main gate. There were a dozen of them and a few of the younger ones even picked up their feet in a soldierly march.

All in all, they were a very worn and weathered pack of cubs. They weren't dirty — far from it, they swam in the lake twice a day — but each was tanned or sunburned by the long days outside, their running shoes puffed dust with each step, their hair was matted and knotted against their heads, fingernails were bent and broken, and bandages were pasted here and there on elbows, noses, knees and shins.

Six days before all the cubs had gathered at the cub hall in Caraway, where a school bus waited to haul them to camp, though some of them jumped around so excitedly they seemed to have enough energy to walk all the way there. Tom was the kind of boy who made lists. He had one that contained every single item he was taking to camp.

"Flashlight . . . candles . . . matches . . . string . . . jack knife . . . swimming suit . . . hunting knife . . . running shoes on my feet . . . rubber boots in my duffel bag . . . sleeping bag . . . " Tom mumbled as Dennis and Kim followed along, more or less. They each had a week's worth of clean clothes too, and of course Tom's had name tags sewn on every item. Kim smiled as Tom checked it all, organized it, and struggled to make it fit back in the bag.

Cubs had a motto: "Be Prepared." It made for heavy packs.

When the bus headed north out of Caraway, it stayed on the highway for a good long while, then turned down wide dusty gravel roads. When cars rushed past, they immediately disappeared into a giant spreading cloud of dust.

Then the gravel turned to packed sand and the bus began lifting up and down gentle hills, soon to be wending its way down a narrow road, also sandy, where the trees bent in to touch each other. Finally, they drove under a high wooden gate and into the wide athletic field.

Camp! It was wonderful.

"We're here!" they all yelled as they piled out of the bus and stretched and yawned. Sparkling through the trees was the shiny surface of the lake, on both sides of them, since the camp was on a small peninsula. A pleasant breeze turned over the leaves on the trees and carried the fresh smell of the lake their way, along with the odour of food. They had disembarked beside the cookhouse — and at the right time too.

"Dinnertime!" Baloo had announced and the cubs surged inside. There was food galore and it was good. Kim had been jammed together with Dennis and Tom at a long wooden table covered with a paper tablecloth; the boys consumed everything in sight. The only thing they hadn't liked was the milk, which came from powder in boxes with water added.

"Ewwww — I'm gonna barf!" Dennis yelled at the top of his lungs after he tasted it. He stuck his tongue out and rolled his eyes wildly. "It's milk, not gasoline," said a voice from far down the table and they all laughed. But Kim agreed with Dennis's reaction. He could hardly drink the stuff.

Then the boys helped clear away all the dishes — many would be on washing and drying detail later — and sang with one voice:

There were beans! (beans!) beans! (beans!)
As big as submarines,
In the store! (in the store!) In the store! (in the store!)
There were beans! (beans!) beans! (beans!)

As big as submarines,
In the Cornermaster's store!

My eyes are dim, I cannot see,
I have not brought my specs with me!
I ha-ve no-ot brought my-yy specs! With! ME!!

Tommy had leaned over to Dennis and yelled through the din, "It's Quartermaster, not Cornermaster!"

"Oh shut up!" Dennis yelled back and added a huge greasy burp for good measure. "Who cares?"

They were all in Cabin Five, Kim and Dennis and Tummy Tom, along with several younger cubs. "Top bunk! First dibs!" Kim had called out when they entered the cabin, and he charged across the floor and flung his duffel bag up onto a bunk to claim it. Several others did the same, though Dennis was squeezed out at the door and had to settle for a lower berth. Kim naturally wanted to be up high, but he soon discovered it had distinct disadvantages. Every time he wanted to sit on his bed he had to climb up the creaking metal bunk frame, which had sharp cutting edges and often hurt his hands.

And it was stiflingly hot up there at night, too hot to stay inside a sleeping bag, which suited the mosquitoes just fine. There were lots of exposed backs and arms to bite. It was also a very long, tortured journey down off the bunk at night to venture outside to pee, which happened to every cub in the cabin at least once a night.

"Wanna trade?" Kim offered to Dennis after two nights of upper-bunk torture. He knew he had to make up an excuse to give Dennis a reason to go for it.

"Stubbed my toe. Hard to climb," Kim explained, and it was partly true. He had several stubbed toes from walking barefoot on the meandering path beside the cabins, where there were gnarled tree roots everywhere.

"Sure!" Dennis replied, making a face that signalled he thought Kim was a little crazy to give up a top bunk so easily. They switched their packs and clothes in a flash. Dennis instantly appeared hanging upside down over Kim's new bunk to declare loudly, "I like it up here! I'm the King!" He licked a bit of foam from the side of his mouth and retracted upward.

Kim smiled and let him brag. He knew Dennis would never admit it if he thought he got the short end of the deal, but in truth Dennis was a pretty apt top bunk-dweller, because he efficiently hunted down most of the mosquitoes with his flashlight just before lights out and whacked them dead against the cabin roof. The rest of the upper-bunk cubs joined him, drawing patterns with their lights on the inside of the vaulted roof. It was fun to watch, but it lasted only a minute or two. Cub camp was exhausting and when Baloo or Akela rapped on the door for lights out, it was lights . . . out . . .

Crafts and contests were the order of the day for most of the week.

"What do you want to make, son?" was the question that greeted Kim and the others from the Crafts Instructor each morning. Kim didn't really like crafts, but it was impossible to decline and best to just pick something to make, like the sign he designed and sanded and varnished. "Wipe Your Feet!" it declared firmly and he hung it outside the door of Cabin Five, to very little effect, since no one did any such thing.

In the afternoon, the contests started.

Some were official, some weren't. Rope Climbing was an official contest, one that Kim was particularly bad at, so he got quite used to the sight of Dennis and the other more nimble kids hauling their way right to the top. "Naaaaahh," Dennis would call from twenty feet up, while hanging on with only one hand. Kim was relegated to the company of the likes of Tommy, who couldn't climb a rope to save his life or anyone else's.

The Log Balance was another official contest. It was pretty simple: there was a big fat log on a wooden stand and two cubs edged toward each other from opposite ends. The winner was the one who batted the other one off, a drop that was fortunately not more than three feet and onto soft grass.

The entire cub camp played off in the Log Balance and Kim, Dennis and of course Tommy soon lost out, along with all the other cubs who later made up the Red team. They were quickly sent spinning to the ground by the older boys.

Kim proved, however, that a younger cub could win one of the big official contests, though his method turned out to be controversial.

Kim actually won the Greased Watermelon Hunt.

It was also pretty simple: a watermelon coated with thick grease was thrown into the swimming area and all the cubs dashed in to see who could grab it and haul it to shore.

"Charge! Geronimo! Attack!" yelled the throng of cubs who dove in when Baloo heaved the greased watermelon off the pier into the deep part. The churning mob of screaming cubs reminded Kim of films he had seen of piranhas devouring a dead cow in the Amazon. They really went at it. The greased watermelon was submerged for a few seconds under a layer of thrashing boys, then it popped to the surface like a dolphin and rolled around. Instantly another clot of boys leapt on it, kicking, elbowing, screaming and laughing.

"We'll get clobbered in there!" Tommy screamed next to Kim, as they both looked on from shallow water. "Murderized!"

Dennis was in the thick of it, but losing to older boys. Kim decided to give the main fight a try, too. He was soon elbowed in the side of the head and knocked underwater for a few seconds, where someone stepped on his back. Recovering, he backed away to shore as the watermelon was urged by the heaving mass toward shallow water. A big kid grabbed it in a bear hug, but it popped straight up out of his arms and plunged beneath the surface, followed by a half dozen cubs who dived at it like ducks, tails up.

The strongest big kid emerged with the melon grasped in his arms and made a final surge for the shoreline — just then to be nailed from the side by another, bigger kid who thudded into his ribs head-down and caused the melon to eject into space once again.

Right in front of Kim! He scooped it up, staggered three steps to dry land, and rolled the greasy watermelon on the sand. He won!

"Hey!" some of the big kids complained, since it was obvious they had done the heavy work and Kim had claimed the prize, which was the honour of cutting the watermelon in half and slicing himself the first huge piece.

But it was fair ball and Kim was the legitimate winner. He just had to put up with the name-calling, but he shrugged and thought to himself that he was sort of used to it.

"Well done!" Akela roared from the sidelines. Kim could tell he liked the display of resourcefulness, if that's what it was.

The cubs weren't so sure that Akela and Baloo and the other adults approved so much of their *other* games, especially the main pastime at cub camp, the game called The Splits.

The Splits made use of the big long hunting knives that every cub had strapped to his belt.

All of this was before now, not a long time ago, but some things were different. Kids were allowed to do more then. They could take off on a Saturday morning and not bother coming home until suppertime, and nobody went looking for them. Computers hadn't been invented yet. Seatbelts had, but not everybody wore them. The Beatles were around, but they were quite new. There were only six teams in the NHL: The Montreal Canadiens, The Toronto Maple Leafs, The Detroit Red Wings, The Chicago Blackhawks, The Boston Bruins, and The New York Rangers. Kim liked Montreal.

Later, "Kim" would become mostly a girl's name, but then it was pretty well reserved for boys. Allergies were rare. Kim had heard of asthma, but didn't really know what it was. He didn't know anyone who had it.

In Alberta, the main highways were paved, but most of the other roads weren't. Television had been invented, but there were only two channels and they were in black and white. The Flintstones were new then and were on at night, instead of the morning, and adults watched them too. Nobody wore bike helmets and nobody locked their bikes, because nobody wanted to steal them.

It was before now and some things were different: Kim and all his friends at cub camp had *huge* hunting knives in leather sheathes that hung by a strap from their belts. The blades were six inches long, and fat and sharp, certainly the master of any branch and of many small trees, for most of the cubs had used their knives to cut and peel a sturdy walking stick that was as tall as they were.

Thwack! Whap! The sound of knives thudding into trees and the sides of cabins was heard throughout the camp — though not when Baloo and Akela were around! Knife throwing was not allowed. Neither was The Splits, because it involved knife throwing, but it went on constantly anyway.

"Wanna play?" was all Dennis had to say to Kim and they would start. They stood facing each other really close, almost nose to nose.

"You go first."

"No, you."

"Uh uh."

It didn't matter who said it. They each wanted the other to start.

"Flip a coin," would be Kim's next move.

Suppose he won. That forced Dennis to go first. Dennis would throw his knife to the ground, trying to stick it a good distance away. Suppose he stuck it. Kim would then have to stretch his legs to reach the knife. He was "split."

But if he could stick *his* knife even further out, Dennis would have to "split" to reach it. And if it was too far, Kim won. If Kim failed to stick his knife, Dennis got another try and of course would attempt to "split" Kim way beyond his legs' reach.

They played The Splits every time they had a spare minute, hundreds of games, but as Kim led the Red team under the wooden gateway and out of the camp, there was one particular contest he remembered.

He and Dennis had been "split" about as far as each could go. They were spread out like hockey goalies making a split save, actually lying on the ground with their toes extended as far as possible. And they were tied.

"Give up?" Dennis had asked.

"No!" Kim said hotly.

"Tie!" Dennis demanded.

"Maybe," Kim replied as he hefted his knife in his left hand. He lifted himself up on one elbow and spotted what he was looking for about ten feet away.

Mud!

The perfect landing spot for a hunting knife!

Kim took aim, then gently flipped his knife end-over-end through the air. The blade flashed brightly in the sun . . . then *stuck* deep down in the mud!

"Da winna!" Kim cried. He rolled out of his split position and leapt to his feet like a victorious boxer.

"Cheater!" Dennis yelled immediately.

"*What?* How did I cheat?" Kim was angry. Dennis had no right to say that. "Take that back!"

"Cheater!" Dennis repeated and Kim pushed him hard enough to knock him backward.

"Hey, you guys . . . " Tom said.

Kim advanced on Dennis and was ready to keep it up, but Dennis turned half away and loudly conceded, "All right, you didn't cheat . . . But you're tricky."

"That wasn't a trick," Kim retorted.

"It was lucky."

"So? Lucky isn't tricky."

"I say you're tricky," Dennis maintained. "Look at the Greased Watermelon Hunt."

"That was strategy," Kim said. "Besides, it was too cold to go in the lake."

"*I went.*"

"So you're half fish. You've got cold blood."

"Tricky . . . " Dennis had repeated as he turned away again. He'd say it, but he wasn't prepared to fight for it.

Well, let's hope I'm tricky, Kim thought as the Red team trudged out of camp to play Capture the Flag against the Blues. Tummy Tom was already wheezing a little in the heat and a few of the smaller boys didn't look too resilient either. Dennis was striding along, heartily swinging his walking stick and soundlessly mouthing the words to a song.

Let's hope we've all *got a few tricks up our sleeves,* Kim said to himself. *We're going to need them.*

There was no sign of the Blue team ahead of them. Dennis hummed louder and it became clear the tune was *The Ants.* Soon they were all quietly singing their favourite walking song:

The Ants go marching one by one,
Hurrah, hurrah,
The Ants go marching one by one,
Hurrah, Hurrah . . .

Ahead of them the road bent gently through the trees. "We're getting close to the turn-off for the ball diamond," Kim noted.

They had been out along this road many times, because hiking and marching and finding your way were exercises the cubs practiced over and over again. Kim was especially good at it, because his sense of direction held even in the midst of the thick, bewildering forest. They were taught to use maps and compasses and make drawings of where they had been and where they were going, but he didn't need them most of the time. The sun and the shadows of the trees seemed to guide Kim without error.

Baloo had noticed it too on one of their previous marches. The one where they had discovered Barefoot McGranger's farm.

They were on a nature walk with Baloo, the longest hike they took during the entire week, lasting a good four hours in all. The group of cubs had explored to the farthest reaches of the domain occupied by cub camp, taking in the gravel pit, another smaller lake, sand hills, and vast stretches of leafy green forest. There were roads, but they didn't follow a pattern that made sense. Often they meandered into the trees, became rutted, then petered out into mere paths leading nowhere. Perhaps they had once been logging trails.

"Where are we, boys?" Baloo asked often during this expedition. "Which way's camp?" Few of the cubs could meet the challenge. At times it seemed as if only Kim and Baloo actually understood their location. Kim knew they were a long, long way from home base when they tramped down a rambling pathway that led into an open field.

Barefoot's place.

Baloo certainly knew it was there, because he had been at the camp for years. Kim saw it next, though many of the cubs on that hike wandered up with their eyes fixed on their shoes and had to be stopped before they passed the big sign at the edge of the property, the one that read: KEEP OUT!

Kim had seen the chickens and goats then, and the ramshackle farmyard with the little house, built right into the hill, that had grass growing on the roof. He had noticed and remembered the water well and the pulley. But he hadn't seen Barefoot so his appearance was left to Kim's imagination, except for the part about no shoes.

"That's Barefoot McGranger's place," Baloo had remarked. "Seen him here for years. 'Guess he's not around today."

"Is he dangerous?" one of the other cubs had asked.

"Oh no. Old Barefoot just wants to be left alone."

They all agreed with that idea. Barefoot's deserted farmyard was the very definition of "creepy," and they couldn't wait to get out of there!

"Which way's camp?" Baloo had asked and Kim had jerked his head in a southeasterly direction. Baloo grinned and his gold tooth showed. "That's right. Let's be getting back," Baloo had said. They needed no encouragement and had set off at a steady clip.

And now they marched again, the Red team, in the game of Capture the Flag.

> *The Ants go marching four by four,*
> *Hurrah, hurrah.*
> *The Ants go marching four by four,*
> *Hurrah, hurrah,*
> *The Ants go marching four by four,*
> *The little one stopped to close the door,*
> *And the all go marching down*
> *To the Earth,*
> *To get out,*
> *Of the rain,*
> *Dum dum dum . . .*

Kim and Dennis didn't know it, but for them it would be a long, long journey back.

Kim's Trick Goes Wrong

The ball diamond was about a half-mile from the camp and it seemed a good place to hide the Red flag. Not right at the diamond, but behind it in the clearing. The Reds hustled across the weedy infield and plunged into the brush.

"Right here," Kim declared at an open spot. "Perfect. Dennis, cut a pole for the flag."

Dennis quickly produced an okay flagpole by whacking down a little tree, stripping it of leaves and branches, and hacking off the end. They tied the Red flag to it.

"The rules say you have to put the flag out in a visible location," Kim said, looking around the clearing. "Do you think this is good enough?"

Tom turned a complete circle and declared in a deep, official voice: "Qualifies!"

"We've got twelve guys. We'll split into three groups. How many does that make each?" Kim directed the question to a young cub.

"Four."

"Okay," Kim continued, "the most important thing is to capture their flag."

"No kidding," said Dennis, looking impatient. Kim ignored him.

"So first we have to find out where their flag is. One bunch of four can stay right here and defend our flag. Okay?"

A few kids nodded.

"The second bunch should sweep around this area about a hundred yards out, to catch any of their scouts that come close. Okay?"

More nods.

"But *don't* tell where our flag is if you're killed, or even if you kill one of them, because they can still talk to their other guys even if you take their ribbon. Okay?"

Kim was encouraged. His team seemed to get it. They just might have a chance, if they all worked together.

"I'm going to take three guys with me. Tom, Dennis, and you," Kim said, pointing at a small cub. "What's your name?"

"Christopher."

"Christopher, and we'll go out and see if we can locate their flag. If we get a chance, we'll grab it! If it's too heavily protected, we'll come back and think of a way to capture it. Okay?"

The kids nodded and said "sure" and organized themselves into groups. Kim signalled to his trio.

"Let's go!"

With that, the Game was on.

Kim's group hurried out of the clearing and into the forest. Dennis and Kim and even little Christopher quickly settled into a dogtrot, but it was soon clear that Tummy Tom could not keep up.

He ran, stopped, tried to run again, then finally stopped altogether.

"Hey, you guys, wait up," he called from a spot back in the woods. Kim broke off his dogtrot.

"Rest time," Kim said, even though he wasn't tired. He ambled back toward Tom, who was panting and holding his tummy. Dennis joined them, clearly irritated. "Why's he even with us? He can't keep up, no way!"

It was so obviously true that Tom said nothing to object. "Sorry," he panted. "Maybe I should go back to the flag."

"Yeah, maybe," Kim agreed and he quickly blamed himself for picking out the wrong groups. Clearly, Tom should have stayed behind. They all stood around waiting for Tom to catch his breath and stop turning red in the face. The little kid Christopher was back up the path studying something on the ground . . .

Suddenly two kids from the Blue team burst out of the trees and attacked him!

Kim signalled for Dennis and Tom to dive into the cover of the brush, off the path. They all did it before the attacking pair noticed them.

"I give up!" little Christopher yelled.

He pulled his red ribbon off his head and handed it over, saving the boys from the Blue team the trouble. One of them ran into him and knocked him over anyway, just for good measure.

Kim, Dennis and Tom crept up through the bushes, closer and closer.

"Where's your flag?" the Blues demanded.

"You can't ask me that. I'm dead!" little Christopher protested.

"Oh yeah?" one of the Blue kids said. He grabbed Christopher's head in a hammerlock and twisted. Christopher yelped in pain.

Kim was enraged! He signalled Tom and Dennis to move up. It was three on two. Kim wanted to keep looking for the flag and not risk being killed here, but what if they beat up defenseless little Christopher?

But before they could burst out and attack, Christopher blurted out, "It's at the gravel pit!"

Kim and Dennis traded a look. It certainly was not!

One of the Blue kids sneered loudly. "Ya liar, that's where ours is!"

With a final push, the Blues released Christopher and ran off down the path, waving the little boy's red ribbon triumphantly. After several seconds, Kim and the other two emerged from the undergrowth and ran over to Christopher, who had collapsed onto the ground. He was sobbing quietly.

Kim patted little Christopher on the back. "Way ta go! You found their flag!"

"Will I get in trouble for telling a lie?" Christopher wondered, looking up at the three of them.

"That wasn't a lie, that was a diversion!" Tom pronounced.

"That was quick thinking," Dennis put in. Kim could tell he was impressed.

"Okay," Christopher said, standing now and rubbing the tears from his eyes. He even started laughing a little, right in the middle of crying. Kim took him aside and made sure he knew how to get back to camp.

"You did your best for your team," Kim said, by way of assurance, and sent little Christopher on his way.

The gravel pit!

They broke into a dogtrot once more and this time Tom had no trouble keeping up. In fifteen minutes they were there, crawling on their bellies to peek over a ridge into the gravel pit. The Blue flag was there, right out in the open the way it was supposed to be, in a hard-packed flat spot in the middle of the big piles of rocks and gravel.

"They must be pretty sure we can't get it," Kim observed. "It's way out in the open." Dennis murmured in agreement. Tom squinted.

There were only two Blues guarding the flag, but they were big kids, too big to defeat easily, Kim realized. They all looked the situation over for several minutes, baking in the sun. Kim was about to suggest they angle around to the other side for a better look, when he caught sight of some movement far across the pit. Three other Blues trotted up!

Big kids, like the two flag guards. One had two red ribbons on his belt and each of the other Blues had one.

"They've got four!" Tom exclaimed.

"Ssshh!" Kim hissed.

The Blues were talking, but Kim couldn't hear them. He quickly skipped along the ridge, out of sight, and snuck up behind another low pile of sand. He edged as close as he could. The boy who appeared to be the leader of the Blues was talking.

" . . . but they never gave in and said where their flag was . . . "

"What if we get all their scalps, but don't find the flag?" another Blue asked.

"We gotta get the flag or we don't win," the leader said flatly. "Anybody look around the baseball diamond?"

Nobody from the Blues had looked there yet.

"I'm gonna go. Who's coming?" the head Blue asked.

While the Blues were sorting out their plans, Kim quickly skittered back to Tom and Dennis.

"They've guessed where our flag is," Kim said breathlessly. "I think the jig's up, boys," he added. He'd heard that in a movie once.

"What do we do?" Dennis said. He suddenly looked at Kim. "You're the tricky one. Think of something."

Kim already had. He winked at Dennis.

"We gotta move fast. Follow me."

Kim took a peek out at the Blues. They were milling and organizing and appeared ready to go.

"Okay. We're gonna decoy 'em away from our flag," Kim whispered.

"Then what?" said Dennis.

"I dunno," Kim replied angrily. "You ask too many questions! Come on!"

Kim leapt ahead and scrabbled down the gravel slope and started yelling. Dennis followed and Tom brought up the rear. Shrieking and howling, they burst into the open, only twenty yards from the Blues' flag!

The Blues were caught off guard by the sight of three screaming boys descending on them down the rocky slope, each with a red ribbon tied around his head and a sharp stick in his hand. For a second, they just stood there.

It was all the time Kim needed to draw them into his plan. He didn't charge at the flag. Instead he veered away from it, leading Dennis and Tom across the packed bottom of the gravel pit — suddenly with four Blues in hot pursuit!

But Kim and the Reds had a big lead. Kim reached the end of the gravel pit and dashed into the trees. He looked behind him as he ran. Dennis, and amazingly Tom, who chugged along like a wheezing old steam engine, pumping arms and all, were keeping up just fine. They all pelted through the underbrush and came across a makeshift path.

Kim dashed down it and looked back again. The Blue leader was putting distance between himself and his team. Strong and lean, he was running without apparent effort and quickly closing the gap. Suddenly Kim saw Tom dodge sideways into the trees and vanish. The Blue leader ignored him and kept coming at Dennis and Kim.

What's he doing? Kim wondered of Tom's sudden departure. *Probably giving up* . . . was all he could think of in the midst of his flight.

Kim ran. And ran and ran and ran.

He glanced back again. They were in a line now, Kim, then Dennis, then the Blue leader. The other Blues had dropped back and were no longer in the hunt.

They ran and ran. The sun speckled through the leaves overhead. They dodged the big trees and ran right over the saplings and clumps of brush. The leaves made a firm spongy carpet under their feet. They *ran.* A pain grabbed at Kim's stomach from the inside and he had to slow down a bit. Dennis, spitting foam like a racehorse, surged right up beside him. They clenched their teeth and kept running! Trees — watch out — they dodged in and out.

Kim had no idea where they were going. They just ran!

The big Blue kid ran hard too, real hard, slamming the ground with his feet, pumping his arms. He was almost on them! Suddenly Kim dashed to the left and Dennis dashed to the right. They both stopped, gasping for breath, ready to take on the Blue leader, two on one.

The boy ran up to them and danced right around backward so he could see them on either side. But he didn't quite stop. He was still moving, backward now, when he caught his foot on a root and staggered back into a clump of brush — he was in the leaves — then he *just disappeared!*

For a second, Kim thought it was a trick. But no, the boy was really gone.

Kim jumped ahead and poked at the bush.

"Hey!"

Dennis joined him and spread some of the branches back. It was like opening a curtain. Suddenly they were looking out over a *cliff* on one side of a canyon.

There was a sheer drop. Straight down.

"Hello?" Kim called.

Then he looked down. And there was the leader of the Blues, spread out flat on a mossy ledge about twenty feet below them.

He was sideways on a rock. And he wasn't moving.

"Ho-lee smokes!" Dennis gasped.

"Matt!" Kim yelled, for he knew the boy's name. Matt's legs moved a bit, and he rolled a little. They could see him breathing.

"He's gonna fall in!" Dennis screamed.

Just below the ledge that held the boy was a rushing stream. It was deep — several feet — and Matt was perched just above it.

"He rolls in there, he's gonna drown!" Dennis wailed. "Ho-lee smokes!"

Kim looked around. The cliff was a straight drop. He quickly scampered along the edge in each direction, but could not see a way to get down.

Matt rolled again.

"Stay here!" Kim ordered Dennis.

"Where you going?"

"Just stay here! You gotta make a stretcher. You know how? Use your knife — get some saplings — use willow for rope if you need more — know what I mean?"

"I guess so. Where are you going?"

"Make a stretcher! I'll be back pretty soon — as soon as I can!"

Kim peered over the ledge again. He quickly unlooped the bit of feeble rope, twine really, he had on his belt and got Dennis to do the same.

"If he rolls into the water, you gotta lower yourself down real quick and fish him out. If you can."

"Why don't I just do that now?"

"'Cause then you'll be down there and we're going to need you up here."

"Gee Kim, what are you talking about?"

"Just stay here!"

Kim took a final look down at the boy, the boy named Matt. He felt a swell of fear and panic, and obligation, but he felt a twinge of resentment and anger too, for that boy down there, Matt, had not always treated him very well.

That boy was his brother.

"Got it!"

Barefoot was asleep. But he wasn't snoring, so Kim concluded he wasn't in a deep, deep sleep and that was good. He would probably react to the distraction in exactly the way Kim hoped.

Kim crawled sideways along the awful, stinking hardened mud of the pig yard and now dared to rise up a little and creep closer to the little piglets nearby. Dopey from the afternoon heat, they regarded him as neither friend nor foe. They eyed him listlessly as he edged nearer.

Barefoot rolled sideways, scratched his chin in his sleep, and rolled back. And again Kim was prompted to ask himself the question that had popped into his head several times already:

Why not just tell him what happened? Why not just walk into Barefoot's farmyard and say, "Look mister, my big brother is unconscious on a rock ledge next to the stream near here and we need help! Fast!"

But again Kim rejected the idea. He just didn't think Barefoot would go along — the big sign at the front telling everyone to stay away, the way Baloo had quite carefully said Barefoot wanted to be left alone — not to mention the way he looked! Kim was certain the hairy old hillbilly would send him packing. He had actually hoped to find him gone from the farmyard, so he could simply "borrow" the pulley and return it later.

Likewise, he had ruled out trying to run back to the cub camp to ask for help. It was probably three miles. Much too far. And that was another thing: they had gone way off where they were supposed to be! As stupid as it might sound, Kim feared they'd all be in trouble for straying so far outside the accepted limits of camp.

He'd rather try to get out of the jam himself. But so far he was only getting in deeper!

"Sooo-kie . . . " Kim whispered at the piglets, for he knew that's how to call a pig, just as he was used to their smell. Scrounging deep into his pocket, Kim located a few crumbs — he had no idea what they were from, maybe bits of hot dog bun — but it was food and it might lure the little piggies over.

Curious, two of them approached, and in response to Kim's gesture with the crumbs it suddenly became a contest between them to investigate the snack the quickest. Kim drew the first one in as close as he could without moving, then — snatch! He had him!

Time to move fast!

The piglet squirmed and wiggled in his arms as Kim dared to stand up and dash in Barefoot's direction. *Ree, ree, reeee!* the piggy began to squeal and Kim knew he had only seconds left. The pig twisted violently in his arms! Kim scooted wide of Barefoot to the enclosed wire chicken coop — *Ree, ree, reee!* — hoisted the struggling piggy high in his arms and slapped its backside as hard as he could.

"Okay, squeal!" Kim hissed as he tossed it over the fence.

The chickens exploded in feathers as the piglet thrashed among them.

REE! REE! REEE!

"Wha — ?" Barefoot muttered in his sleep.

Like lightning, Kim raced past Barefoot and dove into the high grass at the side of the farmyard. Out of sight, he heard Barefoot scramble to his feet and yell, "What's the matter with you?" to the chickens as if they were unruly school-children and, "What are you doing in there?" to the piglet as if it were a boy stealing peas in a garden.

The chickens pecked at the piggy — producing more, louder squealing — and Barefoot grabbed a broom to sort them out.

"Silliest darned thing I ever saw!" he bellowed and Kim could tell that, freshly awake, Barefoot was not quite in command of his senses.

Kim dashed to the water well and unhooked the pulley.

It clunked, but Barefoot was making too much noise separating the animals to hear a thing. More importantly, his back was turned and it gave Kim the endless, stretched moments he needed to haul all the rope up and out of the well — *good, lots of it* — and unhook the bucket that came with it.

"Got it!" he whispered to himself as he dragged the pulley and rope along behind him toward the fence, the last obstacle. In one quick motion, he hopped to the top rail and prepared to fall over into the deep grass on the other side.

Rip!

His pants caught on a nail. Sitting right on top of the fence — in full view of Barefoot if he turned around — Kim gently backed up a few inches to unhook himself. He squelched the "Ow!" that normally would have made itself heard, because the nail had scratched his bum pretty good. No time for that!

Gritting his teeth, Kim bailed out off the fence backwards and tumbled into the cool grass. He pulled the rope over behind him and slithered, boy and pulley and rope, through the deep grass leading to the trees.

Barefoot was so busy with the livestock, he didn't notice a thing.

And Kim didn't notice his red ribbon fall off his forehead as he cleared the fence.

FLASHES OF SUNLIGHT THROUGH THE TREES

When he was safely out of sight of Barefoot's weird little farmyard, Kim stopped in the cover of the trees and caught his breath.

The forest of leafy green poplars, dotted with pine and spruce, stretched away evenly in all directions. The canopy of branches and leaves above, and the carpet of dead brown leaves and moss below, was seamless everywhere Kim looked and he thanked his lucky stars for his sense of direction, because he knew precisely which route to take to get back to the creek, and Dennis and Matt.

He scanned the sky and reckoned it at north by northeast. About half a mile. Fifteen minutes with the load of the rope and pulley.

He looped the rope in big enough lengths to fit right over his head and shoulder. The pulley fit nicely into one hand and he was ready to make his way back . . .

Thinking all the time . . .

Yes, that boy down on the ledge was his brother.

You have to try to save your brother, Kim told himself. *There's no question about that.*

Brothers aren't always what they're cracked up to be, he added to himself. *Sometimes they're great; other times they're awful.*

Matt was two years older than Kim and big for his age. Kim was entirely normal sized.

What a lousy age gap! Kim thought. He often wished he were anything but two years younger. It would be better to be three years younger, then there would be no reason to treat him the way Matt often did. *Leave the little kid alone!*

Or one year younger, and maybe a little bigger for his age, and Kim might not be such an easy, obvious, and weak target. He could fight back.

Maybe.

Maybe not.

Matt was pretty strong.

Even though he was out cold on a rock ledge by a creek.

Kim hefted the pulley and tried to calculate whether he and Dennis could hoist Matt out of there by themselves. He hoped Dennis had constructed a decent stretcher. As usual, Kim had a plan.

He followed his chosen direction unerringly, slogging through the forest at a steady pace, keeping the sun in the same spot so his course would be true.

Above and all around him, the green and brown world of the forest wavered light and dark as he strode through it, with flashes of brilliant Alberta sun piercing the tree cover here and there and illuminating the underbrush in one spot, then missing it in another, darker place. Clearings and thickets, branches and sky.

Kim looked up.

Light, dark, light, dark, splash, flash . . .

It made him remember everything about Matt all at once.

It was all about their town, Caraway, all the kids they knew as friends, and the ones who were enemies, baseball, hockey, the Pig Farm and the Haunted House, everything getting out of hand, and Kim getting in big, big trouble . . . It was all about that long nickname, that "description nickname" Kim had on him — which was Matt's fault! — the one that stuck on him like an ink stain.

It was all about that.

CARAWAY

"**O**h, so you're from a small town, eh?"

Kim had heard that a million times. It was what people from cities always said when he told them he was from Caraway.

Perhaps they had seen it on a map and could place it, clustered around the intersection where one highway continued west and the other one struck off a right angle, heading north to where the farms soon became less frequent and the tall pine and spruce forest took over. Up north where the big rivers were, the moose and the bear and even, if you went far enough, the tundra and the Arctic Ocean.

It was no use, Kim knew, to try to reason with such people, because they just didn't get it.

It would make no impression to launch into the speech he had prepared for them all those million times. City people just didn't know anything about towns.

"No, you see, it's not a small town, it's actually a *big* town," Kim would say to such people, if he ever gave his speech with a pointer and a blackboard, which he didn't because they wouldn't listen anyway.

"Caraway is *enormous!* Try walking around it. You won't make it. Even on a bike it takes a couple of hours. It stretches two miles one way and a mile and a half the other way. It grows right out into fields! There's an old part downtown, and newer parts across the highway, and even newer parts across the other highway. It's growing like crazy.

"It has the railway main line running through it at an angle and there are three or four sidetracks too, which feed over to the grain elevators, which are the biggest things in town. Huge and fat and full of barley and wheat.

"Across the tracks is the bad end of town. You've probably heard of that. 'The wrong side of the tracks.' Well, Caraway has that," Kim would explain with a touch of pride, though he imagined his pretend audience would be getting restless and bored by now. City people were tough to impress.

The wrong side of the tracks was actually the right side if you wanted to have fun. Kim had several friends over there and he visited often, because a lot of the rules for kids seemed to be turned off in that part of town. He lived way on the other end, and there was lots to do and it was plenty of fun, but the good thing about Caraway was that you could tear around on a bike and drop in almost anywhere you wanted. Any time.

The fairgrounds on the west end of town were a gigantic open place that held the hockey arena, the curling rink, a racetrack for horses and sometimes cars, and the main baseball diamond, along with a few small diamonds. The cubs met there in the wintertime in a hall that had been dragged on skids from somewhere else.

To the north of town there was a grassy field that was used by small airplanes as a landing strip. Nearby — and this was a big reason why it was the wrong side of the tracks — was the town's sewer pond. It was a big man-made lake, but there wasn't lake water in it, no sir. This was where the toilet water went and the entire lake smelled like it too. When the wind blew in from the north, as it often did, the odour was overpowering!

That's why that end of town was known by the kids of Caraway as "Sewer-ville" or "Piss Flats." It *was* a fun part of town. It's just that "fun" had a funny smell to it.

The railway tracks were their own special attraction.

"Train's coming!" someone like Dennis would yell when he heard the unmistakable blare of the train's horn from a few miles out of town. A pack of kids would jump on their bikes and pedal like mad for the tracks. Cutting through alleyways and across deserted lots, it was a quick and simple trip to get there.

"A lot of places in Caraway are pretty dangerous," Kim would tell his pretend audience of city people, who weren't listening anyway, "but the train tracks are probably the most dangerous of all. You have to be real careful.

"There are stories about kids being sucked right under freight trains. Personally, I don't believe them, but you never know. It's best to stay well back."

They did stay well back, after they had carefully placed their pennies and dimes on the tracks as the freight trains thundered toward them. Grain trains often stopped and spent hours pushing sections of cars onto the side tracks so they could load up at the elevators, but freight trains could usually be counted on to barrel right through. They were pulled by two or three, or even four locomotives hitched in a row, each one roaring and powering black diesel smoke into the air.

The sound was deafening, but nothing compared to the horn the engineers blasted when the train approached a crossing — there was one at either end of Caraway — or when the kids could persuade him to let it go. They'd stand by the old, wrecked deserted train station — there were no more passenger trains — and make a pulling motion with their arms. *"Blow the horn!"* it meant.

The sound of those horns was like liquid metal crashing through the air. Like electricity zapping the sky. It rattled your teeth, tickled your tummy, and made your bike shake. It was great!

The train would surge ahead through town without stopping. It was so heavy it actually pressed the tracks into the ground when it passed, especially the locomotives, so that the train appeared to be a giant, angry, attacking worm coming down the tracks. It sank and rose and lunged and buckled on its steel rail tracks and, without realizing it, the kids would back up a few feet. What if it jumped off?

Even *on* the tracks, trains were dangerous, deadly things.

"Remember that guy who didn't see it coming?" kids would often yell to each other as the thunderous freights rolled by.

They all remembered for, incredible as it may seem, a driver in a car had once been hit by a train right at one of the crossings in Caraway. It wasn't the main crossing, which was marked by flashing red lights and a dinging bell, but even so, there was no question the train had sounded its horn.

The only explanation was that the driver was watching another train over on the side track. Whatever. He had driven right onto the tracks and his car was hit and crushed like a pop can, then dragged way, way down the tracks, since the train took a long time to stop.

"Can't believe that guy wasn't killed," everyone always said.

Incredibly, he wasn't. It seemed like a miracle, but the collision was not on the driver's side and, even though the car was completely caved in, the crushing metal didn't reach the driver. Not enough to kill him anyway. The car had been towed to one of the gas stations and all the kids saw the blood on the front seat. A close call, but not a fatal one.

If they hadn't respected trains before that, they sure did now!

And with each visit, if they wanted, they could test the weight of the freights by placing their coins on the tracks. After the trains roared out of town, the boys would poke among the train tracks and the smelly timbers and the rocks to find their pennies, nickels and dimes, flattened right out like pancakes, with the Queen's face smeared sideways — sorry, Queen — and the sailboat, the beaver and the maple leaf distorted in a hundred funny ways. They had heard it was against the law, but it didn't seem like much of a crime —and it was their money! — so they did it anyway.

"So you see, city people," Kim would say in conclusion of his lecture to no one, "Caraway is not a small town. Small towns are to be found nearby. Places like Greely and Mayerville and Croft. Now they are *small.* Why, Greely has about ten houses in it!

Mayerville used to be bigger, but it's shrinking now because everyone wants to live and shop in Caraway, which, as I have already said repeatedly, is not small but big. It has its own newspaper, once a week. Kids arrive by bus from miles around every day to go to school, which is why the high school in Mayerville is now closed. It was sucked right into Caraway High and absorbed completely.

"The kids who arrive by bus are farm kids, a special breed, and the kids who live in Caraway are town kids, or 'townies.' They generally don't mix and usually don't spend any time together after school, since the farm kids have to go home to do chores, like feeding all the animals and driving the big machines. Farm kids are very good at that stuff.

"Town kids also do chores, but not as many. That leaves more time for racing around on your bike in the summer and playing road hockey in the winter.

"So, to sum up, we have seen that not only is Caraway *not* a small town, but a big one, it's also a superior place to live, certainly better than your stinky big city, clogged with cars and traffic lights (we manage without these, completely, though there are a few flashing lights on the highway). It's also better than nearby 'big' towns, especially Hanover, which on first impression might strike you as very much the same as Caraway.

"Not a chance. Hanover is quite a ways away and, to me, the further you get from Caraway, the farther you are from anything that counts. Hanover, therefore, is pretty well nowhere because Caraway is everywhere, and furthermore the best place in the whole province to live.

"And since Alberta is constantly proven to be about the best province in the country, and no one doubts that Canada is the best country in the world, you can understand why we feel that Caraway is, as I said, not only not a small town, but pretty well the best place in the whole wide world.

"Is that entirely clear?"

THE PIG FARM

Kim was joking — mostly — when he made his imaginary speech about how Caraway was the greatest town ever, but he really did feel there were special things about it and he knew for sure there were special places to go.

The Pig Farm was one of them. It was like a strange land where terrific adventures occurred and it was also the location of Kim's biggest misfortune, the one where he got the "description nickname" he didn't deserve.

"Let's ride down to the Pig Farm!" was an exclamation commonly heard in Kim's neighbourhood. Dennis might say it, or Tummy Tom, or Kim, or any number of his other friends who lived nearby, like Bobbie, who was on the next block.

Unlike Dennis, who had a serious side and liked to get things right even if it took him all day, or find the truth about something if it killed him, and Tom, who had the irritating habit of blurting out statements in broad daylight as if he were running onto the stage in the school play to yell, "Send in the horses!" or some dumb thing, Bobbie didn't have a serious bone in his body.

It seemed impossible to get Bobbie mad about anything. When things went wrong, like losing a hockey game or even wiping out on your bike, Bobbie just picked himself up and, with a shrug, continued as if nothing had happened. He was a big kid for his age, which was a year younger than Kim. He never wore anything but a white T-shirt, and most of the time he had a brushcut. He was Brushcut Bobbie.

"Let's ride down to the Pig Farm!" Bobbie might yell, or Dennis or Kim, on a Saturday afternoon or any day in the summer holidays.

It was easy to do, because Caraway stopped right at the end of Kim's street. There were houses and then, kerblam, a field. Boys on bikes could just roar off the road and into the barley or wheat. It was best in the fall after the grain had been harvested and only stubble remained sticking out of the hardened ground. Then they could really tear along!

But the very best way to get to the Pig Farm was with its owner, Mr. White. He was the farmer who kept the pigs, as well as a whole other farming operation. It was one of those things that made Caraway pretty special, as Kim saw it, that Mr. White's farmyard was almost right in town. In fact, Caraway was slowly growing around it, because Mr. White's dad had been one of the first pioneers to reach the area and clear land to farm.

For his farmhouse, he picked a spot where two roads crossed. Years later, those roads became highways, the ones that led west and north of town, so the White farmyard was at the intersection of two busy roads and across from where the town part started. Now Caraway was growing around the farmyard as activity increased on the highways and, in fact, Kim's own house and those of many of his friends were on land that used to be farmed by Mr. White and his dad.

The upshot? They had a really big, really amazing farmyard right next to them, and a huge adventurous Pig Farm in a stand of brush and trees only half a mile away!

The farmyard was vast and spread out, with the complicated-looking farm machines all around it, shining metal grain bins and some old wooden ones too, chicken coops and — it wasn't all good — a flock of turkeys that ran wild all over the entire yard.

The White farm was the place where Kim, though he was not a farm kid but a townie, had learned a thing or two about barnyard animals. Turkeys, for instance, turned out to be one farm creature that would not "scare" away. Go "Wah!" at chickens or cows or even horses, and they'd pay attention and probably run. Turkeys — forget it!

A full-grown turkey stood about the same height as a boy. If Kim and say, Bobbie, got in the way of the flock when it was rampaging its way around the yard, they would soon find themselves eyeball to eyeball with ten of them, all with their incredibly wrinkly and hideous heads darting from side to side.

"Wah!" didn't work. Swinging at them with sticks didn't work. They were just as likely to attack as run away, and more than once it was Kim and Bobbie and the others who were sent scampering across the yard for shelter. Bobbie, as usual, got a big laugh out of it. He was like that.

Mr. White loved to laugh too and was terrific fun to be around. His own children had grown up and left the farm, so when he prepared to set out to feed the pigs and asked for help, he quickly gathered a crowd, Kim, Dennis, Tom, and Bobbie usually among them.

"Who wants to come and get the chop?" Mr. White would say with a smile in his voice, because he knew there wouldn't be too many takers for this job.

"Me," Kim would often reply, since it was fun just to be along and he knew the second part of the journey was worth it. Dennis would often volunteer too, as he was the sort of kid who liked to watch machines work.

Chop was grain that was all chopped up until it was the consistency of sand. They drove over to the feed mill along one of the highways to get it, but Kim and Dennis waited in the cab of the truck while it was being poured from a big long chute, because chop was incredibly dusty. It exploded in a puffy white cloud into the back of the truck.

Behind them they towed the buttermilk wagon, which was a big barrel on wheels all made of dark wood that was made even darker by the constant soaking and spilling of buttermilk. The wagon leaked all over too, attracting clouds of flies that followed it everywhere, including the Creamery where Mr. White and the boys towed it for refilling.

"Do you boys want to help?" Mr. White would ask. There was only one answer to that! Kim and Dennis were trusted to scamper up on top of the wagon, pry off the wooden lid, and fit the hose inside. A sweet and gooey river of buttermilk flowed into the wagon. Kim did not know what buttermilk was, exactly, except that people could drink it if they wanted — he'd tried it and it wasn't bad, though kind of thick tasting — but mostly it was for pigs.

Pigs *liked* chop, but they were absolutely *crazy* for buttermilk.

When they had topped up the wagon and returned, leaking buttermilk all over the roads and bringing with them most of the flies in Caraway, they would usually discover a line-up of boys to go on the pig-feeding expedition.

"Hop on!" Mr. White would call out, the signal for a dozen or so to storm the half-ton truck and buttermilk wagon.

Where would they all sit? Well, two or three could cram into the front seat with Mr. White. It was a springy old seat that provided a carnival-ride bounce every time the truck went over a bump. Anyone was entirely welcome to drop down into the chop in the back and sometimes kids did, sinking almost out of sight in the dusty mess. Achoo!

Some kids even rode on the front of the truck, right on the fender, because it was a very old vehicle and had big, round headlights on top of the fenders and a boy could sit there and hold on as if he were riding a horse. Mr. White didn't mind. He drove very slowly for safety. The old truck had running boards along the sides too and kids could stand there and hang on, holding their hands out into the breeze.

Others clamoured up on top of the buttermilk wagon where they picked a spot on the sticky surface and enjoyed the best view — if they could tolerate the clouds of flies.

"Are we ready?"

"Ready!"

Mr. White would ease the truck ahead, festooned with boys on the fenders, jammed into the cab, slung out wide from the running boards and perched on the buttermilk wagon like birds.

Sometimes Mr. White's dad, the original pioneer, appeared from his house to wave as they departed. He was very old and his house was old too. He had trouble walking and trouble speaking, but when he saw the truck leaving he might spot them and slowly make his way a few steps from his back porch to face the convoy. He would smile at them, a big toothy smile, and suddenly his hand would shoot into the air to give them a wide, jerky wave goodbye as if they were heading off to the high seas.

Leaking trails of sweet buttermilk, they puttered slowly out of the farmyard and headed south to the Pig Farm. When the truck and wagon dipped into a rut in the road, the truck bounced on its old springs and the buttermilk wagon creaked and swayed and the boys all went "Oooowwww."

The pigs knew they were coming.

From their pig sheds, from shady spots where they rested, from back in the trees they came trotting out into the big pig yard as soon as they heard Mr. White's truck come squeaking along. In a minute there were dozens of them crowding at the wooden railing of the yard.

"Sookie! Sooo-kie!" the boys would yell, but it was hardly necessary. Every pig in the entire Pig Farm knew it was meal time. From the biggest sows to the tiniest piglets and every porker in between, they were there and they were hungry, so hungry they crawled on top of each other trying to get to the rail.

"All right boys, chop," Mr. White said by way of asking for help carrying the chop. Most of the crowd preferred to jump up on the rail for a bird's eye view of the main event — the buttermilk — but Kim often helped with the chore of hauling the chop. They scooped it from the truck into big buckets, passed them over the fence, then Mr. White and a few brave boys hauled it to wooden feeding boxes a little way into the yard. Actually, "brave" boys were not really required, because the pigs were not terribly interested in the chop. Sure, they ate it but they weren't prepared to trample each other to get it.

But they were completely crazy, absolutely nuts for that buttermilk.

Mr. White would back up the buttermilk wagon so that the big pipe at the end was over a chute that led to the main feeding trough.

"Can I?" a boy would ask, indicating the big wheel on the pipe's tap, and Mr. White would nod. With a turn of the wheel, the gushing white river of buttermilk began to flow.

"Here it comes, pigs!" Tom would yell.

Squealing, jumping, oinking, grunting, snorting, lapping and gulping for all they were worth, the horde of pigs attacked the buttermilk. They put their faces in it, their whole heads, they dunked their eyes in it and, somehow, some of the smaller ones climbed up on the backs of the others and jumped in the trough, where they splashed and rolled and swallowed. They had a bath and a meal all at the same time.

"Wow . . . wouldn't want to fall in there," Bobbie observed quietly in the midst of the mayhem.

"Think they'd eat you?" Tom asked, fearfully sucking in his tummy for a moment.

"They'd sure give you a good licking," Kim put in, with a little smile at making a pun, which no one seemed to get.

"They'd eat each other if they had to," was Dennis's contribution.

"How can they be so ugly? How can anything be that ugly?" Tom wondered out loud and Kim knew he meant the pigs' noses, for there was perhaps nothing uglier in the entire world than a pig's nose. It was wet and pink and flat, with two ugly holes in it, and pigs jammed them into everything, including mud, dead things, and poop. Those wet noses, fifty, sixty, eighty of them, wiped the bottom of that buttermilk trough clean at every feeding time.

Licking their lips, the pigs would slowly back away and turn and stagger through the mud, buttermilk dripping from their jaws. Some would stop and gulp down some chop from the boxes if they had room left in their bulging stomachs, others would just waddle back into the trees or the sheds. There was a low spot in the yard, as there seemed to be in every pig yard, and there was always water and mud in it. Some of the pigs would lie in it, roll around, and get nicely cooled off. When a breeze passed over the mud, it sent the sickly odour of pigs, their mud and their slop, over to the boys on the rail.

That was why Kim was used to the smell of pigs.

"All right, who's coming back?" Mr. White would ask and about half the boys would join him for the return trip. It was an easy walk across the field back to town, so Kim and many others often stayed behind.

"Hey, let's hunt pigs," Dennis might say. They didn't really "hunt" pigs, not to kill them or eat them or anything, but they did chase them all over the entire Pig Farm, which occupied about half of the whole wooded area they called "the Bush." Behind the feeding troughs and mud hole, the pigs had sheds they could sleep in and a big area of trees that was surrounded by a secure wire fence. They could roam around wherever they liked. Of course, so could the boys.

"Got one!" Bobbie or Dennis or Kim would yell if they had isolated a pig on a trail. Then the hunt was on, but it was just a chase, really, since pigs would "scare" almost all the time and go squealing like crazy in a mad run down the paths through the trees. They always got away.

Once, Kim and the others were exploring back in the trees, looking for pigs to chase, when they came across one down on the ground, still but not sleeping. Dennis and Kim looked closer. The pig was dead and it was swollen way up, its belly distended like a balloon. Flies buzzed around its dead eyes.

"Shouldn't we leave it alone?" Tom asked, hopefully.

"Why? It's dead." That was Dennis.

"Look at how it's puffed up," Kim said warily.

"What killed it, I wonder?" said Bobbie.

"Wasn't us," Tom asserted.

"That's one less pig in Pig-ville!" Dennis yelled, way too loud.

"There's lots," said Bobbie. "Lots and lots."

"Weird how it's all blown up like that," Kim said.

Usually Bobbie was the reckless one — for such a happy-go-lucky kid he often got into pretty good trouble — but that day it was Kim's turn to push it.

He had a stick, as usual, and his hunting knife strapped to his belt, as usual, which he quickly used to sharpen himself a pig poker.

He edged closer to the fly-infested thing and prodded its enormous belly with the sharp stick.

"It's like a football," Dennis murmured, licking at a bit of foam at the side of his mouth.

"A pig skin!" Tom pronounced triumphantly, but was ignored as all eyes were on Kim and his stick.

He poked and poked again. Harder. The pig's swollen belly was surprisingly tough, so he stepped closer and leaned on the stick — hard — and jabbed a hole.

There was a thin airy sound — Theeee-ewww — and the belly quickly deflated. The deadness of it had caused the swelling, of course, and now the gas leaked out.

For a second they all stood there, saying nothing. Then the smell hit them — a disgusting, thick, grapey, spongy, awful smell! Rotten, horrible! Kim almost threw up. Tom staggered backward, holding his hand to his mouth. Dennis and Bobbie gagged and quickly stepped upwind to avoid it.

"EEEEEEWWWWWW!" they all cried out. "That is the worst smell in the universe!"

And it was. The smell of a dead pig.

The Pig Farm was like that. Kim encountered things there he never saw anywhere else. It was like a strange and foreign land where adventures and misfortunes occurred and curious and wondrous events could be observed.

Once, Kim was with Mr. White when one of the huge sows had its baby pigs born. The sow was a gigantic animal, six or seven feet long when she lay on her side, as she had to when the piglets came into the world. Her eyes were the size of Kim's fist and her hairy ears were like small folded blankets. She couldn't move during the birth, so Mr. White helped out as the baby pigs came shooting out of her hind end, really quick: one, two, three, four, five, six, seven, eight, nine. Nine little piglets, covered in slime, but alive! Mr. White caught each one in turn and placed them up at the sow's mouth so she could lick them clean.

Then suddenly the sow rolled — only a little — and crushed one of the piglets. Right dead, right there.

Kim watched Mr. White. He did not seem too concerned. After all, there were still eight left. It happened so fast! Just born and just killed. Just like that.

Later, Kim saw that all the piglets were getting milk from the sow. They were all lined up in a row and sucking from the little pouches on her tummy. They would be fine. Mr. White told Kim to stay clear of the sow and baby pigs. Kim could tell the huge sow wouldn't "scare", no way.

When they didn't have piglets, the sows were out with the other pigs and then they did "scare". The one kind of pig that was kept apart was the boar.

Kim and all the others knew this was a grown-up male — there was only one for the entire Pig Farm — because its balls were easily seen hanging off its hind end. The boar was the biggest pig of all, but confined to its own pen it was an easy target for some of the boys.

"Bombs away!" Bobbie would yell as he aimed a clod of dirt at the boar's balls. Dennis did that too, but Kim thought it was stupid and unnecessary. Besides, the boar had nowhere to run. It was helpless in its little pen.

Still, the boar barely jumped when Bobbie or Dennis scored a direct hit. Perhaps it was too big to hurt. After awhile, the kids left it alone.

But the regular, smaller pigs back in the trees were fair game for everyone. Kim and Dennis put their minds to it over a few weekends and built their own tree house right in the pig yard. Lots of other kids had tree houses, which were fairly easy to construct if you didn't bother with a roof. When the leaves and branches grew back in, they sort of became the roof and a tree house could be pretty well camouflaged.

"Ssssshhh!" they'd warn each other, Kim and Dennis, Tom and Bobbie, as other groups of boys rampaged on the trails below them. Sometimes a group of kids could pass right underneath them and not know they were there.

They might be kids like Matt and his friends, and groups of boys from other parts of Caraway, for the Pig Farm and the Bush attracted dozens of boys on sunny, warm weekends.

And, like cub camp, in fact like most activities and sports in town, there was always a division between older boys and younger ones.

It was a reality, and Kim didn't like it. He didn't like it at all.

RIOT AT THE HAUNTED HOUSE

Thwack!

"Strike one!"

Thwack!

"Stee-rike two!"

Thwunk.

"Nope. That's a ball."

Kim hefted the next rock in his hand and took aim. They were throwing pitches at fence posts in the Bush near the Pig Farm.

Thwack!

"Strike three — yer out!" Dennis yelled when Kim rattled the next pitch off the post and into the nearby trees.

"The crafty leftie caught 'im lookin'," Dennis added, as if he were a sports announcer.

"Of course he was looking. It's a fence post," Tom said, in a massive statement of the obvious.

Kim had another rock and also flung it hard at the fence post, hitting it for the fourth time. Kim and Dennis and Bobbie all played baseball and they all had their strengths, Dennis being a real solid catcher and Brushcut Bobbie able to play short-stop and outfield. They could all hit about equally well, but Kim was definitely one of the best pitchers and he had just proven it again. His friends had thrown rocks at the post and only hit it a few times. Tummy Tom didn't really play sports, though he was sometimes valued as a lineman in football simply because of his size. He still got picked last.

Kim had been a pitcher for as long as he could remember. He was left-handed and from a young age lefties were tried out as pitchers, even if they could barely toss the ball, because lefties were a rare and prized commodity in baseball. They had a natural throw to the infield from first base and as pitchers they could toss from "the other side."

It made Kim like the game of baseball a great deal, because it was one of the few activities in his entire life where being left-handed was both an advantage and a valuable asset to his team. Writing, cutting with scissors, using steak knives or trying to work on school desks designed for right-handers were all tedious and difficult jobs for lefties, but in baseball the tables were turned.

Kim was a southpaw.

What the heck did that actually mean? He always wondered. Nobody called right-handers "Northpaws." And why the bit about a "paw"? He wasn't an animal!

But he would gladly put up with any number of weird names, because in baseball being a southpaw set him apart and put him on the pitching mound, where the action was. It had forced him to become a better thrower than he might have been, to really work on his delivery, and learn to throw strikes.

Thwack! He bounced another rock off the fence post, which was a good distance away. Bobbie threw one and hit it too. He paused and pulled his sweat-soaked T-shirt off his back to let a little air in.

It was a wildly hot summer day in early July, a time of year when the sun was high in the sky even early in the morning. By noon the streets and fields shimmered with heat waves. The barley in Mr. White's field between Caraway and the Pig Farm was green and thick and high. Every day it seemed to grow an inch taller.

In other fields there was clover, a plant that produced acres and acres of white blooms. These were excellent for honeybees, which were housed in beehives stacked in rows along the treelines that separated the fields. Honey farmers raised the bees and put their hives next to the clover fields, and those bees were busy all day long. The fields were alive with them, thousands of bees that floated from flower to flower, loading up on nectar. Clover fields actually had a sound to them, the low buzzing of all those bees.

"Anyone bring any water?" Bobbie asked listlessly. They were in the shade, but still suffering from the heat. Sweat glistened on each boy's forehead and it almost hurt to breathe the air.

"You got any?" Tom asked Kim hopefully, but it was clear nobody had remembered to bring water. The Bush and the Pig Farm were so close to Caraway that it was easy, usually, to bicycle home and have a sandwich and get a drink, so water and food were often forgotten. It happened all the time, but on a day like this Kim wished someone had remembered.

"The pigs have water," Dennis said. "There's a hose there that runs into the water trough. It must come from a well. We could get a drink there."

Kim looked at Dennis like he was nuts but he didn't say it, because he knew Tom probably would.

"You'd drink anything, wouldn't you? Gasoline, pig water. What's wrong with you? You'll get sick and they'll have to pump your stomach again." It was Tom talking, as expected.

Dennis took two steps and socked Tom on the side of the head with his fist, making a Thock! like in *The Three Stooges*.

"Shut up!"

"I'm just saying — "

"You want another one? On the nose?" Dennis held his fist menacingly in front of Tom's face.

"It's a miracle you're not dead," Bobbie observed calmly, speaking to Tom. "What with your big mouth."

Tom was about to prove Bobbie's point by saying something, but he kept quiet and turned away. They were all sitting down in the long grass by now, pooped from the heat and without much to do.

From behind them, back in the Bush, came the distant echoes of boys yelling and chasing. There were a lot of kids around the Pig Farm today, all running and milling in their separate clots and groups. Kim knew Matt was in there somewhere, because when they left the house it was apparent they were heading to the same place.

But it was not even a question that they might go off to the Bush together, because Matt avoided his little brother like a bad smell, or a catchable disease, or a pesky dog that persistently followed him around. Kim didn't really know why, but his brother didn't like him. His brother didn't want him around.

"You guys seen Alan? Or Lloyd?" Kim asked to anyone at all, referring to two other friends of theirs who were often down at the Bush. Kim lay on his back studying the high wispy clouds miles overhead in the blue-white sky. Nobody replied, so he assumed they hadn't seen Alan or Lloyd.

Suddenly, there was a crashing sound behind them. They all propped up on elbows to see a kid they knew, little Rodney, tumble out of the brush and come to a stamping halt in front of them.

"There's something going on at the Haunted House," Rodney panted. His freckled face was badly sunburned already, making it a mess of pink, red, and flecked brown. Rodney was a little kid who floated between groups of older boys and acted, like now, as a kind of messenger kid. He just took it upon himself to run around and report the news back and forth.

"Like what?" Dennis asked in his gravel voice.

"Don't know. Maybe a fight. You should come."

"That's nuts!" Tom exclaimed. "Why go near a fight?"

But Tom was the only one who felt that way. Dennis, Bobbie and Kim naturally assumed a fight was worth witnessing. If that's what was going on.

"Who's there?" Kim asked Rodney. The little kid squinted in an effort to summon the names.

"Dunno. Lots of kids. There's lots of kids here today."

"Is Mr. White there?" Kim asked.

"No. Gone quite a while ago."

"What kind of fight?" said Bobbie.

"Well," little Rodney said, taking a deep breath and retrenching, "maybe not a fight. Just a lot of kids running around, you know, with sticks."

Rodney was usually pretty reliable — enough so that kids sometimes issued him a full message about what they were doing or when they would be home, and he could repeat it to someone, say a mom, almost word for word — but he seemed to have dressed up his account this time by using the word "fight."

Bobbie immediately lost interest and fell back into the grass.

"Hey Rodney, did you see anyone with a big container of water?" That was Tom's main concern.

"Yeah, but I think it's all gone."

"Darn."

"I had some though."

"So *tell* me about it, why doncha," Tom whined. Hearing about water and not having any was the worst of all.

Rodney suddenly bounded back into the trees as quickly as he came, calling over his shoulder, "Okay — you're gonna miss it."

"Miss *what*?" Dennis called after him, but the little boy was gone. They all had a laugh about Rodney. He was a terrific pest sometimes, but way too useful as a messenger kid to get angry at, for they all realized that if Rodney didn't race around on his skinny little legs with his knobby knees delivering messages, *they* would have to and it would be exhausting. Rodney had made himself a job and he did it well.

Well, fairly well, Kim thought. *What was going on at the Haunted House?*

"Maybe we should go over there and have a look," he suggested.

"There *are* a lot of kids here," said Dennis. "What if he's right? We could get hurt."

"Naw," Bobbie put in. Bobbie never thought anything bad would happen. It made him sort of fearless, though not in a way Kim really respected, because Brushcut Bobbie could become pretty reckless when he got going.

There was a big stack of hay bales not far from where they rested and Bobbie had been the one, a few weeks before, who decided to try parachuting off it with a bed sheet. He held it over his head to catch the air, and just ran to the edge — about six bales up, maybe fifteen feet high — and jumped off.

WHAM! He plunged to the ground like a shot duck. But Bobbie, being Bobbie, just laughed and shrugged and picked himself up. He didn't even sprain his ankle. "Well, that didn't work," was all he said.

"I am *not* going to the Haunted House," Tom pronounced as he struggled to his feet. "In fact, I am going home."

Tom picked up his bike and prepared to head north across the field to town. The other three lounged on the grass and looked questioningly back into the bush, in the direction of the pig pens and the Haunted House. Tom was obviously trying to start a trend in the direction of home and food and water, but just as obviously he was going to be ignored.

"Let's have a look," Dennis growled and he and Kim and Bobbie began to wheel their bikes into the trees in the other direction. With a theatrical sigh, Tom fell in behind them.

It was so hot even the leaves seemed to shrivel and provide less shade than normal. As they plunged through the undergrowth, the sounds of boys became louder. Some were up in tree forts, others running along paths that could be detected by sound but not seen. It was true. There were a lot of kids there that day.

After five minutes of traipsing through the trees, the Haunted House came into view ahead of them.

It loomed high into the air, two solid storeys of dark wood, with vacant gloomy windows and a peaked roof. It presented a pretty scary sight to anyone who might wish to be scared by it, but it wasn't haunted at all.

In fact, it was an old log pioneer house. The timbers were solid and dark brown in colour, with the cracks between them filled with white cement. At the corners the timbers were notched together tightly in the old-fashioned way. The windows had old-fashioned glass in them that bent the light in wavy patterns. Thin wooden partitions divided the windows into smaller sections of fours or sixes.

For some reason, Kim could not remember when or why, the kids had started calling it the Haunted House, perhaps to give it some extra importance, or scare little kids, or just to cause trouble, but no one seriously imagined it was haunted. No one claimed to have seen a ghost there and most of the kids, Kim thought, would probably say they didn't believe in ghosts anyway. He didn't. The only really fair way to test out the whole idea would be to sleep overnight in the "haunted" house and wait for a ghost to show up. And Kim didn't think anyone was about to try that. Too scary, ghosts or no ghosts.

Besides, he had heard some real ghost stories from his mom and they were pretty darned frightening and convincing — stories about people suddenly speaking languages they didn't understand and could not have learned from anyone around them, stories about sausages running up and down walls, stories about people biting into their food and finding it filled with needles. All of those things had happened, or so it was said, in southern Alberta when his mom was a little girl, years ago.

It was Kim's opinion that such people were probably just imagining things, or perhaps people back then weren't as smart as they are today. His mom pointed out that these stories always seemed to involve what she called "excitable teenaged girls." That meant she didn't believe them either.

There were no teenaged girls near the Haunted House. Just a great number of boys. The "fight" that Rodney had advertised turned out to be nothing more than a big, rambling game of tag, though it looked pretty rough at times.

"Let's stay back here," Tom advised and for once they heeded him.

"There's your brother," Dennis added, pointing out Matt who was involved in the tag game, which wasn't really normal tag at all, but involved quite a bit of heaving of mud clods and sticks. There appeared to be two groups, one with Matt in it and another with a bunch of boys Kim didn't recognize.

Bobbie had an older brother, too, and without a word he ran off to join him at the edge of the action.

"Gee . . . it's turning into a mud fight," Kim noted. "Maybe they were fighting before. Maybe that's what Rodney meant."

Sure enough, instead of "tag" between the two teams, for that's what they seemed to be, the sides had taken to pelting each other with clumps of mud and even a few small stones.

"Ouch!" they heard a few kids yell when the missiles scored direct hits. They were right out in the blinding sun and heat. The intensity of the contest was rising with the temperature.

It was one of those "fun but not fun" exchanges, the sort that had left Kim in tears so many times when he and Matt began a tussle that turned into a wrestle, which in turn became a short, brutal flurry of punches with Kim always on the losing end.

With rocks and mud flying through the air, Kim suddenly thought of balloons. He'd had the thought before — of a balloon when you blow it up and it gets bigger and bigger, stretching itself out. Another puff and another, and the balloon expands and expands, and its skin becomes thinner and thinner.

Blow in more air and the balloon gets stretched so thin it becomes transparent. It is huge and tender and delicate, stretched to the limit. And if someone pricks it with a pin — KABOOM! It explodes! It just takes that one pin prick to create an explosion.

Boys are like a balloon, Kim thought. *When their energies are expanded as big and wide as they can go, when they're stretched to the limit, it just takes one more jab and KAPOW! Those boys blow up just like a balloon.*

Boys are like that, Kim thought. *Boys are like a balloon.*

"I still want to see if that water from the well is clean," Dennis said as they watched the back-and-forth of the mud fight.

"I don't believe you!" Tom said in exasperation. "You'll get sick!"

"Aw, let's have a look," Kim said and his opinion held sway. They began to shuffle off past the Haunted House toward the pig sheds. Kim didn't care at all about the well or the water, because he was quite sure it was filthy and undrinkable, but he instinctively wanted to get away from the older boys and their play-fight.

Dennis led the way and Tom quickly followed, not to have a taste of water he was sure was dirty, but apparently also with a wish to put some distance between himself and the older boys. Kim lagged back a little. It was too hot to run. There was a light wind and even it was hot. It gathered into little cyclones here and there and tossed up whirling clouds of black farmdirt dust, making it momentarily hard to see.

Later, all the boys agreed about what happened next. They all heard it and saw it.

There was suddenly a near-accident out on the road. They didn't know how close a call it was, because they were too far away, but it certainly made a big commotion. They all heard the loud blare of a car's horn, then all eyes turned to see the car swerve around a pokey old farm truck going the same direction, then swerve hard the other way to avoid a car coming toward it. BEEP! They all heard it.

The car that beeped, and the other car, quickly drove out of sight in either direction, but the driver of the old farm truck must have swerved in the excitement too, because he suddenly had trouble controlling the vehicle and it swayed side to side, and dug into the dirt shoulders of the road, throwing up dust. It almost tipped over!

Several of the boys nearest the road ran closer in the scant seconds that the truck was in trouble — Kim could see that Matt was among them — drawn ahead by an unseen hand toward the catastrophe that might unfold in front of their eyes. They were all mesmerized by the sight of the swaying vehicle veering all over the road like a drunken man staggering down the street.

Kim ran ahead a few paces too and stood there, frozen to the spot for a second, then dashed a few steps to his left to get around a tree near the Haunted House so he could keep the truck in view. In the next instant, the driver regained control and straightened the vehicle out. It was out of danger. Then —

SMASH!

Someone threw a rock through one of the windows of the Haunted House.

Kim was near where it happened, but he was around a corner and didn't see who did it. The whirlwinds were more intense suddenly, churning up dust everywhere.

Should he have gone to investigate immediately? Later, he asked himself that question over and over. But it was a savage sound, frightening and reckless, and he instinctively dodged in the other direction and ran right around to the other side. CRASH! Another window was shattered, back from where he had come.

Then SMASH CRASH CLATTER! Broken glass everywhere — but he still couldn't see who was doing it.

Scared now, Kim retraced his steps and ran hard back the way he had come, emerging on the side of the house where most of the boys were, the older ones, the younger ones, and kids he didn't even recognize. And they were going crazy!

The fury of the mud clod fight had been turned on the Haunted House. Suddenly, instead of two groups of boys taunting each other with insults and hurled stones and sticks, their fierce energy had become focused like the burning point of sunlight through a magnifying glass and the Haunted House was getting it — it was really getting it!

SMASH SMASH!! More windows were broken on the main floor and even some up high on the second floor. Kim stood in amazement. He had no words in his throat. His arms and legs were paralyzed. He was horrified! And helpless!

Bobbie was among the boys throwing rocks. And he could see Matt in there too and several other kids he recognized — as well as a dozen he didn't. They were all bombarding the fortress-like House with stones that bounced off the logs, but shattered the glass in every window they faced. One kid hefted a boulder over his head with two hands and charged the biggest window of all, what was left of it, and crashed the big rock right through to the living room.

Then, like the dusty dirt whirlwinds that had been swirling around them all day, the mob of boys collected itself into a twisting cyclone — "Let's go inside!" someone yelled — and suddenly boys were running in packs toward the doors on the other side. Kim felt himself gathered into the churning rabble and swept around the House with them — Dennis and Tom appeared out of nowhere and they were part of the attack force too — and in a flash they were all at the door with the crashing throng and bursting inside.

They were in the kitchen — the sad, old smelly kitchen — and the mob of boys immediately attacked everything in sight. Kim spilled through to the next room along with Tom and Dennis. The shelves in the kitchen were cleared and smashed in a minute and boys flung the heavy iron stove top covers at the walls. Cupboard doors were pulled off, even if it took two or three kids to do it. Sheets and sheets of wallpaper were ripped down everywhere. There were only a few plates and cups, but they made spectacular crashes when the kids tossed them at the walls or onto the metal stove.

There was no furniture in the living room but there were a few pictures, one a photograph of nothing, maybe a farmer, and it was quickly smashed. Some boys took sticks and ran them around the insides of the windows to clear off the last bits of glass.

"Charge!" a kid yelled as he ran across the floor and drop-kicked a wall. He knocked a good-sized hole in the plaster and soon others were trying it too — wave after wave of boys flinging themselves feet-first at the walls. It was bizarre!

Kim exchanged a worried look with Tom, who had backed into a corner. Dennis was flinging a few things around, and several times Kim had seen Bobbie tossing plates and ripping wallpaper.

In the corner, Kim backed up too and felt something behind him. It was a doorknob on a door that nobody had noticed. He pulled it open, thinking it might lead outside, but instead it was a stairway going up!

"Hey, look!" a kid yelled when he spotted the way to the second floor. Kim and Tom just ran up ahead to avoid being trampled, for the mob of boys surged at the stairway in search of new territory to attack and destroy.

Kim dashed up the stairs and into the attic. It was entirely clear of walls or furniture and he could see the big cross beams that supported the roof. It was airy and might have been a neat place to explore another time, but it had the same stale old smell as the bottom floor and it seemed to be a scent that drove the boys on — in an instant, they started wrecking it!

The windows were largely intact and they became the first target. SMASH CRASH!! Boys with sticks — Kim saw Matt in the middle of it — poked out the windows and cleaned off the sides, as if they were doing a construction job and wanted to make sure they finished it off.

The floor was covered with yellowy-brown newspapers with old dates on them. Kim picked up a few and tried to read what was in them, but quickly gave up and flung them into the air. The mob shredded them with their hands, their sticks, with their teeth, and tossed them, all balled up, out the windows.

The attic was filled with the dust of ripped, shredded yellowy newspapers, and sawdust too, for the floor was covered with it. Boys kicked and threw the sawdust around and a few kicked the walls, but soon it was clear there was nothing left to wreck. A few of them piled down the staircase, then suddenly they were all running down the stairs, through the destroyed living room and the totally vandalized kitchen, and outside into the blinding, boiling sun.

Kim and Tom and Dennis quickly located each other in the midst of the milling mass of kids and, stunned at the burst of violence they'd witnessed, exchanged looks of fear and near-panic.

"Let's get outa here!" Dennis yelled and there was instant agreement. Bobbie was nowhere to be seen. Kim noticed Matt and his older crowd of kids running for the road. Clots of boys were disappearing into the trees all around and, as Kim and the others also took flight, the yard around the Haunted House was suddenly deserted.

The dust still swirled and the hot wind still blew over the pig sheds and the Bush.

As Kim dashed into the trees, he whirled around and looked back for an instant. The Haunted House looked like an old man who had been beaten up. His teeth were knocked out, his eyes were bruised, his bones were broken. He was crying.

Kim and Dennis and Tom raced to find their bikes and rode hard through the paths in the Bush and out toward the little road that skirted the barley field and led back to Caraway.

They just wanted to get out of there.

ARRESTED!

Kim slumped on the edge of the rock-hard bed. Down the hall he could hear the muffled voices of several adults speaking in low, serious tones. Every now and then he heard a kid say something too, but not for very long. Tonight, the adults wanted only short answers.

Kim was in jail.

Quite a few other kids had been in jail as well, perhaps as many as twenty. Earlier, several boys had been sitting out in the hallway and the walkway in front of the cells. Each of the kids had been taken into the office of the Town of Caraway's policeman and interviewed about the events at the Haunted House that day. Moms and dads had crowded into the jail cells too and scolded and interviewed the boys, but almost all of them were gone now.

Kim sat alone on the jail cell bed — it really was as hard as a slab of concrete — and waited his turn. Of course, he had never been in a jail cell before and, all in all, it wasn't too terribly scary, but as he thought about it, perhaps that was because the door was open. If the policeman came back and — CLANG! — slammed the cell door shut, that would be a frightening and ugly turn of events, Kim knew.

But otherwise, jail wasn't too bad. Caraway apparently didn't have room for a real jail, so they used the basement of the Town Hall. There were two cells. Kim was alone in the one with the door open, where other kids had been earlier, and the other cell was actually occupied by a criminal and its door was locked shut. Kim had viewed the criminal on his way into the cells and he didn't seem too dangerous. He was asleep, actually, and snoring rather loudly with his face tucked firmly into the far corner of the cell.

Kim was wide, wide awake.

There had been a pause of about two hours after the gang of kids had fled the wrecked Haunted House before the phones started ringing. Word of the riot and the destruction spread quickly, between moms and dads, and questions were sharply put to boys all over the neighbourhood. Inspection tours had been organized among parents and, in the fading light, they had all seen the extent of the damage to the old house. Kim did not know if Mr. White had seen the destruction on his property, but with every ounce of sincerity in his body, he hoped not.

How the heck did that happen? he asked himself. *How could we have stopped it? Could we have stopped it?* He wondered if it would have made a difference if he had raced to the front of the Haunted House when he heard the first window shatter. He didn't really think so, for the riot was as ferocious as a berserk dog and probably could not have been restrained. It bugged him anyway and he felt deeply ashamed that he was a part of it. Mr. White was their friend! How could they do this to him?

His thoughts were interrupted by the sound of footsteps down the hall.

The tall Town Cop appeared in the doorway and, without a word, motioned for Kim to follow him. Caraway had only one policeman, the Town Cop, who was someone's dad, but Kim didn't really know the family. There were Mounties in Caraway too, but they didn't patrol inside the town.

He followed the Town Cop down to a small desk by the doorway to the jail. His mom was sitting there, not looking terribly pleased, and Kim could see his dad walking back and forth out in the hallway. He realized that he was the last kid there. It was late, and finally cooler after the wicked heat of the day. A nice breeze slipped into the basement from a nearby open window.

"Okay Kim, could you just sign your name here for us?" the Town Cop asked, pushing a pencil and a piece of paper toward him.

Kim quickly signed his name and put the pencil down.

He could tell the Town Cop and his mom had drawn a conclusion from that, but he couldn't imagine what it might be.

"Now Kim, tell us in your own words what happened out at the farmyard today," the Town Cop asked.

"In your own words," his mom repeated.

Kim told them everything, and in great detail too, since he could remember the day vividly. He knew they were upset by what had happened, and he was too.

"Is Mr. White mad?" Kim asked them both and his mother informed him that Mr. White was not in town that evening and had not yet been told what had happened to the Haunted House.

"That's why we're trying to get to the bottom of this," she added.

"Now Kim," the Town Cop said, "I want to hear how it all started. Can I hear that part again?"

Kim went over it all again, pretty well the way he had related it before. His dad was leaning in the doorway now. When Kim finished he looked at all three of them — they were all silent for a good long moment — and the thought hit him hard, taking his breath away.

They don't believe me.

He was sure of it. He could tell by the way they were looking at each other! They thought he was lying!

"What's the matter?" he asked after he could stand it no longer.

The Town Cop cleared his throat and sat back from his desk.

"Well, it's like this, Kim. We've questioned every boy we can find about what happened today. That house was a little more valuable than perhaps any of you understood and it's a shame it's been wrecked."

Kim nodded. He certainly agreed it was a shame. He felt very ashamed to have been even an accidental participant in its destruction.

"All the kids remember the cars almost running into each other out on the road, and the old truck there that swerved back and forth," — the Town Cop checked his notes on this — "and a second after that, the first rock was thrown that crashed through the window of the house."

Kim nodded along. That's what he remembered too.

"Well," the Town Cop said sadly, and now he leaned forward again over his desk, "I've got three or four boys who said the kid who tossed that rock was you."

WHAT?

Kim looked at the Town Cop like he was crazy. He looked at his mom, who was shaking her head slowly back and forth and sucking air through her teeth.

"I didn't do that!" he protested. "I just told you I was behind the house! I heard the window smash like everyone else!"

"I've got kids here who say they saw a left-handed kid toss the first rock through that window," the Town Cop said, tapping his notes for emphasis and pushing the sheet of paper Kim had signed toward him. "They think it was you. And you *are* left-handed."

"There were probably lots of lefties out there!" Kim retorted. It was ridiculous! He was being framed!

"The only one anybody saw was you." This was his mom speaking now.

"It was windy and dusty. Did any of them tell you that?" Kim said, being kind of smart-alecky.

"Yes, they certainly did," the Town Cop said in a very irritating, overly reasonable way.

"Some of the time I couldn't see at all! How could *they* see?"

"We've gone over it all several times," the Cop said. "The only name I get is yours, Kim. 'Left-handed kid put the first rock in. Looked like Kim.' They all say it."

"*Who?*" Kim demanded. "Who says it?"

His mom sighed loudly.

"Well, your brother, for starters."

THE KID WHO THREW THE ROCK

Two days later, Kim and Dennis sat on the curb of one of the cross streets downtown.

In happier days, they might sit at a bench along Main Street and watch the people and cars go by, but now they were officially weirdoes and outcasts, both of them, and they felt it best to stay off the beaten track.

Dennis had been The Kid Who Drank the Gasoline for some time now and his "description nickname" showed no signs of fading. It was like an ink stain, as Kim knew, and it was almost impossible to get rid of it.

For the first few hours in the day following the destruction of the Haunted House, Kim was known as The Kid Who Started the Riot, but apparently that description nickname proved unsuitable to those who specialized in such things, meaning just about every kid in town. There were kids who didn't quite know what "riot" meant, even though they had been right in the middle of one.

So as the hours passed that first day, and it turned into another day, Kim's description nickname had been revised into something simpler, a catchier phrase, and one that, Kim knew, would stick to him all the better because it was easier to remember.

He was now The Kid Who Threw the Rock.

To make matters worse, Kim *did* have a habit of tossing rocks and little pebbles at whatever targets he could find. It was part of being a pitcher, he reasoned, but it didn't do him any good *at all* right now.

As he and Dennis sat there on the curb, Kim was picking up little stones and tossing them into the street at other little stones. It's just what he did to kill time.

But now, when kids passed and even grown-ups, they gave him a look, as if to say, "Yeah, there he is, that's The Kid Who Threw the Rock."

He was getting pretty fed up with it. Three kids went by, two in a wagon being pulled by a third, and they all looked over at him from way across the street. That same *look.* Without thinking, Kim stood up and rifled a small rock onto the street so it bounced among the wheels of the wagon. The three kids hustled out of there as fast as they could go.

"That's not going to do you any good," Dennis warned.

"*I know,*" Kim retorted. He was just plain angry. Dennis took another look at the kids with the wagon, who were way down the street now and talking and pointing back at Kim. Suddenly Dennis laughed.

"What?" Kim demanded.

"On the other hand, you've got a *reputation* now. Look at 'em! They're afraid of you. Of both of us."

"I don't want kids to be afraid of me."

"Why not?"

"I just don't! I don't want to be a bully."

"You're not a bully and you never will be. There's a difference."

Actually, Kim knew he was right. There was a difference and his new, dangerous reputation might even do him some good with older kids some day. All he had to do was pick up a rock! Mostly, however, he just felt lousy.

"It's so unfair," he said as he sat back down on the curb.

"Yeah."

"What did you see?"

Dennis thought for a second, then continued in his gravel voice, "Well, I sure didn't see you toss no first rock. By 'time I got back from looking for the water hose, lots of kids were throwing rocks."

"What do other kids tell you?" Kim asked, hoping for an answer different from the one he'd been hearing for two days.

"Well . . . they say it was hard to see, with the dirt and dust and all, but they think it was you who chucked the first rock. You know, being left-handed 'n everything."

Great, thought Kim. Suddenly being a southpaw had no redeeming features whatsoever.

"But I don't get why they blame it all on you," Dennis said. "You didn't wreck the house any more than me 'n' Tom. Sure, we were there, but we weren't the leaders. It's just that they think you started it."

"Yeah," Kim muttered. "Boys are like a balloon . . . "

"Huh?"

"Boys are like . . . oh forget it," Kim said hastily.

"That sounds kind of kooky," Dennis said, shifting a little down the curb from Kim and looking at him strangely.

"It's like this," Kim said firmly. "It's true, we didn't wreck the Haunted House. Big kids did. Heck, *Matt* was right in there and lots of his friends too. And there were kids there I didn't even recognize — and I think one of them threw the first rock, by the way — but adults don't care who did it, they care who started it."

"Yeah, that's right."

"And once they think they know who it is, they hold him responsible."

"Yeah, like you're responsible for what thirty kids did. You're right. It's unfair."

"*Totally* unfair," Kim said with great emphasis, and loudly enough to be heard by an old lady passing on the far side of the street, should she care to take note of his protests.

"Yeah but . . . " Dennis continued. Kim knew what he was going to say. "It's totally unstoppable too — the blame, I mean. Getting the blame is as unstoppable as trying to stop the kids wrecking the Haunted House once they got going."

"Yeah."

"My mom says 'once the toothpaste is out of the tube, you can't get it back in again.' It's like that," Dennis observed.

"Yeah, it's like that," Kim agreed.

"What did Matt say?" Dennis asked. Kim scowled. This part really bugged him.

"He said he told me exactly the same as he told the Town Cop."

"Which was, like, what . . . ?"

"Which was that he chased out toward the road when the accident almost happened, then stopped and looked back right when the House was all sort of whirled around with dust, and it was hard to see. But he could see a little bit — and the sun was shining brightly into the dust, sort of, at the right angle to see this kid — me, he said — run up to the house and chuck a rock right through the window."

"But did he see your face?" Dennis asked.

"He was quite far away by then. I've thought about it. But he looked back and saw this left-handed kid — me, he said — toss the rock through the window."

"But his face, what about his face?"

"Well, *exactly*," Kim said, as if he'd proven something. "Matt said he saw this figure, this kid — me, he says — throwing the rock but he was turned away from Matt, more or less. Mostly he's sure the kid was left-handed."

"So he didn't see your face," Dennis said flatly.

"I don't think he saw the kid's face, no," said Kim. "He just drew a conclusion based on which hand the kid threw with. He's pretending to be responsible by pointing the finger at me."

"Yeah but . . . " Dennis continued and Kim knew where he was going.

"But other kids reported the same thing, yeah, yeah, I know," Kim put in. "I think they all cooked it up afterward. Think about how much damage they did, all those kids. They were going to be in serious trouble. They needed someone to blame, right?"

"No kiddin'."

"So they decided to blame *me*, since I'm a southpaw and they know darn well that adults hold the one who started it responsible for everything that happened later."

"That really stinks," Dennis said. "Worse than pigs."

"Tell me about it."

"They're deflecting the blame."

"You wanna believe it."

"You think we're gonna go to jail?"

"We've already been in the jail, Dennis."

"Yeah, but I mean for good."

"Naw. They were just trying to scare us."

"Worked."

"Yup."

"I figure it's like this," Dennis said, drawing a pattern in the dust with a little stick. "If it was your word and mine and Tom's, say, against any other batch of kids, we might pull it off. They might believe us. Or at least give us the benefit of the doubt."

"Yeah."

"But the big problem here is that your own brother says it was you. I mean, you gotta think your own brother would know who he was looking at, right?"

"No kiddin'."

"So when Matt says it was you, that kind of carries a lot of weight."

"Tell me about it," Kim replied, disgusted and angry and helpless.

The stain was on him firmly now, like the stripe down a skunk's back.

How could he ever get rid of it?

In the Nick of Time

When Kim arrived back at the top of the cliff, Dennis was on the verge of panic. He saw Kim coming through the forest, lugging the pulley and rope, and ran up to meet him, dancing around anxiously like a little kid who had to pee.

"Hurry up!" Dennis snapped.

"I *am*!"

"He's almost rolling off into the creek!"

Kim dashed to the lip of the cliff and could immediately see that Matt had moved quite a bit. He was definitely closer to the creek — and still out cold.

"I was ready to drop down there if I had to," Dennis reported and showed Kim his emergency descent rope, tied to a tree. "But I figured it was better to leave him if he didn't actually roll into the water."

"Okay," Kim panted, catching his breath. Where's the stretcher?"

"Right here."

Dennis dragged his creation over to the lip of the cliff. It was a large, light frame of poplar and willow saplings lashed together with bits of rope and flexible green tree branches. There was a gaping slash in the forest where he had cut the wood.

"Good job, Dennis," Kim said. The stretcher was excellent. It was just what they needed and Kim realized Dennis was probably the best friend he could possibly have along in this mess. He came through in a pinch and he wasn't a quitter.

"All right, here's the plan," Kim said quickly. "We need to hang the pulley out a ways from the cliff. We can use that branch." He indicated a sturdy limb nearby and Dennis set to hacking off a length of rope sufficient to suspend the pulley.

"We thread the rope through the pulley, attach the stretcher, and I'm going to ride down with it and tie him on. You'll have to lower me. Think you can do that?"

Dennis nodded curtly. "No problem. It's a pulley. There's a mechanical advantage." Kim smiled a bit and nodded back.

"Right. And you can loop the rope around a tree to help you."

Dennis squinted. "Yeah. That makes two pulleys when you think about it. You make the tree into one too."

"Right," Kim replied and smiled again. All the time Dennis spent watching machines was paying off!

"And that might work when we hoist him up," Kim continued. "Or maybe you can pull from up here and drop the rest of the rope down to me and we'll both pull. Then we get me back up and we're off."

Dennis nodded. He had the rope he needed to attach the pulley and, with one sure toss, looped it over the protruding tree branch. Using a stick, he snared the dangling rope and had the pulley secured in an instant.

"Ohhhhhhh . . . awww . . . " A sound reached them. Matt! He was moaning and rolling around quite a bit now.

"He's been doing that," Dennis observed. "Let's hurry!"

They quickly tied the stretcher on and lowered it over the edge of the cliff. Kim tested the system for weight and it seemed strong enough. While Dennis held the rope — looped around a nearby poplar tree for the additional advantage — Kim slung himself onto the stretcher.

"Okay, let 'er go — easy!"

"Here goes, here goes," Dennis replied, playing out the rope.

In a second, Kim was dangling out over the ledge, twenty feet up. He swayed and dropped little by little as Dennis let out the rope.

"You okay?" he called up to Dennis and heard a "yup yup" back, but it was still obviously pretty heavy for one boy to handle because Kim felt himself dropping a foot or two at a time. It wasn't a smooth ride.

"How close?!" Dennis yelled.

"Can you hold it?"

"Uhhh — yeah!" Dennis yelled again just as the stretcher and Kim plunged a good four feet.

"Easy!" Kim hollered.

"I'm trying!"

There was another sudden drop. But Kim held on and he was soon in range where he could handle a fall right to the rock if he had to, though it might be hard avoiding a crash with the stretcher and Matt.

"Okay? Okay? You there yet?" Dennis called out.

"Five feet . . . four . . . three . . . " The end of the stretcher touched the rock and Kim followed it down. Dennis managed the last bit very smoothly and Kim was able to alight on the rock as if he had been lowered by a huge construction crane, not one boy grappling with a rope and pulley.

"Perfect! I'm down!" he cried and in a moment Dennis peered over the top, grinning. So far, so good.

Kim immediately scooped a few handfuls of water from the creek and splashed it on Matt's face. It made his brother roll and react a little, but it did not revive him. He tried a few more with the same result. He checked Matt over too, but could not detect any broken bones. His legs, arms, neck, hands, fingers — all were okay.

"Check his head," Dennis called from above and Kim nodded. He was just about to do that. There were no marks or cuts on Matt's face. He felt back around through his hair.

"Hmm. He's got a big bump on the back of his head."

"Must've just dropped backwards and then hit his head."

"Yeah. Good thing there's moss here. It cushioned the fall."

"Is he breathing all right?"

"Yeah. Just a sec. I'm going to try something."

Kim grabbed Matt's head firmly by the hair and slapped him hard on the face.

"What you doin'!" Dennis cried.

"Just trying to wake him up. What do you think I'm doing?"

"I dunno. Trying to get even, maybe."

Kim didn't bother replying. He splashed more water on Matt and had a good, long drink himself.

"Can you bring me some?" Dennis asked.

"Sure. How? You got a container?"

"Naw." As usual, they had forgotten any sort of canteen.

"I know," said Kim. "I'll soak my shirt in the creek and tie it to the stretcher and you can wring it out to get a drink."

"Yuk."

"Take it or leave it."

"Okay, do it. That doesn't mean I'll drink it."

"I thought you'd drink anything."

"Yeah, I could use a nice glass of gasoline about now."

They were both passing the time to see if Matt would revive. Apparently not. Kim splashed water on him for a third time and looked for hopeful signs. Matt moaned a bit and rolled around, but he was still out.

"You think he hurt his brain?" Dennis asked bluntly.

"I don't know. I hope not. He's really loose, like a rag doll. If there was anything wrong with his neck, we wouldn't move him but I think we can try this."

Kim went to work binding Matt to the stretcher. It was difficult and sort of weird rolling his brother around so that he could be fit onto the frame of tree branches. He had to tie Matt in several places to ensure he wouldn't fall off.

"Now," Kim wondered out loud, "how do we make the whole contraption stay level?"

"You can't," growled Dennis from above. "Don't even try."

"No?"

"No. I've seen loads on real cranes rigged so that they're tipped about half upright. It's steadier than trying for level, which you can't get anyway unless you have two points of attachment and even then, it doesn't work."

Kim was impressed. "So what do I do?"

"Make a tie near one end, then loop the rope so it picks up near the other end."

Kim did what he said. Matt's head didn't roll around, because there was a little nest of leaves from the stretcher branches to cradle him. He was packaged up like a doll in a crate.

"Okay, let's see," Dennis called. He vanished and began to haul on the rope. Kim guided the stretcher up from the rock until it was almost off the ground. The whole load rose at a promising angle, with Matt's head up, and tipped about halfway off the vertical. It worked! Dennis was right.

"Looks good!" he called up the cliff.

"Okay, that was a dry run," Dennis called back. He eased off on the rope and the stretcher returned to the ground.

"Now for real," Dennis said from the top. "I'm going to throw you the tail end of the rope. I'll pull up here and I'm using the tree again. You pull down there and try to fasten it somewhere, okay? The two of us should be able to do it."

Kim nodded okay. In an instant, the end of the rope appeared.

"Ready?" came the sound of Dennis's voice.

"Ready!"

The rope snapped taut as Dennis yanked on it. Again, the stretcher was hauled up off the ground and stabilized in its half-tilt position. Kim grabbed the rope and pulled hard.

Suddenly Dennis let go and the stretcher fell toward the ground! Kim caught it just in time before it slammed onto the rock!

"*What are you doing?*" he screamed.

"What are you doing? You pulled the rope right out of my hands!"

"I thought you wanted me to pull it!"

"Just anchor it — don't yank it!"

"Okay, okay!"

It took a second to cool off their tempers and get started again. The stretcher rose from the ground for the third time, and on this attempt Kim didn't pull hard on the rope. He realized that Dennis must be able to handle the entire weight himself, what with the help of the pulley and by using a tree too.

There was nothing strong enough to secure the rope to, so at first Kim wrapped it around his waist, then quickly changed his mind. You should never wrap a rope around yourself, he knew.

"Hang on, Dennis!" he called and quickly extricated himself. He could hear Dennis cursing him over the delay, but their progress promptly resumed. The stretcher with Matt strapped to it inched upward past Kim's head.

"It's swaying!" Kim warned.

"Can't help that. Steady it."

"I'm out of hands!"

"Try!"

He did the best he could. Matt was about halfway up, but the whole load was twisting now due to some imbalance in it. Kim decided they just had to see it through.

Up and up it went, a rope tug at a time. More and more, until Matt's head was even with the top of the cliff . . . then the length of the stretcher passed it . . . and finally Matt and the frame made of tree branches were twirling in the air at a point higher than the lip of the cliff. The pulley squeaked loudly as it pivoted around.

"Uh . . . we've got a problem," Kim called loudly from down on the ledge.

"What?"

"Well . . . how are you going to haul him in without letting go of the rope?"

"Good question."

They both pondered their difficulty for a time as Matt hung there, suspended in the air out over the cliff. Kim peered upward and prayed that the branch would hold while they figured out their problem. He thought he had felt it give a little, and heard a few cracks too, though maybe he imagined it.

"I can go around this tree a few times and tie it off up here," said Dennis.

"But you'll need some slack to reel him in," Kim pointed out.

"Yeah, you're right. You'll have to loop the rope around something down there and control the slack."

Kim looked around again. "There's nothing here. Just smooth rocks that won't hold a rope."

"Oh boy."

"Yup."

They both considered it a bit longer, then Dennis called out, "You're going to have to hold it yourself."

Kim exhaled sharply, but he knew Dennis was right. He would have to act as the counterweight.

"All right," he called back, "I see what you mean."

"Put the rope around your waist," Dennis said.

"You're not supposed to do that."

"I know. But if you let go and I'm not holding on up here, whammo, the whole thing will fall all the way down, right?"

"Yeah, you're right."

"Come on — let's get him up here! This is taking too long!" Dennis suddenly yelled.

"All right, give me a second." Kim quickly twirled into the rope with two complete turns. And he looped it around one arm too. He was now the counterweight.

"Ready!"

"It's going to pull you up the cliff! Are you ready for that?"

"Yes — ready!"

"Okay . . . here we go . . . Now!"

The rope above Kim snapped taut as Dennis let go completely. Kim was suddenly hauled up the cliff face violently — he had to kick his feet into it to hold himself. Above him, the stretcher dropped an equal distance.

"*Hold on!*" Dennis roared.

"I *am!*"

Kim grabbed at the cliff with his free hand and dug his feet in as hard as he could. He was slowly being dragged up the cliff — he couldn't hold it! — and then he was tipped right upside down, "walking" up the cliff as he tried to maintain the counterbalance.

He could see Dennis reach out with a long stick and snare the stretcher. He coaxed it to the edge and got it settled onto the lip, then pulled it hard to land it completely.

The action hauled Kim a few more feet up the cliff — upside down.

"Okay, he's here!" Dennis yelled.

"Don't untie it!" Kim screamed. "I'm upside down ten feet off the ground!"

"Oh."

"Hey, I've got an idea," Kim continued breathlessly. "Just pull the stretcher further back little by little. It'll haul me up. I've got to get up anyway."

"Gotcha!"

Dennis instantly understood what Kim was trying to do. He dragged the stretcher away from the pulley and the cliff face, which yanked on the rope and dragged Kim higher and higher. Kim continued "walking" up the cliff almost upside down, using his weight and his legs to adjust his ascent.

"You there yet? Dennis asked.

"Just about. Keep pulling on it."

Dennis hauled the stretcher even farther back and was greeted by a strange sight at the lip of the cliff. Kim's feet appeared first from out of the canyon, followed by the rest of him.

"Steady, steady, keep it going," Kim called. It was working wonderfully! Kim "walked" right up over the lip of the cliff, using the assist of the rope. At the last second, he jumped a little ahead and he was there! They were all there!

"'Kay . . . " was all Kim said. What a complex system of ropes they had created! Dennis fell back, exhausted, and looked it over too. Kim was looped with rope that was in turn looped around a tree before it traveled to the suspended pulley and back to the stretcher. It was like they had bound themselves in a big artificial spider's web.

They were too tired, however, to celebrate.

Kim unlooped himself and Dennis untied the stretcher. They both sat on the ground, catching their breath.

"Darn it," Kim said at last.

"What?"

"I forgot to soak my shirt to get you a drink."

Dennis sighed and licked foam from the side of his mouth.

"Your shirt's soaked anyway, but even I won't drink sweat."

"Yeah. Good job, Dennis."

"Yeah, you too."

"Three Miles. Let's Get Started."

Their rest break was understandably short. Matt still showed no signs of coming around. It's like he had slept through the entire escapade to avoid the work and now he was going to sleep through the trip home too.

Dennis had constructed the frame so that the ends had handholds sticking out that they could grab, just like a real stretcher. They tested the load and it was very heavy.

"How far to camp, you think?" Dennis asked.

"Three miles. Let's get started."

"Impossible. We'll never get that far."

"Yeah, you're right. We've got to hope we run into some kids, or at least come to a spot we recognize and one of us can run ahead," Kim said. "I mean, the big danger was him being on the ledge near the water. We've solved that. Now we're going to need some help."

"No kiddin'," said Dennis. "What about all this stuff?"

They looked back at the pulley, still dangling over the edge of the cliff, and all the rope and branches strewn around.

"We leave it. Maybe we can get it later, I dunno. Let's go."

They put their backs into lifting Matt and the stretcher and immediately knew they'd be lucky to haul it half a mile.

"How much does he weigh, anyway?" Dennis called over his shoulder from the front.

"I dunno. Too much."

"Tell me about it."

They soon discovered they could carry the stretcher for about two minutes at a time and that was all. Then they had to set it down and give their aching arms and shoulders a rest. Also, they would switch positions. Sometimes it even helped to be at the front and walk backwards, just to change the way the weight felt, but all in all, it was tiring, difficult work.

"Ahahahahahah . . . " Dennis began to wail after awhile. He wasn't really in pain, but it helped to be able to say something. Kim just put up with it, the pain and the wailing.

"Ahahahahahah," Dennis moaned. "When do we get to stop?"

"We just have to tough it out, Dennis."

"You got any tricks up your sleeve?" Dennis asked from the back.

"No sleeves. No tricks," Kim replied. It was hard to talk very much when they were underway.

"Why not? You're the tricky one."

"Stop saying that. And don't mention the Greased Watermelon Hunt again, either."

"What about last winter? At Beaches' Pond? With my dog? You were pretty tricky then!"

"Okay, maybe. But in a good way."

"Hey, I'm not saying you're tricky in a bad way. I'm just saying you're tricky."

"Okay, okay."

Kim agreed with Dennis only to put an end to the conversation. It wasn't pleasant to be called "tricky," but as he thought about the incident Dennis mentioned, he realized that perhaps Dennis was right.

Fresh Ice at Beaches' Pond

It had occurred at the beginning of the winter before. It was late November and the nights had turned very cold, and the days too for that matter. The sun dipped lower in the south every day and everybody knew there would soon be snow, lots of it, and the shatteringly cold days of deep, dark winter.

"Hey Kim!" Dennis had whispered in class at school. "Beaches' Pond is frozen!"

Dennis sat in the row across from Kim, and slightly ahead of him. In those days, kids at school sat in desks in rows and could not talk in class, but there was a lot of whispering and sign language that went on, and the girls passed a lot of notes around.

Kim nodded back as if to say "I know" and put his head down to continue studying fractions. They could get in a lot of trouble for talking in class.

Later, they met in the hallway.

"Let's go test the ice after school," Dennis suggested and they quickly agreed to meet near the highway with their bikes.

Beaches' Pond was beside the highway that ran north out of Caraway. It was actually a dugout, a huge, long excavation made when the highway was constructed. Big road-building machines had scooped countless loads of dirt and clay that was used to build up the highway. That was years earlier and now the dugout had become ringed with reeds and bulrushes and resembled a natural pond. Red-winged blackbirds lived in the growth along the shore and every summer there were a few families of ducks there too.

Why it was called Beaches' Pond? Kim had no idea. There was certainly no beach and the banks were steep and slippery so nobody went there in the summer. Too dangerous! But when winter arrived, Beaches' Pond was the biggest open-air skating rink around.

They could have walked, but Beaches' Pond was most of a mile north of town and more like two miles from where they lived. They had a choice: a long cold walk or a short cold bike ride. They slung their skates over the handlebars of their bikes, balanced their hockey sticks sideways, and headed north.

"Come on, Biff!" Dennis had called to his dog. Biff was big and black and, being a good dog, would trot right along beside them without wandering into traffic.

"Aw, there's already kids there," Kim observed as they approached the pond. He loved being the first to arrive on a patch of fresh, clear ice.

"Must've got a ride," Dennis said, for there were no bikes. "Lucky." The other kids had been dropped off from a car and would be picked up again later. Dennis and Kim always seemed to take the hard way.

The other kids were sitting on frozen clods of mud at the side of the huge pond and lacing up their skates. The pond was a wonderful sight, gleaming in the sun like a sheet of steel. It was frozen, rock hard, but there was almost no snow yet, just a little dusting of white visible out on the black fields beyond.

The ice was a clear, clean surface. No one had skated on it yet and there wasn't a single mark on it.

Kim and Dennis traded a glance, for they each understood that they wanted to be first! They hurried as they laced up their skates, but still the other kids beat them. A little boy, about six years old, ventured slowly out from the shore. Then he stopped and returned. The other kids skated out too, but they didn't go far.

Kim looked at Dennis again. He whispered. "Hah! They're scared. They're going to stay close to the side . . . "

Dennis nodded and grinned, then added, "You think it's thick enough?"

"Well, we'll find out, won't we?" Kim replied, though underneath their conversation was a current of fear. The first, fresh ice of the year was terrific — but was it thick enough?

The other kids, or their dads, had broken a hole through the ice about twenty feet from shore. Water still oozed out of it and was freezing around the edges. Kim and Dennis, with their skates on now, went out to inspect this test hole. As they got close, the ice made no sound. A good sign.

Kim bent on one knee and took off one of his mitts. He plunged his bare hand into the freezing water and felt down the side of the hole.

"I'd say about four inches," he reported to Dennis, as he shook the water off quickly and jammed his hand into his armpit to warm it up.

Dennis tried too.

"More like five," he said.

"Hmmm," said Kim. He wasn't sure.

They had to be careful, because it was known, for sure, that Beaches' Pond was very deep. In the summer, if you threw a big rock way out, it went "spe-LUNK," the sound that indicated deep water.

Kim and Dennis both knew if they fell through that ice, and could not be rescued, they would drown. The absence of skate marks anywhere far out meant that no one had gone all the way around, or across the middle, to test the ice. But the other kids had been dropped off and just *left* there. Surely their parents wouldn't do that if it was dangerous . . . And they had broken a test hole. Did that mean it was okay?

Kim and Dennis had their hockey sticks, which would probably help in case of a breakthrough, and there were the other kids nearby to run for help, but they were a long way from the edge of Caraway and even quite a ways off the highway.

"We better stay close to shore," Dennis said.

Kim nodded. The brilliant, low-angled sunshine lit up each plume of their steamy breath.

"And let's stay together," Dennis added.

Kim nodded again.

"Did you bring a puck?" he asked.

"I thought you were bringing the puck," Dennis said.

Kim sighed. Neither of them had brought a puck, but it didn't matter much. Beaches' Pond, because it was so big, was more for skating than hockey. They could always shoot around a chunk of ice or a frozen piece of dirt. What they really wanted to do was skate all the way to the end and back!

But was it frozen, enough, to hold them?

Kim skated a little way beyond all the other kids. He turned a big smooth curve and his skates cut into fresh frozen ice.

GAR-RUNK, went the ice.

"Watch it!" Dennis yelled.

Kim quickly scooted closer to shore.

"I don't know," he said. "I thought I could feel it move."

It was Dennis's turn. He ventured out about as far as Kim had and turned a circle to come back.

The ice emitted more sounds: spanning, cracking, shifting sounds that were hard to describe. Sort of like metal wires being stretched to the breaking point. And GAR-RUNK.

Dennis skittered quickly back to the shore next to Kim.

"Gee," he said in a worried voice.

"Hard to tell if it's adjusting to our weight, or about to break," Kim observed.

"Yeah. Maybe we should go back."

Without answering, Kim took another big, curving turn out on open ice.

GAR-RUNK!! went the ice, louder this time, and Kim quickened his speed to shore. He was losing his nerve to go for a big sweeping skate. It just seemed too dangerous.

Then a strange thing happened.

Biff the dog was on the ice too, and was chasing the puck in the other kids' hockey game. Suddenly, he lost interest in that and rejoined Kim and Dennis. And he started to chase Kim!

"Hey Biff! Stop it!" Dennis called, but the dog ignored him.

"Biff, go away!" Kim ordered the dog, but Biff kept chasing him. It was strange, because Biff was usually friendly and easygoing.

It was simple to get out of the way. Kim could turn and Biff couldn't. When the dog yelped and woofed and charged, Kim just let him get up some speed, then cut a corner one way or the other. Biff skittered along the ice, pawing with his claws and churning his legs as he tried to stop, the way the cartoon characters on TV did when they ran off a cliff. Since he could not get any traction, as if he were on a waxed floor, Biff slid quite a long way before he could stop and get going again.

"Biff! What's wrong with you?" Kim called to the dog, but he charged at Kim again.

"Dennis!" Kim yelled in frustration, and Dennis called again, but the dog ignored his owner's commands.

"Maybe it's the skates!" Dennis called. "They're making him kind of kooky!"

It was sort of funny at first, but Biff really seemed angry. He looked like he would bite if he ever caught up to Kim, so there was nothing to do but keep skating to draw Biff along, then dodge out of the way and watch the dog go flying out onto the ice.

GAR-RUNK, went the ice, this time because Biff was out on a new spot.

"Hey . . . wait a sec," Kim said under his breath.

Biff was a good-sized dog. He probably weighed as much as a kid!

Kim skated to a new part of the pond and Biff charged after him. Kim suddenly cut a hard turn out of the way and Biff careered past him out onto a fresh patch of ice.

GAR-RUNK went the ice — but it didn't break.

Kim repeated the move and was able to slingshot the dog out onto another untested part of the pond.

GAR-RUNK the ice moaned again as Biff clawed at it helplessly.

"Hey, what if *he* falls in?" Dennis called, then quickly changed his mind. "Aw, he's a dog — he could swim long enough for us to get him out."

So Kim did it again. And again. Each time, the ice seemed to complain like a living thing — but it held firm.

"Biff the Explorer!" yelled Dennis triumphantly, now very proud of his death-defying dog. "What a neat trick!"

Kim was able to check the entire pond. Finally Biff lost interest in charging Kim and went over to chase the puck again.

Every time I do something clever he thinks it's a trick, Kim thought to himself as he watched Dennis skate, but he smiled too. Dennis was like that.

The huge, flat, gleaming pond stretched away from Kim. He skated hard now, swishing left and right. He went all the way to the far end, which was a hundred and fifty yards at least, and swooped in a big, big curve around it.

The ice still groaned and gar-runked, but Kim knew it was just adjusting to his weight.

Beaches' Pond was frozen! Frozen good and solid, and thanks to that crazy dog Biff, Kim and Dennis had been the first kids to skate it, end to end.

The Super Cub

"**R**est!" Dennis called out. They both set the stretcher down in a hurry and stepped away from it.

Their arms and shoulders were on fire! Kim rolled his head around and tried to lift his arms over his head to move the muscles around. He couldn't. His stretched-out arms wouldn't go that high. He wished he had a chunk of that Beaches' Pond ice to cool down his forehead.

"Ohhhhhawwwww," Dennis moaned. "How far do you think we've come?"

"Not very far," Kim answered matter-of-factly. "Good thing it's basically flat," he added, trying to look on the bright side.

"Yeah," Dennis agreed. "A hill would stop us cold."

The forest was level and undisturbed by deep gullies or steep rises, but they still had to avoid thickets of underbrush and fallen trees. It made for a lot of detouring along their path and it was a challenge for Kim to keep them on their steady southwesterly bearing. He had to do it, however, since he was sure that Dennis didn't really give their direction any thought and was relying on him.

After letting the pain in their arms take them over for a minute, they both gravitated back to the stretcher, not to pick it up again, for it was far too soon, but to have a close look at Matt.

"Think we should pry his eyes open?" Dennis asked.

"No."

"Poke him?"

"Go ahead."

Dennis prodded and poked Matt gently. No response. He also blew air over his face and Matt subconsciously rolled the other way to avoid it — "That's a good sign," Dennis said — but he didn't wake up.

Kim looked at his older brother. *Boy oh boy*, he thought, *too bad you don't have a badge for flying. You could have swooped down to that ledge and landed like a bird. Instead — this.*

Matt's arms were bare, because they all wore T-shirts, but Kim could easily visualize Matt's cub sweater, the kind they all wore throughout the winter when they attended their weekly cubs' meeting.

Matt's sweater was special, because it was adorned with the most badges and the most stripes of any cub in the pack. He had so many proficiency badges that the sleeve of his sweater was a solid, crusted tube and their mom had been obliged to start sewing them on the other arm too.

Matt was a signaler, an observer, a woodworker, a swimmer, a guide, a team player, a first-aider, a canoe man, an explorer, a hiker, a camper, a knotter, an athlete, a marksman, a prospector, a tracker, and more.

Kim, on the other hand, was a guide and a reader.

Matt also had two stars on his cub cap. They were supposed to be like two wolf eyes boldly looking out. Kim had no stars and that meant, as a cub anyway, he was blind.

The clincher, however, of Matt's complete supremacy in the Caraway cub pack was his status as a senior sixer. The leaders in the pack were called sixers, which meant they had two yellow stripes on the left arms of their sweaters and were in charge of a group of cubs.

But Matt had *three* yellow stripes. Akela had promoted him to senior sixer, the only one in the Caraway pack, and that made him the top cub. The pack was his kingdom and there, he was the ruler.

There were constant challenges to Matt's position, not so much over the formal markings like the sixer stripes, but in the never-ending series of contests and games that were the meat and potatoes of every cub meeting. This was before now, and some things were different. Contests weren't staged to make everyone feel good and pronounce each participant worthy just for showing up. They were designed to produce a winner and, more often than not, it was Matt.

Chicken fighting was a popular contest in the cub hall, perhaps because it could easily be staged inside on the bare hardwood floor.

To chicken fight, the cubs hopped around on one foot, holding the other foot up with one hand. That left one hand free to go on the attack. The strongest boys with the best balance lasted the longest. Kim might knock over one of the tenderfoots before someone Matt's age, or Matt himself, hopped by and sent him flying to the floor. Then he sat in a circle with the other defeated cubs and cheered until only one was left hopping around. If it was Matt, as it often was, Kim cheered loudly because he was proud of his brother, even if his brother was never very thrilled to have him around.

Matt had other duties that Kim, and most of the other cubs, were not allowed to perform. He was the sixer who took down the flag and folded it up when cubs was almost finished for that week.

The cub pack had given in their ten cents of dues. They had told about the good turns they had done that week or, as Kim often suspected, had made up a really good story about a good turn they had done! Sometimes he had to resort to that himself.

And, finally, all the cubs promised to "Be Prepared."

They had squatted and chanted "Dib! dib! dib! dob! dob! dob! I'll do my best!" in a big circle. All that was left was to sing *God Save The Queen*, take down the flag and walk home.

O Canada had been invented by then and it was — at least Kim thought it was — the official national anthem, but there was another song that the cubs sang a great deal: *God Save The Queen*.

It often produced a few snickers around the circle of singing boys, because it was hard to imagine Queen Elizabeth in any danger.

"God save the Queen *from what?*" Dennis might whisper over to Kim in the middle of the song. There was a picture of the Queen at the front of the cub hall and, as in all her pictures, she did not seem particularly happy, but not sad or frightened either. She just stared across the room at the big hairy moose head on the other wall. The moose stared back. Kim often thought they should sing *God Save The Moose*, since of course it had been shot and stuffed before it was mounted on their wall.

There was another funny part in the song and Dennis, Tommy, and even Kim sometimes pretended it was raining when they sang "Long to-oo reign oo-ver us . . . " as if the Queen were raining on them. They all knew reign meant "rule", but they did it anyway, always very careful to make sure Akela and Baloo didn't see, for they would not be amused.

Besides, Kim wasn't really sure about those words. Did the Queen rule over them? What was she doing in Canada anyway? She was English.

And she was *everywhere*. It was always that same picture, where she wore a banner like Miss Canada, which was odd because she was really Mrs. England.

It was in the Post Office, the Legion Hall, the cub hall, every single classroom in school, the principal's office, the Curling Rink, even over the candy stand in the Arena. And she was on the back of every coin and the front of every dollar and the face of every stamp. Queen, Queen, Queen! It was a Queen-erama!

Kim would sigh at the end of cubs and salute anyway. The cub salute was special and it was neat — left-handed. They had to be the only kids anywhere who saluted like southpaws!

He sang along with the song and saluted the special cub salute, as his brother Matt, the Super Cub, lowered the flag. It was a different flag than now, too, a British one called the Union Jack, an explosion of blue and red and white crosses and slashes. Matt folded it in a special way and placed it in a wooden chest where it would stay until next week, when the cub pack would meet and howl and chicken fight again . . . "Ready? Kim — you ready?"

It was Dennis talking. Kim realized he had been daydreaming, but who could blame him? There was another painful slog ahead.

"Yeah, ready," he said. It was his turn on the front of the stretcher, so he got in position and, on Dennis's signal, they both lifted the load. It was as crushingly heavy as before and instantly the pain stabbed into both shoulders.

"Where's that Giant when you need him?" Dennis said from behind him.

"Who?"

"The Giant? Remember?"

Kim smiled as he stepped forward. Then he winced as the weight pulled on his arms and he decided to relive their encounter with the Giant last winter as a way of forgetting about the trial of hauling Matt through the forest.

"Remember?" he called back to Dennis. "Who could forget?"

THE GIANT

Kim had heard of the Giant long before he ever saw him.

"He's as big as a grown-up!" some kid wailed.

"You only come up to his shoulder!" another yelped.

And when Kim finally encountered the Giant, he saw it was true.

There he was, standing outside the Arena with a group of kids, and he was a good foot taller than all of them. He was as tall as a grown-up — and not skinny, either — and he was exactly twelve years old!

Kim and Bobbie had hauled their hockey bags toward the Arena with a feeling of dread, pure dread, trailing behind them like a rag on a string. It was their day to take on the Giant.

"Why do we have to play these guys, anyway?" demanded Dennis in the dressing room. "They're not even in our league."

"Yeah, who comes up with these exhibition games anyway?" Bobbie said loudly.

"We're gonna get creamed!" someone whined.

Kim sank down on the bench in the dressing room. It was true. They were gonna get creamed. He did not feel like a Giant killer and nobody else looked like they did either. His teammates all pulled on their hockey uniforms rather slowly that afternoon. "Caraway Cleaners" read the lettering on the front, because they were sponsored by the local dry cleaning business.

On the ice in the warm-up, the Giant seemed to be in the wrong game. He was bigger than the referee! He was huge!

He turned out to be a gentle Giant. He was not rough or dirty. He did not trip or crosscheck. He didn't have to! Whenever he got the puck, Kim's team just got out of the way. The Giant skated up the ice and shot, a clean, hard shot from his long, straight stick.

If he hit the net, it was almost certainly a goal. The goalie was Kim's friend Lloyd and, understandably, he cringed visibly inside his equipment each time the Giant bore down on him. He actually seemed to shrink.

A few times Lloyd dared to make a save off the Giant's shots and they could hear him yelping in pain from beneath his makeshift mask. But most often, he just got out of the way and once he even turned around and ducked. He was being a chicken, but no one blamed him.

After the first period, the score was eight to one for the Giant's team and one of their players — guess who? — had seven goals.

It was pretty quiet in the Cleaners' dressing room. They were experiencing a distinct shortage of team spirit. Kim caught his breath and remembered the story of David and Goliath. He looked around and did not see a slingshot. Just as well! He didn't have the courage to face the Giant alone anyway and, all together, the Cleaners barely had the courage to go back out on the ice.

All the adults in the crowd, however, were very impressed by the Giant. More people than usual had turned out to see Kim's team and they were witnessing a good old-fashioned drubbing.

At the end of the second period, it was fifteen to two and the Giant had twelve goals. Bobbie and another of Kim's friends, Alan, had scored for the Cleaners, and Kim had an assist on Bobbie's goal. A comeback was unlikely but Alan yelled, "Come on, you guys!" in the dressing room. They all knew they could do better.

They *did* have scoring chances when the Giant was on the bench, and soon in the third period they had two more goals. Alan made a nice pass to Kim and he just shot it at the net. It slipped between the goalie's pads. Then Alan got a breakaway and made a crafty deke to score, so it was only eighteen to four at that point.

Then it happened. The Giant was back on the ice and nobody dared go near him. No, he wasn't mean, just so darned big he only had to give the opposition players a shove and they went flying.

But Alan wasn't giving up, and Kim and Bobbie, his linemates, were doing better too. They were shooting hard; they were starting to click. It made the Giant try harder, too, and the consequences were soon evident.

On one play, he just plain ran Bobbie over. Just crushed him. Then he collided with Kim and sent him flying through the air. He cruised behind the Cleaners' net, chasing the puck and bumped — only bumped — Alan from behind.

Alan was a little small for his age, though a scrappy and tenacious player. Next to the Giant, the size difference was even more pronounced. Alan fell face-first into the boards. Crack! In a flash, he lost a tooth. One of his big front teeth was broken right off, halfway down. Kim came to a stop beside them just as the whistle blew and Alan fell to the ice. Blood poured from his mouth. Thinking quickly, Kim scraped up a pile of snow with his skate and offered it to Alan, who jammed it in his mouth to try to stop the bleeding and quell the pain. The snow quickly stained bright red.

The Giant stood there and looked upset. It was not his fault, that much was plain, and Kim realized instantly that this sort of thing happened to the Giant, and his opposition, quite often.

This was before now, and some things were different. Kids did not wear masks over their faces. They wore mouthguards, but they were on the outside, held onto the helmet by a strap. Alan's strap had slipped and that's why his tooth was broken off. The coach and the referee helped him off and he gave in to the pain and was crying.

Kim turned circles on the ice and seethed with anger, but he felt helpless and afraid too. What could he do? What could anyone do against a Giant?

The final minutes ticked off the clock and Kim and the rest of the Cleaners just tried to stay out of the Giant's way. When the buzzer sounded to end the game, Kim was never so glad to get off the ice in his life.

The final score was twenty-one to four or, as some of the kids joked later, Giant eighteen, Cleaners four, because the Giant scored eighteen goals.

"The Cleaners got cleaned," Bobbie joked afterward in the dressing room. Nobody laughed.

Lloyd, the goalie, tore off his equipment and threw it in his bag.

"That was the stupidest game I ever played!" he said in a loud voice. "Look at this!" Lloyd held up his arms for everyone to see. They were covered with blue bruises.

He swore and added, in colourful language, how dumb the coach was to arrange a game like that.

The coach, Mr. Barnaby, did not come into the room right away. When the door opened and closed, Kim and the other Cleaners could see him out in the hallway joshing and joking with the other coach about how the Giant was an amazing player and would "Go a long way."

Kim quickly took off his equipment and stuffed it in his bag. Dressing rooms were wet, stinky places after a game and he just wanted to get out of there. He knew he was supposed to say something like "We'll get 'em next time!" but he didn't have the heart for it. Instead, he wondered how much Alan's mouth hurt.

As Kim lingered near the concession stand, waiting for Dennis and Bobbie, the Giant's team left their dressing room and headed for the door. They would be driving back to their town soon with a huge, lopsided victory under their belts. Most of the kids were laughing and joshing around, but Kim noticed that the Giant was rather quiet. He didn't seem to be having much fun and, instead, looked quite lonely.

Maybe he feels guilty that he broke Alan's tooth, Kim thought. He hoped so.

In a few minutes, Dennis and Bobbie joined him and they all walked out with their sticks and skates slung over their shoulders, and their hockey bags too. Kids didn't get driven around to games very much then. They had to walk. It was already dark, even though it wasn't suppertime yet. Kim could even see the Northern Lights glowing near the horizon.

"Hey, know what?" Bobbie said out of nowhere. "We actually beat that team!"

"What are you talking about?" Kim said. Bobbie could be a real wiseguy sometimes.

"That big guy scored eighteen goals. It ended up twenty-one to four. Take away his eighteen goals and they really only got three. We won four-three!"

The Switcheroo

Even now, Kim smiled at Bobbie's twisted reasoning. Old Brushcut Bobbie could come up with an "angle" like that on lots of things. It was a kind of talent, Kim realized, to always be able to see things differently. Especially if you could imagine a twenty-one to four loss was a win!

They slogged slowly along with the stretcher between them.

Kim could hear the sound of Dennis panting behind him. Both of them had fallen silent, because it was too tiring to carry the load and talk at the same time. It was sunny and hot too, but luckily the canopy of trees overhead provided almost unbroken shade. Now and then they had to cross an open clearing and, in a few moments, the sun baked them like bread.

Kim tried to breathe evenly and prayed to be cooler. He was sweating all over and it helped cool him off, a little, and he also tried to imagine he was cool, that a nice breeze was making him cool, and that he wasn't so darned hot!

He tried to adopt Bobbie's tactic of making something seem the opposite of what it was — so he deliberately placed himself back in the coldest day of his entire life.

Ninety Below

That day, it had taken Kim a few minutes to discover how cold it really was, because at first he couldn't see the thermometer.

The window that afforded him the view was completely frosted over — on the inside. Getting a thermometer had been Kim's idea, because he liked to check the temperature, and the device was safely out of the sun on the north side of the house where it should be.

Normally, he could just drag over a chair and stand on it to get a reading, but this morning it wasn't so easy. Kim had to hold his hand against the ice on the window, and blow warm breath on it, and wipe it again, to make a little hole in the ice. Then he could see through.

It was pitch black outside, even though it was eight o'clock in the morning, and it would be pitch black for almost another hour, but Kim could read the thermometer by the light from inside the house.

He had to look way at the bottom to find the red mercury. It was down there at forty-five below. Celsius degrees had been invented, but nobody used them yet. Temperatures were listed in Fahrenheit degrees, though forty-five below is about the same on both scales. Very, very cold.

"Pretty cold," Kim mumbled to himself. He noticed something else. The bare branches of the trees outside were faintly visible and they were vibrating back and forth really fast. The windows were good and tight, so they didn't shake, but obviously there was a howler of a wind out there, coming straight out of the north.

Kim retreated to the kitchen and quickly crawled under the table where one of the heat vents was located. When the furnace was on, which was pretty well constantly in such weather, it blew nice warm air up his back.

Kim stayed there for a few minutes before getting some breakfast. *That's probably the warmest I'll be all day*, he remarked to himself.

"Let's see what the radio says," his mom said to nobody in particular and switched it on to get the forecast. His dad had already left for work, walking, because on a day like this it was difficult to get a car started and keep it warm.

As usual, the radio's weather information was for the large city further south, so it didn't reflect what was going on in Caraway. The radio said it would be no colder than thirty-five below in the city. Then it added, "Colder in outlying areas." *That must include Caraway*, Kim thought.

"With northerly winds thirty to fifty miles per hour," the radio continued. It was right about that part.

"You'd better put on your long johns," Kim's mom said. Snow suits hadn't been invented yet.

Kim didn't really like wearing long underwear — long johns — because they were not comfortable once he got back inside. They were hot and tended to get wet and soggy, but he could tell the suggestion was "not for discussion." Kim glanced outside and saw snow whipping straight sideways down the street. Long johns suddenly seemed like a fine idea.

Kim went downstairs to get dressed to go to school. The house was quite warm, but not the basement floor. He skipped over the cold tiles to the bedroom he shared with Matt and got his toes onto the carpet. Warmer!

As he dressed, he did a quick calculation. A few years before, the weather report had started talking about wind chill. It was a recent invention, apparently. Generally, all you had to do was add the temperature and the wind speed together. So it was really simple: the temperature was forty-five below. The wind was, say, thirty miles an hour. So the wind chill was seventy-five below.

Matt came in to the bedroom and also began searching for his long johns.

"Dad said the radio said the wind is blowing at forty-five miles an hour," Matt reported. It seemed that, in what amounted to a weather emergency, Matt was willing to talk to his little brother more than usual.

Kim put on two pairs of socks and the addition snapped together in his head. That meant it was *ninety below*! He considered a third pair of socks, but knew it wouldn't help. Too many socks actually made you feel colder somehow. He would tough it out with two pairs.

Matt was first out the door. His school was further than Kim's and in a different direction and, even in such extreme conditions, there wasn't really any thought given to them walking together. Kim would be on his own and he knew it.

He thanked his lucky stars that he only had to walk one long block, cross the highway, and he would be there, on the school grounds at least. It would be straight into the wind. If he could get that far, he would make it.

At the door, Kim's mom checked his tuque and pulled it down a little further. His parka did not have a hood. She wrapped a scarf around his face, then opened the door for him, pushing hard against the wind to do it. Wham! The door blew shut again.

The second Kim was outside, the cold attacked. It froze the skin on his cheeks and made water pour from his eyes.

That's dangerous, he said to himself.

At forty below, you could see water freeze on an ice rink. It was as if a sweeping hand of cold passed over it and, presto, it was frozen.

Kim knew the same thing would happen to his tears. They would freeze into ice in a snap and then do the same to his skin. At ninety below, he wondered if the frozen tears might glue his eyes shut.

Kim immediately turned away from the wind and wiped his eyes. He thought he got all the tears, because he could see them frozen on the outside of his mitts. Cold invaded his parka from the loose underneath edge and ran up his back. The wind knifed through his tuque. His ears hurt. The rubber outsides of his boots froze stiff.

He had not taken a single step.

There was no time to lose. Kim clamped his hands over his ears, because he was sure he'd get an earache unless they had extra protection.

He started walking backward toward the street.

His mitts kept his ears warm, but raising his arms created another problem. It made his parka shift up and now a painful tickle of wind licked at his waist. He hunched over and kept slogging backwards.

The wind was strong and stiff and constant. He felt like he was pushing backward into a wall. It made a steady hissing and howling noise, but he could safely cross the street facing backward because in this weather cars made a much louder noise. He could hear them crunching on the frozen snowy streets from half a block away.

No cars, Kim said to himself. He strode backward across the street.

The long way was up the front of the street, along the sidewalk. The short way, the route he usually took, was up the back alley. It would take maybe a minute less.

He took the back alley.

What if he fell and started to freeze?

There were lights on in most of the houses. Kim figured he could always run to one and pound on the back door to be let in.

There was also the ghostly blue-green glow of the street lights. There were a few in the back alley, so he felt safe enough.

However, there was more snow than he had counted on, blown down into the alley by that forty-five mile an hour wind from the north. Kim struggled along backward, lifting his boots high on each step and plunging them into the snow. He kept the backyard fences steady on his left side and tried to make a line with his steps. That way, he knew he was going straight. On the other side was a park, and he didn't want to wander out into it and start turning circles.

His waist was freezing! For a few seconds, he took his mitts off his ears, so his parka would shift down and warm up his waist. But only a few seconds. Searing cold knives stabbed into his ears — he quickly put his mitts back over them. He also had to jam his wrist against his scarf now and then to warm up his face. He had to gulp a mouthful of air for each breath, warm it up in his cheeks, then breathe it. He didn't dare breathe through his nose.

He had passed most of the houses along the alley and the rattling of the crosswalk sign told him he was close to the highway. He took a peek each way, receiving a cold slap on the face each time.

Even the cars looked careful in the cold. Just like him, they crept along very slowly, apparently afraid to expose themselves to the wind by going fast.

There was only one car to stop for him when he arrived at the crosswalk. He angled sideways enough for the driver to see him.

He couldn't see inside the car — the windows were almost entirely frosted over on the inside — but he knew he was spotted, because the car slowed to a stop. Its tires crunched on the frozen snowy road with a painful, awful sound.

Kim skittered backward across the highway, sliding a bit with each step, but not too much. That would surely open other cracks in his armour and let in more icicles of wind. The snow swept over the highway like a sheet being pulled over it, again and again.

"Almost there," he muttered to himself. "Just another minute through the parking lot then — inside!"

Then he noticed nobody *else* was there. No town kids coming from other directions. No school buses bringing in the farm kids. Only a few lonely cars near the door.

Kim reached it and wrenched the door open with both hands. A huge suction of wind held the door back, but he got it open far enough to reverse the suction and use the wind to propel himself inside. He had to pull the door shut against the seething breath of the building, which suddenly seemed like a living thing.

He plunged through the second set of doors and immediately took off his tuque, his mitts, his scarf and his parka, tossing them to the floor. The only thing colder than being outside in ninety below weather was being inside in freezing cold clothes!

But where was everybody? He was early, but not that early.

Mr. Carruthers, the principal, appeared at the far end of the hallway. There was a janitor, too, and one teacher, Mrs. Knowlton. All three wore their parkas inside.

Mr. Carruthers made a flipping motion toward Kim, as though he were fending off an eager puppy.

"Go home! Go home!" he called. "School's closed!"

Mr. Carruthers and Mrs. Knowlton briskly disappeared into the main office. The janitor, who was not so worried looking, stopped near Kim and shook his head. But he had a smile on his face.

"None of the buses could run. Boiler's iffey. Nothing to do but go home," he said, giving Kim a wink.

Kim knew the wink meant, "You're lucky — you get the day off," but he didn't want the day off, really. He liked school, and staying home on a day this cold was very boring.

It would be too cold to be outside and, during the day, the television programs on both channels were awful. He decided he would undertake a very large drawing.

He plunked on his tuque, tied on his scarf, and prepared to head back out into the blizzard.

Again, the wind rushed at him like a demon, but he hunched down and stepped quickly. This time he could see ahead and the wind was with him. He was at the highway in half a minute and, taking a quick look each way, easily skittered across the icy surface with the howling gale blowing him like a sailboat.

His boot holes in the back alley were still visible, although the storm had almost filled them with fine, windblown snow. Plunking his boots into each one, almost running now, he quickly retraced his steps.

It was easy! The wind drove him along like a parent's hand hurrying him somewhere, late, and there was even a glimmer of light in the whitish grey swirling cloud that passed for sky that day.

Kim reached the street he had crossed first and then he made his big mistake.

He started running. He had only a few steps to go — why not run?

He plunged ahead — only a few seconds left — and suddenly his carefully insulated crouch was destroyed and the searingly cold air grabbed him everywhere! It was on his stomach, up his back, inside his tuque, and freezing his lungs!

Mistake! Kim screamed to himself, but now he was committed. He kept running and made the other side of the street. He lunged up the two little steps to his own walk and put his head down for the charge to the door. But he caught one boot on the other and crashed face-first onto the sidewalk! His tuque was knocked off!

In an instant, his entire head froze. Kim grabbed the tuque and jammed it over his skull as quickly as possible — his ears were exploding — and crawled three feet before rising up and throwing himself on the outside aluminum door. He pried it open, digging one of his boots into the gap and, fighting the wind for every inch, squeezed in and kicked the other door open as soon as he turned the handle.

In winter, it was pretty close to criminal to leave a door open, so Kim eased the outside door shut — the wind helped — then put his back into shutting the thick, inside door. He fell backward against the stairs leading up to the kitchen entrance and shed his parka, tuque, and mitts.

"What happened to you?" his mom said, entirely unconcerned, as she appeared above him.

"'S cold," was all Kim could manage.

"Watch you don't freeze your cheeks," she replied, stooping to hold her hands against his face for a moment. Her palms felt like hot irons.

Kim used his own hands to warm his toes, which were dangerously chilled, but not frozen. He dreaded frozen feet, because it hurt like crazy when they warmed up again. More than once he had found himself outside, dancing in the snow to cool off frozen feet that had started to warm up. *That* was agonizing.

No sooner had Kim rewarmed himself than the two back doors opened again and a strange, frosted, ghost-like figure appeared: Matt. Kim yielded the space so his brother could get out of his parka and boots.

Their mom glanced outside, past the thermometer, and into the blizzard wind.

"Cold?" she asked.

"Naw," Matt said. "Not really."

OFF COURSE!

The trick was working. Kim felt cooler than before, quite cold in fact, almost as if he were standing in the basement in front of the open door of the freezer . . .

"Kim! Kim — set it down!" Dennis yelled from behind.

"What?" Kim asked dreamily.

"You're waving around — put the stretcher down!"

Kim suddenly tripped and almost fell. Dennis was right. He was going to fall over!

"Easy . . . easy . . . put it down," Dennis said in a coaxing voice. Kim did what he was told. He was in no position to argue. They set the stretcher on the ground and Kim stepped away — then fell right to the ground.

"You okay?" Dennis asked, hurrying over to him. "You were staggering from side to side like you were gonna faint."

"I was thinking about something," Kim stammered. "Something cold."

He put his hand on his forehead, which was actually burning hot. His arms and shoulders were so sore they almost didn't feel like anything anymore.

"Take a rest. You were delirious," Dennis said bluntly, then his gravelly voice softened a bit. "I don't blame you."

They sat on the ground for a few minutes, too tired to say anything. Kim had never been so exhausted in his entire life. After a time, Dennis spoke.

"How much farther you think it is?"

"Don't know."

"How much longer you think we can carry him?"

"Not very far."

"Yeah."

Kim looked his older brother over. Matt was still unconscious, though occasionally he shifted around. *Wake up!* Kim screamed inwardly. *We're at the end of our rope, Matt!* He resented his brother intensely at that moment. Matt was always so in control, always running things, always right — except about who threw that rock — and when he was wrong, he could still enforce his opinion, because he was bigger.

"You think he'll remember this?" Kim asked.

"I hope so!" Dennis retorted and Kim managed a little grin, for he felt the same way. *You* better *remember what we're doing for you*, he said soundlessly to Matt.

Kim struggled to his feet to get a sense of where they were. He walked a few paces each way and suddenly it hit him . . . "Hey!" he said, scrambling up a tiny rise nearby. It gave him a view — of a little pond!

"Hey, there's a pond here!" he called back to Dennis.

"Yeah!" Dennis yelled and in a flash appeared, running, toward the little body of water, which was more like a dugout. The water in it was brown-coloured. Dennis didn't care. He charged headlong toward it, paused to remove his shoes and socks, and ran in until he fell right over.

"It's great! Come in!" Dennis called, but Kim hesitated, not because the water was dirty, although it certainly was, but because the pond meant something very bad to him.

They were *not* where he thought they were. They were off course!

"Whyn'tcha come in?" Dennis yelled. "Cool off!"

Dennis splashed around like a duck, not at all concerned that he was getting all his clothes soaked and stained. Finally, Kim joined him, reasoning that he might as well take a dip. He too removed his shoes and socks and plunged in. The water was fantastic! But . . .

"Uh, Dennis," Kim said after they had both splashed each other furiously.

"What . . . ?"

"This pond isn't where it's supposed to be."

"What do you mean?"

"I recognize it. I was here last year on a march."

Dennis looked at him, concerned.

"I'm afraid I got us lost."

"How can we be lost if you recognize the pond? That means you know where we are. You always know where you are!"

"Well, I think I do. I was wrong."

"Okay, so what?" Dennis didn't seem too concerned now. "So where are we?"

Kim sighed.

"We might be further from camp than when we started out."

"*What!*"

"Sorry . . . "

"Kim, that's really bad!"

"I know. Sorry. But look, I'm not really sure. I think it means we didn't go in a straight line, the way I wanted to. We've probably taken a bend, like this." Kim held up his arm and bent it at the elbow about a third of the way into his chest.

Dennis licked his lips and squinted. "But you know where we are now, is that right?"

"Yes. I'm sure now."

"You're *sure?*"

"Yes."

"Well," Dennis shrugged, determined not to be bothered by the news that he had just hauled Matt the long way around, "that's okay. That's better than being totally lost."

"Sorry."

"Oh, stop saying that! We're not really worse off than before."

"You got a talent for looking on the bright side."

"Good for me," Dennis smirked. "If you don't look on the bright side, you're looking on the dark side and then where are ya?"

"In the dark."

"Exactly."

Dennis slogged out of the "pond," which was really more of a mudhole after all. "Let's wet down Matt. We shouldn't let him get too hot."

They drip-dried themselves, then dried their feet completely so they could put their socks and shoes back on, dry, since squishy feet were the worst. Then they soaked their shirts and traipsed back to Matt and gave him the once-over.

Kim was amazed that Dennis was so forgiving for his incredible error in directions. He was supposed to be the kid who never got lost! The kid who always knew where he was! He told Dennis so.

"Look," Dennis replied, "we've been chugging through the trees for at least an hour, we're both hotter than a two dollar pistol — I heard that somewhere — and despite the fact that you are supposed to know your directions, you're in a place you've hardly ever been. And you still recognize this mudhole from last year. That's not bad."

Kim appreciated the long speech from Dennis. He was not a kid who bothered to say that much about most things, so Kim could tell he really meant it. That, or he was getting worried. Dennis wasn't finished, either.

"You can get fooled by things. You can think something is one thing and it's the opposite. You can fool yourself or other guys can fool you. Remember last winter at the wrestling match?"

"Yeah!" Kim said loudly. "We were both fooled!"

"Seriously fooled," Dennis said. "Remember?"

"Yeah . . . " Kim replied, and he realized that Dennis was probably running stories and memories through his mind too, to get his thoughts away from the pain in his arms, shoulders, and neck.

"Well, that's what I mean," Dennis said. "The Crusher and Moby Joe had us going, right?"

"Yeah, sure did."

"So don't worry about it."

"Okay."

"You got your direction now?"

"Yup."

"Okay, let's go."

Dennis was at the front this time, with Kim at the back. They hoisted the stretcher and Kim gave Dennis his heading, and off they went, bent under the load with Kim — perhaps as Dennis had intended — remembering their encounter with The Crusher and Moby Joe.

THE CRUSHER VERSUS MOBY JOE

The Crusher slammed onto the wrestling mat right in front of Kim.

"Look out, Crusher!" Kim screamed, but it was too late.

Moby Joe stomped up beside The Crusher and kicked him in the ribs. The Crusher moaned and rolled around in pain.

Kim couldn't believe it. He kicked him right in the ribs! No fair!

But the referee did nothing. He had a little silver whistle in his mouth, but he didn't blow it. He just walked around, looking stupid. What good was a referee if he didn't do anything?

"Get up, Crusher, get up!" Kim yelled.

"Kick him again! Kill 'im!" Dennis yelled, even louder. He was next to Kim and they were both right beside the wrestling ring, so close they could lean in on the white canvas mat.

It was The Crusher versus Moby Joe at Wrestling Night in Caraway. And The Crusher was losing.

Would he ever get up? He rolled and moaned some more, while Moby Joe strutted around the ring like a rooster.

Kim couldn't *believe* that Dennis was hoping for Moby Joe. Their friend Lloyd was also there and *he* was on Moby Joe's side too! It was all so unfair!

"Crusher, get up!" Kim screamed again, only a few feet from The Crusher's ears, but the big wallowing wrestler seemed to be deaf. His eyes were closed tightly and his face was all scrunched up in pain.

"Aw, he's fakin' it!" Lloyd sneered. "He isn't hurt. Get up Crusher, you fake!"

The Crusher and Moby Joe were travelling wrestlers and this was their first time in Caraway. It was also Kim's first time at a wrestling match and he was pretty sure it would be his last. He didn't like it — so unfair! But it was impossible to turn away and Kim, like Dennis, took a feverish interest in the outcome.

Suddenly Moby Joe stopped his strutting. He lunged backward toward the ropes across the ring and leaned into them with all his considerable weight. The ropes bowed back, like a slingshot, then they hurled Moby Joe through the air and he landed right on The Crusher, hitting him a terrible blow to the head with his fist! Moby Joe's fat body sent a thumping BO-OOM echoing around the hall.

Kim was sickened by the sight of The Crusher's suffering, but yells and cheers came out of the darkness behind him and Dennis and especially Lloyd screamed in delight. The entire hall was dark, except for the wrestling ring, which was brightly lit, so bright that it almost did not seem real. But it was. It was horribly real to see The Crusher get hurt so badly right in front of Kim's face.

"Get up, ya big galoot!" someone yelled from the darkness and Lloyd joined the chorus.

"Come on Crusher, ya fake, get up!" Lloyd hollered and it finally set Kim off. He had to do something! He couldn't climb in the ring, of course, so acting strictly on impulse he turned to Dennis and Lloyd and said through clenched teeth: "I bet you The Crusher's going to win!"

They squealed in delight and Lloyd made a face and sort of stuck his tongue out at Kim. "Okay — it's all fake anyway!"

"Is not," Kim muttered to himself. He wasn't really sure, but Lloyd kept saying it was and Lloyd, being from across the tracks in Caraway, often knew about such things. Kim and Dennis took it seriously. It certainly looked real. Unlike some things that adults cooked up for kids, like Santa Claus and the Easter Bunny, this did not rely on creatures or events you couldn't see. It was right in front of them! And even in the un-real glare of the blinding lights, Kim was sure he knew horrible pain when he saw it.

Now The Crusher grabbed his stomach and moaned like he was going to throw up. Moby Joe paced around the ring like a bear in a cage. He even snarled. Then he grabbed The Crusher's arm. He pulled The Crusher up and The Crusher somehow staggered to his feet and wobbled forward. Moby Joe flung The Crusher into the ropes! The ropes bent like a slingshot again and hurled The Crusher back into the center of the ring, where Moby Joe jumped in the air sideways and threw a cross-body block. He hit The Crusher in the chest and they both crashed to the mat! BOO-OOOM!!

Moby Joe bounced right back to his feet. The Crusher slapped onto the canvas and bounced and stayed there, moaning again.

Lloyd and Dennis cackled with delight! Kim couldn't believe how unfair it was!

Moby Joe stomped right beside them, growling. He didn't see them, but Kim stepped back anyway and pulled his hands off the canvas. Surely Moby Joe would crush his fingers — and laugh! — if he stepped on them.

Kim noticed Moby Joe's boots as he tramped by, because they were a strange sort, a kind Kim had never seen before. The Crusher wore them too. They were black and laced right up to the knees. Their wrestling shorts were black and tight and shiny. Both Moby Joe and The Crusher were hairy and, in a strange way, fat but not fat. They both had brush cuts and mostly looked like the guy on *The Three Stooges*, the big dumb one.

The Crusher sat up and rubbed his head. He twitched like he had something in his eye. Suddenly a woman leapt into the ring. She had been around before, but Moby Joe had scared her off into the crowd. Her name was The Divine Madeleine and she had black eyebrows, red lipstick, and black bushy hair. She wore a shiny blue bathing suit costume and the same big black lace-up boots. She was The Crusher's friend and she was there to help him.

But no! Moby Joe turned and saw her. He roared over to chase The Divine Madeleine out of the ring again. She retreated through the ropes, but stayed at the edge of the ring, hanging on. She tried to reason with Moby Joe, but he refused to listen and growled at her some more.

The Crusher stood up finally, but he was wobbly. He shook his head like a dog trying to get away from a horsefly.

"Look out, Crusher!" Kim yelled, but again it was no use. Moby Joe came up behind The Crusher, threw a hammerlock on his head, and ran him into the corner of the ring where the ropes came together. The Crusher's whole body shook and he teetered backward, then his knees buckled and he fell flat on his back. His arms were stretched wide. He looked dead.

"Finish him off!" Lloyd yelled, though Moby Joe hardly needed encouragement. He boinged off the ropes again and flopped like a fish right on top of The Crusher, pinning him down. The referee dropped on all fours beside them and whacked his hand on the canvas.

"One . . . two . . . thr — "

But he didn't finish, because The Crusher came to life at the last second and snapped himself like a rope and bounced Moby Joe off! The Crusher got up! He looked okay!

"Yay, Crusher!" Kim yelled.

But Moby Joe was still strong and he paced around behind The Crusher, ready to leap. Then suddenly The Divine Madeleine ducked between the ropes and kicked Moby Joe in the back of the knee!

He fell forward just as The Crusher ran across and elbowed him in the stomach! Moby Joe fell over flat on his face!

"Yeah! Yeah!" Kim screamed, making a face at Dennis and Lloyd. Dennis was upset, because the tide had turned, but Lloyd thought it was all hilarious and laughed so hard he turned red.

The Crusher pounced on Moby Joe, yanked hard on his arm, and magically Moby Joe rose and was led around like a rubbery rag doll. The Crusher hurled him into the ropes. Moby Joe slingshot back out and The Crusher flung him across to the other ropes. Moby Joe rebounded again and

The Crusher leaned into the ropes to pick up speed for himself.

They were both sling-shotting across the ring, each going a different direction, but crisscrossing and missing each other. Then The Crusher adjusted his bounce and collided with Moby Joe, *hard*. They bonked heads and a hollow POCK! echoed through the hall, like the sound of two curling rocks hitting each other.

Moby Joe crashed to the canvas so hard he shook the entire ring. He was down!

Kim yelled wildly. The Crusher pounced on Moby Joe. The referee was there.

"One . . . two . . . three!"

It was over! The Crusher won!

Cheers and catcalls issued from behind the boys, from the dark, smoky crowd that filled the hall. People smoked a lot in public then and didn't give a hoot how much smoke they put out. By the time an event like Wrestling Night in Caraway was over, a flat blue cloud of smoke filled the Town Hall. It floated gently up and down about five feet above the crowd, sort of like the surface of an upside-down lake.

The Crusher was triumphant now. He stalked around the ring with his arms raised high in victory, creating eddies in the lake of smoke. Moby Joe, apparently stunned by the turn of events, could barely manage to sit up. He rubbed his head groggily, and didn't know where he was. The Divine Madeleine offered her hand to help him up, but he growled at her and she retreated.

"Get up, ya bum!" someone hollered from the darkness.

Slowly, with many exchanges of taunts among themselves and with the crowd, the wrestlers exited the ring. It took a good ten minutes, because several times they began yelling threats to each other and looked as if they'd go at it again.

Finally, when it appeared to be really over, Kim, Dennis and Lloyd went downstairs to the concession stand to get a pop. They were so worked up by the spectacle they had witnessed, they acted out the whole match all over again, but without tossing each other down.

"Boys," the man behind the counter said firmly and they settled down.

"Aw, The Crusher cheated," Dennis said flat out. "He had The Divine Madeleine working for him behind the scenes."

"Fake," said Lloyd.

"You're just mad 'cause you lost the bet," Kim retorted. The "bet" was for nothing, of course, except maybe bragging rights when they all told the story at school the next day.

"I'm going home," Lloyd announced as he noisily sipped the last of his pop up the straw and carefully returned the bottle to the man behind the counter. "See ya, suckers."

Lloyd found his parka on the coat rack and skipped up the stairs. He backed into the bar to open the doors and waved at them as a swooshing gust of frigid air blew into the entranceway. Kim and Dennis could feel it from twenty feet away. Winters were colder then.

"Let's help with the chairs," Kim had suggested and Dennis quickly nodded agreement. They ran up the stairs to the main hall.

It looked different with the lights on. The wrestling ring was still in the middle, but it didn't seem as important, especially since some men were beginning to take it apart. Even the hovering bank of smoke was less solid, less threatening with the glare of normal light piercing it.

There were dozens of chairs to be put away and Kim and Dennis pitched in. They did not expect any money. It was fun to help — noisy, clanging and boisterous — and when the floor was cleared off, they had their reward. It was a smooth, hardwood surface that was quite slippery, almost like Beaches' Pond. They took their shoes off and ran from one end to the other in sock feet, then slid to a stop. It was fun! Once, Dennis slid so hard he fell down and kept sliding on his pants.

It was quite complicated getting the ring apart, but several men were working on it and they were almost done. Kim thought he recognized one. Wasn't that The Crusher? He looked closer. It was! But he looked different. Very different, really. He was just a big man with a brush cut, helping take the ring apart.

A lady was supervising the job, but Kim did not recognize her. Then he listened closer. She *sounded* like The Divine Madeleine, but she didn't look like her, not at all. She also looked very normal. The black eyebrows were sort of like The Divine Madeleine's, but she wore no red lipstick and her hair was short and brown, not black and bushy.

Kim pointed her out to Dennis. "Isn't that The Divine Madeleine?"

Dennis studied the woman closely for a few seconds and also listened to her voice.

"Yeah, I think it is," Dennis concluded. "She must have been wearing a wig."

The ring was in pieces now and the men were carrying it out the back door of the hall. Kim and Dennis felt like part of the job now and tagged along to see it loaded.

In the back alley, there was a large pick-up truck with a long trailer hitched to it.

The two boys hung around in the doorway and felt refreshed by the cutting cold outside. Snow had begun to fall in big fluffy flakes. The last pieces of the ring were loaded and the doors of the trailer bolted shut.

A man arrived at the door from inside, who Kim recognized as one of the officials who ran the hall. With him were The Crusher and the lady who was probably The Divine Madeleine without her wig. They were joshing and joking. They all shook hands and the man from the hall handed The Crusher an envelope.

"That's the money," Dennis said and Kim nodded.

The Crusher opened the door of the truck, the lady got in, and the Crusher followed.

Kim took one step into the alley, away from the heat of the doorway, to see who else was in the truck. The snow, heavier now, made it tough to see. He peered close. The driver was Moby Joe!

Kim grabbed Dennis's arm and thrust his friend ahead so he could also see.

"Hey!" Dennis said, scowling in disappointment. He and Kim traded a quick look and they immediately knew Lloyd was right. It was a fake!

They stared down the alley again and could see the three people in the front of the truck. They were certainly *not*

152

disagreeing the way you would expect after they had been tossing each other around the wrestling ring.

Suddenly the whole alley turned red from the truck's and trailer's brake lights, then they turned onto the street and were gone.

Kim and Dennis had trouble looking at each other. They were both too embarrassed and ashamed. They had thought it was real and now they felt stupid!

"That Lloyd . . . " Kim muttered and he realized Lloyd would have lots of fun reporting to their friends that Kim and Dennis had been taken in.

"Yeah, we better show him a real wrestling match tomorrow," Dennis put in, which was not a bad suggestion. Lloyd was a big kid, but no fighter, and a few minutes rolling on the ground with Kim and Dennis on top of him might just keep his mouth shut.

"I don't get it," Kim said. "How can they do that? And what about all the adults here? Do they know it's a fake? They were cheering like it was life and death."

"At least it didn't cost too much," was all Dennis had to say.

They were both standing out in the alley, with snowflakes, now hard and falling in darting bits, bouncing off their shoulders. They shivered from the cold and ducked back into the open doorway. The man who ran the hall was there, with two other men.

"What did you think of the show there, sonny?" one said. Kim did not like being called "sonny'" and he could see they were probably going to rustle his hair, so he quickly ducked out of reach.

"I thought it was pretty unfair," Kim replied and was greeted by deep chuckles. Kim knew they would laugh, he just knew it.

"What he means," Dennis growled, "is that it was all a fake."

The men laughed much louder and Kim had answered his question. Clearly, the adults were in on it too. Had they been the only two in the entire hall who took it seriously?

The man who ran the hall wasn't finished with them. He stepped back and spoke like he was old and wise. "Well, I'm sure you'd agree it was a heck of a show, in any event."

They said nothing and ran back into the hall instead, sliding again on the bare hardwood floor and charging hard now for the exit doors. They grabbed their parkas off the hooks and flung them on in one motion and slammed backwards into the horizontal bars that opened the doors to the street.

It was a freezing cold snowy night, the kind where sound carries a long way. The street was silent until Kim and Dennis ran right down the middle of it, yelling at the top of their lungs, *"FAKE!"*

THE ROAD BACK

Kim smiled to think about it even now. They had felt the only way to get revenge on the wrestling match was to denounce it all over town.

"Fake . . . !" Kim said and he could see Dennis's shoulders shake ahead of him, as he laughed at the recollection. "Fake!" Dennis called back.

"Break!" Kim replied in a rhyme and they set the stretcher down again. Amazingly, his arms didn't hurt quite so much as before. *I might be getting used to this*, he thought.

Dennis turned around, also looking refreshed, and said, "I wonder how many other towns The Crusher and whathisname, Moby Joe, pulled their trick on — "

He didn't get to finish. Suddenly Matt said something!

They both leaned close to hear it — Matt muttering in his unconscious condition — "*Who's that? Who is that? Watch out!*"

His head rolled back and forth and he said it again. "*Who's that? Who is that? Watch out!*"

"Matt, wake up!" Kim yelled at him from close range. "Wake up!"

But it didn't work. Matt rolled a bit more and stopped muttering.

"Wonder what that means?" Dennis said. "Who's that? Who is that? Watch out!" he repeated.

"Yeah," Kim said vacantly. He had no idea. He just wished Matt would come to. It was pretty worrisome. His brother must have been knocked out for a good two hours now. Panic spiders ran around inside his stomach; he tried to squeeze them still.

"I'm going to check ahead," he said as calmly as he could. He was afraid about Matt's condition, not about where they were, for he was pretty sure of that now. His stupid direction error had cost them valuable time and distance, and they would have to make it up, but Kim was certain now of their location.

Mind you, Kim, he said to himself in a sarcastic voice, *you were sure before, weren't you?*

However, as he walked ahead into the trees, Kim did recognize where they were. The forest was less dense here and, as he expected, he could see paths in a few places. Further along, he knew, they should encounter a small road that, if they followed it for some time, would lead to a larger one, and another one, then camp.

The discouraging part was the distance. At their present pace, it would take them at least twice as long as they had already been walking.

Kim stared ahead into the trees and, setting his resolve — for they had no choice — was about to turn back to rejoin Dennis.

Wait a second! He could see a movement way ahead!

Kim crouched and peered. Was it a bear? That's all they needed!

"A deer, probably a deer," he mumbled to himself, for deer were often spotted near the camp. There were stories about bears in these woods too, but he usually found that, with persistent questioning, the stories turned out to be just that — stories.

The movement continued and Kim waited patiently. It was far away, right at the point where the trees and brush closed in like a curtain and cut off his view. He strained to see . . .

It was a kid!

"Hey! HEY!!" Kim screamed. He dashed ahead recklessly — he had to reach this kid!

Kim charged as fast as he could go, cracking the branches he stepped on and slapping leaves out of the way and still yelling as loud as he could.

In a flash he was face to face with one of the Blue team! He knew the kid by name: Greg.

"Hey, Greg!" Kim blurted out breathlessly. "Thank God — you gotta help us!"

Greg responded by dodging in next to Kim and knocking him over.

"What are you doing?" Kim screamed.

"The game's still on!" Greg yelled. He was still wearing his blue ribbon and he quickly searched for Kim's red one.

"You're dead," Greg announced. "No ribbon."

"Forget that stuff!" Kim screamed.

"You're trying to trick me!"

"I am not! Look, Matt got knocked out, we've been hauling him through the woods on a stretcher. You have to help us!"

Greg looked at Kim with suspicion.

"Where?"

"Over here! Come on!"

Kim ran back toward the stretcher, dragging the reluctant Greg behind him. Suddenly Dennis appeared walking from the other direction.

"Dennis, Dennis, Dennis! We've got help!"

Dennis broke into a grin and ran up to them, yelling for joy.

"Ya-hoo! We're gonna make it!"

"You're dead too," was Greg's only comment, as Dennis's red ribbon was long lost in the forest somewhere.

"Forget that stuff," Kim said again. "Come and see Matt — he's unconscious — maybe we can haul him together and make better time — "

Kim breathlessly led the other two back through the trees to the stretcher. Dennis was yipping with glee!

They raced up to the spot where they had left Matt — and the stretcher was *empty!*

"Huh . . . ?" Dennis said, flabbergasted.

"You guys . . . " Greg remarked, disgusted at what appeared to be a tall tale.

Kim was dumbstruck. Where was Matt? Was he dreaming this? It was impossible!

"What's going on?"

It was Matt's voice. They whirled around and there he was — standing over in the shadows!

"Matt! You okay?" Kim yelled, as he and Dennis ran over to check him out.

"Yeah, yeah . . . " Matt mumbled. He rubbed the back of his head and seemed a little dizzy, but otherwise unaffected by the fall, being knocked out, and the long journey on the stretcher.

"You fell," Dennis said. "You were chasing us and you crashed through some bushes and fell down onto this ledge."

"You were knocked out," Kim added. "For probably two hours. We got you off the ledge and we've been trying to carry you back to camp!"

Kim and Dennis looked at each other anxiously, and at Matt.

"You're really heavy," Dennis added.

"I just remember being in the gravel pit, protecting our flag," Matt said. "Then you came running in," he said to Kim, "and we chased you out of there. That's it."

Matt shrugged and smiled a bit at Greg. "Who's winning?" he added as an afterthought.

"I don't know," said Greg, "but these two squirts are dead. Where's your ribbon, Matt?"

"I dunno."

"I made this stretcher with my knife and some rope, and we've been carrying you quite a ways," Dennis said sternly. "We got a bit lost, but then we got back on track, and now Greg is here. We're gonna make it back!"

"Of course we are," Greg said in a real irritating, arrogant way and then it hit Kim, hit him like a brick. That same feeling . . .

They don't believe me!

Kim stepped right up to his big brother's face and hissed at him: "Don't you remember? We saved you!"

"I just told you what I remember," Matt said curtly. "Besides, if I was out cold, like you say, *what else* could I remember?"

"But before that," Kim seethed, "when you fell down to the ledge. What about that?"

"Nope."

"I think they broke the rules," Greg said.

"Go sit on it!" Dennis yelled.

"Aren't you that kid who drank the gasoline?" Greg said with a snicker. Dennis picked up a clod of dirt and flung it at him, but missed. Greg ignored the attempt, just as he was ignoring their story.

"How far to camp?" Matt asked his teammate.

"It's a ways, but not too bad," Greg replied. "You guys gonna bring that thing or leave it here?" he asked Kim and Dennis, indicating the stretcher. The way he talked to them, Kim wanted to kick his head in!

Dennis looked his creation over. Obviously, he was proud of it.

"What are we going to tell them?" Dennis asked Kim, jerking his head toward camp. He meant Baloo, Akela, and everyone else. Kim came to a horrible realization. They couldn't tell them anything!

"I don't get the feeling they're going to believe us," Kim said quietly to Dennis and his friend, very discouraged, nodded in agreement.

"I guess we leave it," Dennis said in a small voice.

"So," Greg announced loudly, "I consider you two captured by me — "

"You don't have our ribbons!" Dennis spat back at him.

"Doesn't matter."

"Yes it does!"

"Look, I've got my ribbon and you two are missing yours. That makes me your captor."

"It does not and you know it," Kim said flatly. "You have to have our ribbons."

"How are you gonna get back?" Greg asked in his irritating way. "It would help to know the way."

"I know the way," Kim asserted. He pointed into the woods. "Through there."

"Okay," Greg conceded.

"Now that we don't have to haul my brother on that stretcher — which we did for about a mile and a half — we will be just fine," Kim informed the big kid. "Matt, can you walk all the way back?"

"Yeah, sure. Why not?"

"You feel okay?"

"Yeah. A bit dizzy."

"Aren't you wondering how you got way over here?" Kim asked, a hint of sarcasm creeping into his voice. He realized immediately that was a mistake, because it put Matt on the defensive.

"Not really," came the reply and Kim could tell the conversation was over. Matt drifted over to join Greg and they started walking away.

Kim and Dennis took a last look at the stretcher, gathered up their other belongings, and followed them.

TOMMY'S TRIUMPH

Finally unburdened by the weight of Matt and the stretcher, Kim and Dennis fairly skipped and ran the mile or so they had to cover to reach their destination. Kim still chafed from Matt's complete misunderstanding of what had happened, but there was no way he could bring Matt around to his point of view.

"Look, I was running after you two and that's all I remember," Matt said flatly, more than once. Obviously, he was getting tired of discussing it and when Kim pushed him on the subject, Matt jumped to conclusions like, "You must have tricked me" or made provocative comments like, "Why'd you tie me onto that thing anyway?"

As maddening as it was, Kim felt defeated. For now, at least, he had to drop the whole thing and, besides, the second they arrived at the main gate it was clear there was a big commotion going on at camp. The Red and Blue teams were gathered together, separately, on the playing field and most of the boys were discussing something with great agitation, throwing their arms this way and that, and pointing here and there.

From among the clot of younger boys on the Red team, Tummy Tom emerged and ran over to them, all but bursting

162

with something to say. He reached them and gasped, *"We won!"*

Kim and Dennis were so surprised they almost asked "Won what?" but he had to mean the game of Capture the Flag! Tom danced in a little circle, shaking his head like a circus clown, and his tummy bounced up and down. He was one happy kid! Dennis and Kim smiled at the sight of him.

"How?" Kim finally asked.

"When you two guys decoyed the Blues out of the gravel pit, they all chased you, right?"

They nodded, not yet ready to tell Tom what had happened to them.

"Yeah, and I saw you peel off into the trees," Kim recalled.

"Cor-rect," Tom replied. "No way I could keep up, so I thought it was best to dodge out of the way . . . "

"True," Dennis said.

"But I circled back to see who was left at the pit to protect the flag. One guy! There was only one guy left! So I let him settle down after all the excitement, and snuck up behind him while he was sitting on the ground, and snatched his ribbon!"

Tom triumphantly held up a Blue ribbon. Dennis and Kim nodded with approval. They were impressed!

"So he was dead," Tom continued breathlessly, "and I just grabbed the Blue flag and got out of there as fast as I could. This kid could still talk, of course, so he tried to run off and find some other Blues to stop me, but I got away first and ducked into the trees!"

Tom was in the middle of a full-scale dramatic re-enactment now. He mimed his actions of hiding and running and dodging his way back to camp as if he'd been exploring in the Old West and discovered the Pacific Ocean or something.

"I laid low as long as I had to! Once I even crawled on my stomach! Then, when I got near enough, I made a break for it! Two Blues saw me at the last minute, but I was already at the gates. I ran flat out to Akela's desk over there and turned in the flag. We won!"

"Neat," said Dennis, which was how kids said "cool" then.

Tom was plain out of breath. He gulped some air and wheezed, "What happened to you two?"

Kim couldn't help but laugh a little. His arms and shoulders hurt even thinking about it. Dennis smiled too and licked his lips.

"Tommy, you wouldn't believe it if we told you," Kim said.

"So the diversion worked," was all Dennis had to say. Tom nodded and chose a spot in the sky where he directed his next words, one arm raised in triumph: "I'm Tom the Flag Capturer!"

In a blaze of glory, he returned to the rest of the Red team, who cheered his arrival. Kim and Dennis had a little giggle over that.

The Blues were milling around in exactly the same way they had before the game began, but this time, instead of loud boasting directed at the Red team on the subject of how they were going to clean up, they were crafting excuses for why they lost. Kim could hear the blame being handed out, the accusations and defences, the finger-pointing and the whining.

They had lost to a pack of little kids. They had to figure out why!

Kim could see Matt and Greg in the middle of it and he was sure — *certain* — that a pretty good excuse story was in place by now as to how Matt had been decoyed from the flag, lured through the woods and, who knows, bonked on the head and tied to a tree or some such thing!

Matt was not inclined to make up excuses himself, but Kim knew he would not have to; the other boys would do it for him.

"Gee, do I wanna go for a swim . . . " Dennis said, looking longingly through the trees toward the lake.

They were about to ask permission, when another commotion occurred at the main gate. A man who bore a resemblance to a scarecrow was there gesturing and yelling at the adult who had come to meet him. The "scarecrow" pushed his way in. It was Barefoot McGranger stalking into camp!

Instantly, Kim and Dennis turned away from Barefoot. But the hairy, dirty hillbilly had no interest in the cubs anyway. He went straight to the desk and cornered Akela and Baloo.

Kim and Dennis retreated to join the other Reds. They could hear Barefoot complaining loudly about something, but couldn't make out the words. Then Dennis peered closer.

"Look at what's in his hand," he said to Kim.

A red ribbon.

"Oh oh," Kim mumbled. He realized he wanted to hear exactly what Barefoot was saying, so he ambled around the edge of the playing field, looking very casual, until he could make out the words. He bent over and retied both shoes very slowly.

" . . . little hooligans must've been there 'n this proves it!" Barefoot snarled, holding the red ribbon in Baloo's face as evidence.

" . . . somehow nabbed m' water well pulley an' a good length of rope!" Barefoot continued.

Baloo and Akela spoke in soothing tones, trying to settle Barefoot down and, perhaps, gain some time to figure out what had happened. Kim could tell they were concerned, but mostly they wanted to get Barefoot to cool off and stop yelling.

After fifteen minutes of words and gestures back and forth, Barefoot left the camp compound, picking his feet up quickly through the dust and gravel like an angry rooster. He could walk right over rocky ground and stones and not feel a thing.

" . . . nothing but trouble since this camp come here!" were Barefoot's last words as he skittered away. Smiles crept across the faces of a few boys after he was gone, for all in all Barefoot was not nearly as scary in the middle of civilization as he was on his strange little farm. He didn't belong and his white, hairy legs were rather ridiculous poking out of the bottom of his cut-off pants.

"Assembly!" Akela called loudly and the smiles vanished.

All the cubs gathered in a big circle in the middle of the sports field. Even though there was no real order to it, the assembly had most of the Red team on one side and the Blue team on another. Akela and Baloo walked into the middle and looked around at all the boys.

"The game went very well and congratulations to the Red team for capturing the flag," Akela began. There was no cheering of any kind. Cubs in assembly stayed quiet and listened.

"It's a nice and fitting end to a good week here. You've learned a great deal and had a lot of fun, no one has gotten seriously hurt, and you've preserved nature as well."

Kim and Dennis looked straight ahead at Akela.

"However, we have had a complaint from Mr. McGranger, who as you all likely know, has a farm off past the edge of the area we use for the camp.

"Apparently, he has suffered a loss of property from his farm, namely a pulley and some rope, and he feels that perhaps one of the cubs from the camp had something to do with it."

Akela held up the red ribbon Barefoot had found.

"This was discovered just outside the fence around his property. Now, I'm not making any assumptions here. Just because it's a red ribbon doesn't mean a boy on the Red team dropped it. It could have been one of the Blues who had a captured red ribbon in hand.

"And I'm not going to accept or lay any blame here without firm proof that a cub from our camp was involved. However, I do agree with Mr. McGranger that it's all a little suspicious."

Kim recalled that Barefoot's words had been just a little stronger. "Stinks to high heaven," was what he had said.

Akela fell silent and looked around the circle at all the boys. Baloo spoke next.

"So if any of you boys, especially on the Red team, know anything about this, anything at all, we want you to step forward now."

Nobody moved. All the cubs glanced around at each other, all of them wondering who could be involved.

Baloo kicked at a bit of dirt.

"Are you sure, boys?"

After a second, Kim stepped forward into the circle. He could feel Dennis's eyes squeezed on him like a pair of pliers and almost hear him crying out, *"You're not gonna tell 'em, are you?"*

Akela marched over to face Kim, looking very serious indeed and, Kim noticed, quite disappointed. Baloo joined him, also looking grim. Kim looked at the ground. All eyes were on him. He couldn't help but feel quite mischievous, because he knew the longer he waited, the more they would accept what he had to say. So he drew it out for a long, long moment.

Finally he spoke, directing his words at Akela: "I was sort of the captain of the Red team, sir, so um . . . I'll try to find out what went on."

It took Akela a second to respond. That was not what he had expected to hear, apparently.

"Uh . . . okay Kim, you find out what you can and report back to me and Baloo."

Kim nodded and returned to his spot. Dennis kept his face pointed straight ahead, but his eyes followed Kim back to his spot. Kim, for his part, with his back to the adults, gave Dennis a wink.

Dennis, Kim said to himself, *you are probably right after all. I can be pretty tricky when I have to be . . . !*

Kim turned around and faced Akela and Baloo again. There was a small pause, then Baloo broke into announcements:

"Swim time in ten minutes . . . Cabin Two has latrine duty . . . Cabin Six will do the dishes tonight . . . general clean-up as tomorrow is the last day . . . "

His voice faded away in Kim's mind, replaced by a single thought:

What do I do now?

BAREFOOT AND THE PULLEY

After thinking about it overnight, Kim decided on a course of action. He vowed to do the best he could to put things right with Barefoot's pulley and his missing rope.

Kim told Dennis his plan and got his cooperation. There was another swim time on their last full day in camp, so when Cabin Five was changing into their suits, Kim lingered and allowed Dennis to lead all the other young cubs out the door in a "Charge!" to the lake.

"Go ahead, go ahead," Kim told them all, pretending he couldn't find his towel. Instead, he kept his clothes on, slipped out of the cabin, and headed up the trail toward the cookhouse and playing field.

A quick detour behind the cookhouse led him to the front gates and in an instant he was trotting down the main road — on his way back to Barefoot McGranger's farm.

Swim time was scheduled to take one hour and Kim calculated he could just make it to Barefoot's and back in that time. He carried with him a pencil and piece of paper, for he had no intention of speaking to Barefoot directly. He would leave him a note.

He settled into a dogtrot and covered ground efficiently. He was still tired from the terrible exertion of the previous day, but Kim was driven by a special energy that grew out of a sense of desperation to straighten out the mess as much as he could. That, and plain old fear, gave him the strength to keep going.

Sooner than expected, he was closing in on Barefoot's odd little farm. Kim slowed to a walk to catch his breath and to give the place the once-over. He edged forward through the trees.

The pigs, goats, and chickens were scratching away at the ground, and ambling on top of the roof, just like before. There was no sign of Barefoot.

Kim sat cross-legged on the ground to compose a note of explanation. What should he say? He was halfway through it in his head when a thought occurred to him. *Barefoot probably can't read!*

He certainly looked like the type who had never gone to school, so Kim decided to draw a map and illustrate where the pulley had been left. Would Barefoot figure it out? He hoped so.

Kim had considered going all the way to the cliff again, and hauling the pulley and rope back to Barefoot's, but he wasn't sure he had the time or the endurance. He also didn't want Barefoot to see him approaching the farm with the missing implement. That would prompt a lot of explaining that he didn't want to do!

He completed his drawing. There appeared to be no choice but to attach the paper to the fence that surrounded the property. There was no other location where Kim could be sure Barefoot would see it. He crept forward, hunched over, though he had seen no sign of the hairy, creepy owner at all. *Probably asleep again,* Kim said to himself.

He quickly finished the job and stepped back, satisfied that he'd done the best he could to help Barefoot, and put the matter to rest for himself.

"Done," he murmured and turned away — right into the end of a pitchfork! Poked at him by Barefoot McGranger!

Kim almost pooped his pants! Terror clenched his teeth together, *hard.*

"Whater yew doin' here, kid?" Barefoot growled, his eyes narrowed to snaky slits.

Kim couldn't speak. He backed against the fence wire and felt it dig a pattern into the skin between his shoulder blades. The long curved prongs of the pitchfork followed him back and stayed three inches in front of his mouth.

"What ya got?" Barefoot seethed and he snatched the paper from Kim's hand. Kim remained motionless as the hillbilly scanned the diagram and directions. He was close enough Kim could smell him and it was quite a whiff. Phew!

Barefoot scowled.

"Why'n heck don't ya write it out?" he said. "I kin read, ya know!"

"Sorry," Kim said, very quietly. "Didn't know that."

"So you took it!" Barefoot roared. "You stole m' pulley!" He stabbed the pitchfork through the paper and Kim was sure it would go through his ribs next.

"Why, boy, why? What I ever done to you or all that pack o' little monsters that roam around here half the summer?"

Kim's brain was blank. He had no words.

"Can't a man be left alone? Is that too much ta ask?" Barefoot's voice was growing louder and angrier. "Tell me boy, tell me!"

Kim decided to take the plunge. It was his only chance.

"Sir, I needed the pulley and the rope to rescue my brother. He fell off a cliff and hit his head and was out cold and we thought — me and my friend Dennis — we thought he might roll into this creek and drown. We had to act fast.

"I'm really sorry about borrowing the pulley," — Barefoot's eyes narrowed again and it was plain he didn't appreciate the description — "yes borrow, sir, because as you can see, I fully intended for you to get it back, it's just that there wasn't any time and we needed it right away."

"Why'n't you come to me for help at the time?" Barefoot demanded.

Kim swallowed and took a deep breath. "I was afraid, sir. I wasn't sure you'd help. Or believe me."

"So you jist decided to snatch it," Barefoot concluded and he pressed his teeth together in a grizzled snarl.

"Yes, sir. I'm sorry about that, sir," Kim said quickly.

Barefoot backed up a bit and scratched his head. Now that he was so close to the grimy farmer, Kim could make out a human being underneath the hair and the dirt. He was slightly less scary than before — but only slightly. He still smelled pretty bad, though.

"You better stop callin' me sir, kid," Barefoot mumbled. "I won't know who yer talkin' to."

"Okay."

"Your own brother, you say?"

"Yes, si . . . yes."

"Well, a man has to take care of his brother, don't he?" Barefoot added, looking off into the distance rather dreamily for a second. "That's one thing you just hafta do."

Kim decided to take another plunge. "Well, my brother and I don't get along too well, sir — sorry — and even though we were able to get him up off the rock and back to camp, he still doesn't believe what happened."

"He don't?"

"He don't."

"Darndest thing," Barefoot replied and Kim could tell he was taking a genuine interest. "Why not?"

Kim blurted out the whole disaster between himself and Matt in about a minute and a half. Barefoot stood there listening closely. He lowered the pitchfork and nodded along as Kim sketched it out and he seemed, if Kim were not mistaken, to be quite sympathetic to the problems of having a big brother.

"All right, look kid," Barefoot said, growling again and suddenly raising the pitchfork up once more in a menacing way, "I'm still not sure I believe ya. Let's go see if m'pulley's where you say."

In an instant, they were bouncing through the trees on Barefoot's clunky old tractor. It was the smallest, loudest tractor Kim had ever seen, not the huge modern kind Mr. White had for plowing and raking his vast fields, but an ancient, rattling thing that Barefoot drove like a bumper car at the Exhibition. He plain rammed over little trees and bounced and clanged over small ridges and through little ditches. All the while, operating it with bare feet.

"Hang on!" he yelled over the rumbling engine, which belched a steady plume of black smoke into the air. Kim barely needed the advice. He was hanging on for dear life anyway!

"There, right there!" he yelled after only a few minutes and Barefoot chugged the tractor to a stop just short of the clearing where the rescue had taken place.

It was just as Kim and Dennis had left it. There was rope everywhere, looped around the trees in their complicated mechanical arrangement, and the pulley still dangled from the branch.

Barefoot turned off the tractor and quickly inspected the scene. He ventured to the edge of the cliff and looked down to the rock ledge. Kim did too, and he shook his head. It seemed like a bad dream, the whole nightmarish fall Matt took, the way he had been splayed out across the rock, not moving, and the frantic effort to get him back up.

"Huh," was all Barefoot said. He strode around the area and retrieved all of his rope and the pulley, saying "Huh" some more and nodding his head as he compared the reality to the version Kim had told him.

"It's like you said," he finally concluded. "Tough job. Your brother should be thankin' ya."

Kim nodded but thought, *Not too likely, is it?*

"All right," Barefoot continued, "You done what you had to do. I don't blame a man for that, nor a boy, neither. Let's go."

They loaded up the rope and pulley together and Kim found a secure spot where he could grip the tractor fender with both hands for the crashing ride back. Off they went!

Again they bashed like crazy people through the trees and Kim was amazed that the tractor didn't topple over on its side. Barefoot, however, just pointed it straight ahead and mashed most obstacles in their path. He actually sat back and steered with one hand! He appeared to be talking to himself and musing about what had happened.

In no time they were back at his farmyard. Barefoot wheeled the tractor to a stop and tossed the rope and pulley over the fence, sending chickens squawking in all directions.

The tractor continued to puff black smoke at an idle as Barefoot spoke to Kim over the noise: "All right, kid, I ain't gonna cause no more trouble with the camp 'bout the pulley. You done the right thing comin' here to try'n set it right, just like you done the right thing helpin' out your brother. He owes you one or two and you can tell him I said so."

Kim nodded and began to get down off the tractor, but Barefoot stopped him.

"I'll run ya back."

"Okay," Kim called over the noise. It was a terrifying prospect, but he was way late now and running out of energy too. He took up his spot once more.

Fortunately, there was a finished road for much of the journey and Kim was able to quell his fantasies of flipping into the ditch at high speed. As they approached the ball diamond he yelled, "This is good, this is good!" and Barefoot throttled back the tractor and coasted to a halt.

Kim bounced off the fender to the ground. In his heart, he just wanted to run, but he figured he'd better say thanks.

"That's okay, kid," Barefoot replied. "You watch yerself, now. You come off lucky this time, seems to me."

Kim nodded. He had to agree with that!

Barefoot revved the rattling old machine and a blast of black smoke erupted like a belch from a volcano. He rammed the gearshift forward and the entire tractor shook.

"Come 'round see me next year if yer back," the hairy farmer yelled over the roar, then he fixed his eyes forward and the tractor lurched ahead and he was off.

"Sure will," Kim said, just loud enough that it was clear he had replied, but not so loud that Barefoot could hear him.

All in all, he rather doubted he would call on Barefoot again.

How To Put Out a Fire In a Big Hurry

The chilly fresh water of the lake never felt so welcome in Kim's entire life. He plunged in from the dock and swam out to join Dennis on the raft.

They were surrounded by boys leaping and diving into the lake, then rocking the raft like a piece of cork when they climbed back on. Some of the more acrobatic kids could run a few steps and execute three-quarters of a forward somersault on their way into the drink.

"What happened?" Dennis called over the din.

"I'll tell ya later," Kim called back, then added, "It worked out," so Dennis would not be concerned.

Kim stood up on the pitching raft and stepped backward toward the edge, calling back to Dennis just before he jumped: "You won't believe it!"

He fell back into the churning, cool water and Dennis quickly followed with a cannonball, sending a plume of spray exploding skyward.

Later, when Dennis heard it all, Kim could tell he wasn't quite sure whether he should believe it — the encounter with Barefoot, the peaceful retrieval of the pulley and the rope, Barefoot's strange friendliness — but Dennis was exhausted, like Kim, and all he could say was, "Good enough for me."

Kim nodded. He felt that way too. They were back in Cabin Five on a late afternoon rest break before their final camp meal and campfire.

Kim and Dennis didn't have much to do except take orders, which suited them just fine, for the final campfire was a Tummy Tom Production.

Ever since he had pulled off the victory for the Red team in Capture the Flag, Tom had been in his glory. No one in the camp was left unaware of any aspect of his conquest. The ladies at the cookhouse had heard the story told in a highly elaborated fashion, Baloo and Akela were regaled in great detail, all of the younger cubs knew the story by heart and even the older ones, most of whom had been Blue team members, had put up with Tom's blow by blow re-enactment several times.

Tommy had told the story at breakfast, during games on the playing field, while swimming, again at lunch, and to anyone who would listen back in Cabin Five.

It was one of the few times in Tommy's entire life when he had been the kid who swooped in with the decisive move and won the day. Tom was never the one who scored the winning goal in street hockey or hit a double just when his team needed one in baseball, so all the cubs forgave him for revelling in his triumph.

He was bragging, that was for certain, and bragging was not something any real athlete was supposed to do, but Tom was allowed his day in the sun. It was all pretty funny to watch!

Kim and Dennis merely hoped that Tom would continue to gloss over the part of the tale that dealt with the "diversion" to draw Matt and the others away from the flag. They didn't want too many questions asked about that part and, they realized, neither did Matt.

Tom, however, could be relied upon to concentrate on his role, and no other, in the heroic victory over the Blue team. He was Tom the Flag Capturer!

"We need more firewood than ever before!" Tom commanded to the Cabin Five cubs, as they sat on the steps taking his instructions.

"You three," Tom pointed to a clutch of small cubs, "can sharpen wiener sticks. We need more than ever before!"

Apparently, it was going to be a rather large fire — "The biggest fire we've had!" Tom proclaimed — and they would give the cookhouse ladies the evening off by roasting hot dogs and eating beans. Later, as they did at every fire, they would sing songs, tell ghost stories and look for shooting stars and the Northern Lights.

As evening fell and the supper hour approached, Tom had every detail under control. The little kids had sharpened at least three dozen wiener and marshmallow sticks. The wieners and buns, relish and ketchup, and cans of pork and beans, were all in boxes down at the fire site.

The fire itself was blazing three feet high and there was a sizeable pile of wood nearby, stacked by Dennis and Kim and the others.

It was mid-summer, so the fire had to be built in the twilight, for it would take far too long to wait for darkness at this time of year. Evening, twilight, dusk — call it what you will — stretched for several hours and a deep blue band of light illuminated the northwestern horizon well into the night.

The weather was good: clear, pleasant, and not too cool. The mosquitoes could be kept at bay by a combination of insect spray, smoke from the fire, and long pants and kangaroo tops with the hoods up — that, and a quick hand to slap them.

Kim and Dennis found a spot on a log around the leaping flames, just close enough to be warmed, but not so close that they might catch a spark.

"Did you get a hot dog?" Tom demanded as he did the rounds of boys sitting on the logs. The flames were reflected in his glasses and lent him a devilish look.

"Yeah," said Dennis. "One. Are there more?"

"Two each," Tom replied crisply. He moved on.

"And I bet he counted 'em too!" Dennis chuckled.

Across the fire pit a few cubs began a low chant that reached their ears.

> *Beans, beans, the wonder fruit . . .*
> *The more you eat, the more you toot . . .*

Dennis smirked, and Kim too, for they knew Cabin Five would be a smelly place after all these cubs had canned beans for supper!

> *Beans, beans, the wonder fruit . . .*
> *The more you eat, the more you toot . . .*

Dennis stood up and joined Tom near the boxes of food. "When do we get to eat the beans, Tom?" he asked.

181

"Pretty soon, pretty soon," Tom replied in a brisk fashion. His entire body seemed to scream *"Can't you see I'm busy?"* as he bustled about the food area, ensuring that everyone was fed and there was enough to go around.

"Beans're coming," Dennis growled as he rejoined Kim, and they both settled in to wait. The beans were actually "pork and beans," because they came in cans, swimming in brown sauce, and with a small piece of pork in there somewhere, but their name had become squashed together and they were now known to all as "porkenbeans."

Porkenbeans were a staple food at cub camp and, as he waited, Kim put his mind to work trying to recall a day when they hadn't been served them. There might have been one. Thankfully, such a meal was usually followed by an outdoor activity because, as the song said, the more you eat, the more you toot!

Beans must have a lot of energy, Kim concluded, as he whiled away the time, waiting.

Overhead, the sky was growing darker, and over to the east it was almost black, but on the western horizon the glow of the fading sunset still reached them as a pleasant blue. The dazzling planet Venus hung there in the blue-black sky, as bright as a flare. Just below it was the thin slice of the new moon. The rest of the moon was visible as a hazy globe.

Kim looked away and looked back. Venus and the moon both seemed to have slipped lower. He yawned.

"Any Northern Lights?" Dennis asked when he saw Kim scanning the sky.

"Don't see any. Maybe later."

Campfire songs had broken out now among a few groups of kids around the wiener roasting blaze, punctuated by cheering and laughing. Kim didn't really feel like singing tonight. He was too wrapped up replaying the events of the week, over and over again, and sorting out what had happened, when, and to whom, and what it all meant.

He had taken the opportunity earlier to make his promised "report" to Baloo and Akela, simply telling them that he could find out nothing about Barefoot's pulley and rope from among the ranks of the young cubs on the Red team. They seemed satisfied with his efforts and, in any event, he was quite certain Barefoot was not going to return to the camp. They had a deal.

"What are you doing when you get home?" he asked Dennis, who was staring into the fire and watching his hot dog wiener darken in the flames.

"I dunno," Dennis said. "Some baseball games, aren't there?"

"Yeah."

"Darn!" Dennis growled suddenly and Kim saw that the wiener had fallen off the stick. It was a goner and quickly blackened when it hit the orange-red coals at the bottom of the blaze. There were several other objects in there too that he couldn't identify; perhaps they were rocks.

Dennis stalked over to the food boxes to get another wiener.

"How many have you had?" Tom demanded and seemed for a second to be prepared to make a fuss, since Dennis had eaten one and lost his second one in the fire. That put him at his limit. But Dennis just growled and stuck his stick an inch from Tom's tummy, then reached past him to get a fresh wiener.

Kim was still hungry, even though he'd eaten his two hot dogs, and he figured most of the other cubs were the same way.

"Okay, Tom, time for the beans!" Kim called out across the fire and was met with a dismissive wave from the busy organizer. Kim got up to stretch his legs and ambled over to Tom, who was counting marshmallows.

Kim poked his nose into the food boxes and looked around.

"Where are the beans, Tommy?" he asked, since the porkenbean cans were not in the cardboard boxes.

Tom had a hot dog stuffed in his mouth, but he motioned over his shoulder at the fire and said something like, "Nearm, nearm," which Kim took to mean, "Over there."

"In the fire?" he asked and Tom nodded as he turned and swallowed a solid glob of chewed-up bun and hot dog in one final gulp.

"Yup," he said, and burped for good measure. "They're all in the fire. When they're hot enough, we'll roll 'em out and use our knives and open 'em up!"

"I'm first," Kim said and waited for the Tom Triumphant reaction, for Tommy had become quite bossy in his position as Campfire Organizer.

"You'll get yours when everyone else does!" he ruled, and frowned to underline the fact that he was terribly serious.

"'Kay, 'kay," Kim said, laughing to himself. Tom was getting a swollen head, a head blown right up like a balloon!

Kim shambled back to his spot and sat next to Dennis to wait. *Boys are like a balloon* . . . he reminded himself and suddenly he realized he was in no big hurry to get back to Caraway. Why couldn't camp, and a nice night like this, last forever?

Tommy cleared his throat to make an announcement.

"Cubs of the Caraway pack!" he called out. "This brilliant, amazing campfire and supper are brought to you by . . . Cabin Five!"

There were a few whistles and cheers, and a few cubs clapped their hands . . .

. . . and then there was a huge BOOOOM!!

Suddenly it was dark. The fire was completely out. Fire logs with glowing sparks on them were scattered a few feet from the fire pit. Dense white smoke filled the air. And beans — there were beans everywhere!

Globs of them on Tommy's clothes, on his head, and in his hair. Dennis and Kim had beans splattered on them too — porkenbeans everywhere!

Baloo rushed into the fire circle.

"What happened, boys?"

Tommy staggered about in a daze.

"What happened," Baloo repeated. "Someone get a bucket of water from the lake!"

Tom looked at the brown sauce on his hands and licked a bit of it. At his feet was the blown-open shell of a metal can.

"The . . . the . . . beans blew up!" Tom stammered.

"Did you poke a hole in the cans before you put 'em in the fire?" Baloo demanded.

"Huh?" Tom blurted in confusion. He was changing before their eyes, from Tom the Flag Capturer back to Tummy Tom again.

"You have to do that?"

"The other cans!" a cub called out and the boys around the circle jumped off the logs and backed up a good distance.

Baloo grabbed a stick and rolled the remaining cans, five of them, out of the fire pit. It was hard to see with all the smoke and without the firelight. Several boys pointed flashlights in his direction.

"Here!" Dennis called, leaping ahead with his hunting knife held out for Baloo, who quickly pierced each of the cans as he held them under his boot. The cans hissed loudly and hot brown sauce bubbled out.

A cub appeared on the double with a bucket of water and the sparking logs were all extinguished.

"We can rebuild the fire!" Kim called and he used a stick to poke the coals together into a pile. He bent on his hands and knees, blew hard, and instantly a ball of flame popped into the air like a magician's trick.

"I didn't know! I didn't know!" Tom stammered to no one in particular.

He wandered around for a moment or two, as if he were on the verge of issuing more orders, but his authority had been blown up along with the can of porkenbeans and he knew it. He retreated to a log at the edge of the fire circle and sat down.

Later, as the blaze regained strength and the supper was re-organized, the cubs managed to salvage enough beans to feed themselves. They cleaned up and put the food away. Marshmallows were flamed in the fire and carefully eaten.

It grew darker and the sliver of moon and the planet Venus sank below the horizon. The sky became filled with clusters of steely stars. The Big Dipper curved above them. A few flashing shooting stars fell around them and there was even a thin veil of bluey-green Northern Lights off in the distance.

Kim and Dennis and all of the cubs from Cabin Five joined in the songs, as did all the older cubs, for this was their last night. They sang and chanted and linked arms to sway back and forth around the circle. The bigger, older cubs did too, though they seemed to be making a bit of fun of the whole thing.

One cub didn't move. Tummy Tom put his chin on his hand and stared at the fire. The best day-and-a-half of his life had come to an end and he just wanted to go to bed.

KICKED OUT!

"Do you see him?"

"No."

"Anybody else? You see anybody else?"

"Nope."

"Let's ride a little closer."

"Okay," Kim replied to Dennis, who had been asking the questions.

They were on their bikes, out on the road that led out to the Pig Farm and the Haunted House. Tommy was with them. They had chosen the road so they would be able to see right into the area of the Pig Farm where they might expect to see Mr. White at work feeding the pigs, and perhaps other kids helping him.

Ever since returning from cub camp, Kim had known that sooner or later he would encounter Mr. White. The prospect filled him with dread. Did Mr. White think he was The Kid Who Threw the Rock? Everyone else in Caraway did! As soon as he stepped off the bus, the inky stain of that pesky description nickname had drawn itself down his back again. Camp had been a wonderful interlude, a break from all the worry and shame he felt about how the Haunted House had

188

been wrecked, even if Capture the Flag had become a great deal more elaborate than planned.

Strangely enough, Kim preferred the desperate adventure of hauling his brother through the woods on a stretcher to the nasty game of glances and whispers that seemed to go on in Caraway. Was he imagining it? Or did kids look at him funny? Were adults talking about him, perhaps pointing his way, with a scowl of recognition on their faces?

It would be the worst — the very worst — if Mr. White treated him the same way, for there was probably no adult in all of Caraway who was as kind to kids, and to Kim and his friends in particular.

Kim, Dennis, and Tom had not ventured near the feeding-of-the-pigs expeditions for several days after coming home, because all of them didn't want to "push it." If the news was bad, they could wait for it.

But their curiosity had gotten the better of them and now they were returning to the "scene of the crime," as it were.

"I don't think there's anyone there at all," Tom pronounced flatly as they came right up to the entrance gate off the main road.

"Well, those pigs have to be fed. Everyday. He must be feeding them," Kim put in. "Have you guys heard of other kids going along?"

"It's getting to be summer holidays," Dennis observed. "Lots of kids aren't around." Of course, it had *been* summer holidays for weeks, but he meant it was getting to be the time when families went away on trips, which was true.

"Wait. What's that?" Tom asked. There were noises far off in the Bush, back behind the pigs' area.

"Sounds like kids," Kim guessed and he was probably right. "So there's a few kids here anyway."

"Yeah," Dennis continued. "Let's go in. What's the matter? Why not?"

Kim hesitated. Tommy too. Then Kim realized that he was *not* a criminal, so there was no reason to *behave* like a criminal. Dennis was right. Why not go in?

They passed through the gate and rounded a little corner and there, sort of staring at them like a ghost, was the Haunted House. It looked even worse than Kim remembered and, with a shiver, he realized that more damage had been done. Some of the window shutters had been ripped off their hinges, there were signs of attacks on the logs by big boulders, and there were the telltale, black char marks of a fire that had been set near one of the walls.

Kim's stomach was as thick as mud. To be involved in such a thing and especially to be hung with the blame for setting it off — it was an awful feeling.

Dennis squinted and looked up at the sun, over at the House, and out to the road.

"What did Matt say . . . ?" he asked Kim.

"Say *when*?" Kim shot back, nodding his head sharply at Tommy, who was fortunately looking in the other direction at that moment.

"Oh yeah," Dennis growled, having finally recalled that Tom still didn't know about the rescue, the journey of the stretcher, and the encounters with Barefoot. After Tom went overboard celebrating his victory in Capture the Flag, Kim and Dennis had decided he was, temporarily at least, not reliable and shouldn't be trusted with those particular secrets.

They were both forced to summon the words from memory, since Tom was back in listening range again.

"Who's that? Who is that? Watch out!"

Kim looked over the scene. They were standing about where Matt had been during the rock throwing fight. He would have seen two sides of the Haunted House, but certainly not where Kim had ducked away, just before the first rock went crashing through a window. And then there was the dust . . .

"No way he could see me from here," Kim stated flatly and Dennis nodded in agreement.

"Who?" Tom said.

"Doesn't matter," Kim replied firmly, to end the exchange, though it certainly did matter.

"Who's that? Who is that? Watch out!"

"And why say, 'Who is that?' if it was you? He would know you. It had to be someone else," Dennis said, rattling off the conclusion he and Kim had arrived at, this time and every other time they discussed the beginning of the riot.

"Yeah," Kim agreed.

"What the heck are you two talking about?" Tom asked, though he should have been able to guess, Kim felt. Tommy, however, was venturing toward a post that was sunk into the ground near the House.

As they approached, Kim realized there was a sign attached to the post. They had been looking at it edge-on, so he hadn't noticed it at first.

"What's it say?" Dennis called ahead to Tom.

Tommy stopped in front of the sign and scratched his tummy. "Uh oh . . . " was all he said.

Kim and Dennis rode their bikes the short distance and stopped too. Kim felt his chest press together and suddenly it was hard to breathe.

Tom read it out loud: "Police investigation. Do not enter premises."

That was the main message. In smaller lettering, which must have been put there by someone else, since it was scrawled in handwriting, there were additional words: "No boys at the farm for now. Thanks."

"We've been kicked out!" Tom said, quite a bit louder than needed.

"You think Mr. White wrote that?" Dennis asked, indicating the second part.

"Probably did," Kim said in a small voice. "And I bet we get blamed for this too . . . "

"What do you mean 'we'?" Tom said, quite indignantly, and Dennis rolled his eyes impatiently. Tom could be such a pain!

"You know what I mean," Kim added wearily. "I mean me."

"Why don't you say it then?" Tom said, actually scowling.

"Oh shut up, Tommy!" Dennis snapped at him with unmistakable anger and Tom shrank back, silenced, but only for a moment. It was quite apparent that he felt his humiliation over the exploding beans at the campfire entitled him to rub it in.

"Where are we going to play now?" he said, with his hands on his hips, clenched into fists like a ninny.

Kim and Dennis replied with one voice: "What do you mean 'we', Tom?"

"You know what I mean," he added hastily.

"Why don't you shut up, then?" Dennis threatened and finally Tom stopped trying to have the last word.

"I guess we should go," Kim concluded unhappily as he turned his bike away from the House and the pig yard. Suddenly it all looked sad beyond description.

They made their way through the Bush in the direction of the field that would carry them back to Caraway, using a route that wouldn't break the "keep out" rule. After a few minutes, they picked up the sound of boys' voices.

"There's those kids again," Dennis remarked as they approached the edge of the trees, right near the spot where they had lingered prior to all the trouble breaking out at the Haunted House. Just as they cleared the Bush and broke into the sunlight, they saw a few boys ambling along the tree line, including their friends Lloyd and Bobbie.

Hmmm . . . those two, Kim thought as he observed the pair coming toward him. He readied himself for a problem — exactly what, he didn't know — for Bobbie and Lloyd together often produced difficult situations. They were both the kind of kid who could watch trouble build and build and not become concerned. *They must be used to it and not scared by it,* Kim thought. It made them good hockey players, but not always the best choice of kids to hang around with, which was why he preferred Dennis and Tommy, whose moods so often cancelled each other out.

He wasn't afraid of either of them, just wary. Lloyd — he called him Lips Lloyd because of his heavy mouth — shambled up with his hands in his pockets as though he were scuffling down Main Street with nothing to do. Brushcut

Bobbie, as always, tagged along waiting for something to happen.

"Hi, you guys. We're going home," Tommy stated boldly, hoping to begin and end the encounter immediately.

Lloyd smirked. "Why you going home? You just got here."

"Naw, we've been here awhile," Dennis said in his most raspy voice, and he licked a bit of foam from the corner of his mouth for good measure.

"Spell pig backwards, then say 'funny colours'," Lips Lloyd said out of nowhere.

"Gee you pee funny colours," Tom responded and he actually stuck his tongue out at Lloyd.

"That's 'pug'," Bobbie said blankly, just stating a fact.

"They're pugs, they're pugs!" Lloyd laughed, entirely to himself. He always seemed to think he was saying something funny, and it was always a joke about someone else. Kim desperately hoped Lloyd didn't bring up the time he and Dennis had been sucked in by The Crusher and Moby Joe.

Lloyd shuffled his feet a bit more, smirked and looked at the ground, and Kim could feel it coming — he could just feel it!

"Well, I guess we better get used to hanging around town, eh?" Lloyd said, raising his eyes and squinting, and Kim decided to put an end to the game they were playing. He hopped on his bike and began to pedal away. Dennis and Tom joined him and Kim called back over his shoulder, "You don't like it out here anyway, Lloyd!"

The added sentence, the one he didn't have to say out loud, rang across the space between them. *"So go hang around Piss Flats, why doncha!"* Lloyd must have heard it in his mind

194

because he sent Kim off with his own nasty, pointed dart of a reply. "Because you just got us kicked out o' here for the summer, didn't ya, Kim!"

Can Caraway Days Do It Again?

The next two weeks passed in absolute misery for Kim.

With the Pig Farm and most of the Bush off limits to kids, there was suddenly a townfull of boys angry that one of their favourite hang-around spots was closed to them until further notice. Despite the sign about the "police investigation," nobody heard of anything happening on that front. The Town Cop was not going around questioning kids and, since the night of the first arrests on the case, very little had been done to try to get to the bottom of it.

However, the cloud of blame still hung over the one deemed responsible for starting it all, as if that boy had done all of the damage himself, and there was no question of the identity of The Kid Who Threw the Rock.

At every opportunity, Kim pleaded with Matt to start telling kids — and Mr. White and the Town Cop — that he was mistaken about what he thought he had seen, but Matt could find no reason to alter his version of events.

"Look, it was a left-handed kid, a southpaw, and I thought it was you," Matt told him curtly each time Kim asked about it. "You don't want me to lie, do you?"

"There's a difference between lying and saying maybe you're not sure!" Kim would counter, but Matt appeared to feel it was his duty to stick to his guns. Kim could also tell that the more he pressed his brother on it, the further Matt dug in his heels. It was becoming increasingly difficult to back away from the story that said his little brother Kim was indeed The Kid Who Threw the Rock.

Once, when they were both getting ready for bed, Kim confronted Matt with the intriguing words he had mumbled while semi-conscious on the stretcher.

"Who's that? Who is that? Watch out!"

Matt, of course, viewed the entire rescue saga and the exhausting struggle to lug him back toward camp by stretcher as pure invention on Kim's part, so he had absolutely no comment about the nonsense Kim said came out of his mouth.

Kim felt stuck, horribly stuck.

He couldn't clear his name, he couldn't persuade his brother to cooperate, and he couldn't get kids to stop blaming him for the closure of the Pig Farm and the Bush as places to run around and play.

The summer weeks had rolled from July into August by then and Kim began to pray for the arrival of two particular days in mid-August that held out the only hope that he might get a break and actually have some fun in this entire summer of misery. The riot at the Haunted House was weeks old now and the stale taste of shame and anger had been in his mouth for most of the best, warm days of the year. What a waste!

Disasters and inconveniences had occurred in other areas too: the baseball team he played on with Dennis, Lloyd, Bobbie and Alan (Tom was not a ball player) was on a six-game losing streak and had slipped into the middle of the

Caraway and District League standings. They even lost to Greely, the puny town of Greely, with its pathetic little collection of houses and ball diamond that had weeds growing in the infield, and an outfield that resembled a cow pasture and probably was, since the grass was knee-high in places! Any ball hit to the outfield came to a very abrupt stop at the Greely baseball diamond.

Kim's pitching, normally among the best on the team, had degenerated into a long nightmarish series of walked batters, hard liners smashed through the infield, hit batters, wild pitches and passed balls, and the occasional solid Crack! of a home run sailing way over the heads of his outfielders. His hitting was a mess too, with his strikeout total mounting by mid-season to surpass the number he would expect for the entire year.

The Kid Who Threw the Rock couldn't throw strikes and couldn't hit a beach ball. The rest of the team wasn't much better.

It was that sort of summer. There had been disasters at every turn, but as those two sweet August days approached, Kim began to cheer up a little, for they represented pretty well the best time a kid in his town could have all year.

They were Caraway Days.

Officially, they were the Caraway & District Agricultural Society Fall Fair, but most everyone called them Caraway Days or, more to the point, "the Fair."

Kim loved those two days more than Christmas, Halloween or Thanksgiving. The sweet smell of the long grass, the barley and the hay fields, blew softly through town and, as if a notice had appeared in the newspaper or a bulletin had been sent around to every house, as if all the parents of Caraway and the Town Cop had held a big meeting and conducted debates and passed motions and resolutions, suddenly almost all of the rules controlling the behaviour of children were called off!

You could do anything! It was Caraway Days!

At least, that's how it had been in previous years and, the morning of the first day, Kim hauled himself out of bed early, without having to be called or reminded, because a question burned in his heart and rang around the inside of his head, a desperately important question: *Can Caraway Days do it again?*

He really *really* wanted to forget about being The Kid Who Threw the Rock for a few days and just be another kid hanging around town for the summer. Caraway Days were his best chance.

"See you at the parade, Mom!" Kim yelled on his way out the door after a quick breakfast. He raced to the backyard where his bike was waiting. The day before, he had slapped on his decorations, not much, just a few streamers of orange crepe paper threaded through the wire basket and the spokes. He certainly didn't expect to win a prize, but to ride a bike in the parade, decorations were required.

Kim's mom waved and smiled from the back step as Kim rattled away on his bike. Matt was already off somewhere else and Kim didn't give a hoot. His big brother only reminded him of all the problems. He wasn't even planning on meeting any of his friends at any particular spot, because they would all be there somewhere. That's how it went at Caraway Days.

You just boinged around town like the steel ball in a pinball machine, and there was always another play.

"Dinner will be on the table at noon," his mom called after him. That's what they called lunch in those days.

The parade gathered at the parking lot of the shopping centre on the highway, then proceeded down Main Street. Kim simply rode up on his bike and joined the mass of other kids on decorated bikes. He had not officially entered, but so what? If you weren't going for a prize, no one cared and you could ride along anyway.

The wail of the fire engine siren announced the start of the procession, and the thump-thump-BLARE of the Scottish pipe and drum band settled into its regular rhythm at the head of the column of floats and cars, bikes, horses and kids. Kim's section was back in the middle.

A horse-riding club from out in the countryside was ahead of them, which Kim knew they would all come to regret, since horses had a habit of going to the bathroom in a big way in the midst of parades.

Soon it started. Ahead of them, the statuesque riding horses began to lift their tails and large round lumps of poo began to hit the street with a cadence about as regular as the click-click of the horses' hooves. Click-click . . . plop-plop . . .

That's enough for me! Kim said to himself. Since he wasn't even officially part of the decorated bike section, he was free to leave and he pedalled quickly out of line to avoid the horse dung and zipped far ahead in an instant. He passed the horses — one of the riders, a girl, waved at him from way up high on her gigantic mount — and then zoomed along right next to the spectators.

"Kim . . . Kim!" he heard his mother call. She and a few other moms had carted lawn chairs out to the highway and were enjoying the spectacle, calling out to people they recognized and offering comments and compliments to one and all. Several of the floats had candy-tossers flinging treats into the street and in only a few moments, Kim had his pockets full.

"Brush your teeth after dinner," his mom said off-handedly and Kim nodded along. "Do I have time to go to the grounds before dinner?" he asked.

"Sure. Be back by noon," she waved and Kim was off. It was always good to take a peek at the attractions ahead of the afternoon rush. He directed his bike down the back road that led to the fair grounds on the west end of town, leaned on the pedals, and was there in five minutes.

It cost money to enter the fairgrounds with a car, but kids on bikes just sailed past the ticket booth and right on in. Kim swooshed his bike to a stop at the baseball grandstand and left it there, unlocked. There was already a baseball game underway and people were already milling around on the midway. At the far end, there was a giant Ferris wheel making its slow, majestic turns and all the ground in-between was covered by striped tents and whirling rides.

Kim checked his pockets. For weeks, he had carefully saved some of his allowance and now he had quite a bit of money. He counted it. A dollar and thirty-five cents. That was a pretty good chunk of cash. It had to last two whole days and Kim was sure it would.

He wandered around one of the games and selected a likely candidate for a first try: the five-cent diggers. He jingled his money. Should he try it? He knew things like the five-cent diggers were a waste of money. But it seemed so easy . . .

Just once, he said to himself as he plunked in his five cents.

The glass case lit up and came to life, with the steam shovel rattling. Quickly and coolly, Kim twirled the wheel to swing the shovel over the little box of treasure. Without warning, the steel jaws dropped and snapped together like an infielder's glove on a two-hopper. In a split second, Kim swung it back to the prize slot, with a pack of nickels dangling precariously. They dropped into the slot — thunk! Bingo! He had twenty-five cents!

Another try? Naw! He'd been lucky and he knew it. He lilted down the midway, feeling light on his feet and ready to try anything.

The milk bottle toss was another well-known waste of money. The prize was a silver dollar, which rested temptingly on top of a milk bottle, which was in turn perched on top of two other milk bottles set side by side. All three bottles, forming a little pyramid, were on a stool.

For ten cents, you got two baseballs to try and knock the dollar free. If it hit the ground, you got to keep it.

They let you stand real close, only six or eight feet away. It seemed so-ooo easy.

Ah, hah! There's a trick! Kim said to himself, for it was obvious that the milk bottles were not bottles at all. They were not the glass kind that the milkman left on the front steps, the ones that split right open when the milk was left, unclaimed on a forty-below morning, and froze into a bizarre upward-vaulted white Popsicle. No, no. They were wood — or maybe stone! — for they were heavy, solid things.

Countless times Kim had seen other kids send a hard pitch right at the "bottles," only to see them fall over without even toppling off the stool. The fat, shiny silver dollar, hopelessly tempting, fell straight down and stayed there.

Should he . . . ?

Kim looked closer at the stool. Huh! It had a *rim* on it! No wonder the dollar never fell off!

Should he . . . ?

He passed a dime to the grimy man who ran the game.

"Once," Kim said.

The man passed him two baseballs and took the dime without even looking at Kim.

Kim reared back and threw, left-handed of course, and hit the bottles perfectly in the space between all three. An incredible throw — a better pitch than he'd tossed in weeks in baseball! All three bottles went flying!

The silver dollar fell straight down and landed flat on the stool.

That was a great throw! Kim screamed to himself. *I should have won! FIX!*

He appealed with a gesture to the grimy, potato-faced man who ran the milk bottle toss, but he was still gazing down the midway at something and completely ignoring Kim. Machine noises from the rides filled the air.

Kim turned away and stamped the ground. No fair!

Well, Kim, he told himself, *it's your own fault. If you're stupid enough to hand over your money in a fixed game, they'll take it.*

The silver dollar lay there, shining dully. Kim was so close he could see the canoe. He could see the Indian and the fur trader *in* the canoe.

What the heck, he thought, rolling the baseball in his hand. *Nothing to lose* . . .

Kim reared back and threw straight at the dollar for all he was worth. It was like a three-two fastball where you just hucked it as hard as you could and dared the batter to hit it.

To his utter amazement, he picked that dollar off that stool like a kid shooting a bird off a wire with a BB gun.

The baseball bounced off the stool and thudded into the canvas tarp behind it. The dollar jumped in the air and landed in the sawdust.

Kim was stunned. He got it? Didn't he . . . ?

He looked at the grimy man, who was still watching down the midway, and chewing and spitting bits of sawdust. He spit, bent to fetch the coin, and handed it over. All without once looking at Kim.

"Yeah!" Kim yelled out loud, and he raced away, grinning and grinning, to get his bike. He encountered Dennis before he got there and proudly showed him the silver dollar.

"What a great way to start Caraway Days!" Kim crowed.

Dennis was impressed, though Kim felt forced to point out that he had just thrown his two best pitches in a month.

"Yeah, I guess you're right," Dennis agreed. "Maybe you should be a professional."

"What do you mean?"

"You do better when there's money on the line."

Suddenly it occurred to them that they were standing in front of the dunking tank, which featured members of the Caraway Volunteer Fire Department perched on a little chair overtop of a tank of water. For fifty cents, you got two tries to dunk them by hitting a target with a baseball. Kim and Dennis were about to move on when an elderly man, who had just purchased his two attempts, smiled at them and said, "Here boys, you may have better aim than I."

He handed them the baseballs. Free tries! Kim reared back and threw. He missed by six inches.

"Yup," he said to Dennis, "I've had my best tosses already."

Dennis licked his lips and chucked the ball hard — wham! — right on the money and the fireman was suddenly in free fall, hitting the water with a tremendous SPLASH!! Half the water in the tank gushed into the midway, then the drenched fireman resurfaced to bellow, "Cold! That's *cold!*"

There was a big laugh, though Kim thought he saw the fireman look at them a little resentfully. The old man had been right: he wasn't going to succeed at dunk ball, but boys might!

Laughing and jumping, Dennis and Kim ran off down the midway, then parted company.

Twice on the bike ride home, Kim stopped to pull the silver dollar out of his pocket and look at it. It felt as big as a pancake and weighed at least a pound.

"Maybe I'd better keep that for you," Kim's mom said at dinner. "You don't want to lose it."

Kim agreed. A whole dollar was a lot of money. A silver one, with all that dollar in one coin, well, that was just too much money in one place.

Besides, he had a plan to make some more money that afternoon.

Along with everything else, Caraway Days were one big long baseball tournament. The men's team, the Caraway Continentals, was in it along with teams from far and wide.

The Continentals usually won a game or two, then lost on the second day. On the rare years that they made it to the final game, all of Caraway turned out to watch.

Kim hoped to play for the Continentals one day. He didn't mind the prospect of playing for a team named after a car, because a Continental was a very big car, after all. So he had heard. Kim had never actually seen one. During the fair, the Continentals' games were a way for Kim to line his pockets.

After a quick dinner — "Thanks, Mom!" — he cycled back to the fair grounds, left his bike again, and staked out a position behind the high, white wooden grandstand where the spectators sat to watch the ball games. The structure also housed the hamburger and hot dog stand, and there was a steady stream of customers coming and going. It all smelled very tempting, but Kim wasn't there to eat. Along with five other boys, he fixed his eyes on the high lip of the grandstand, waiting for a foul ball to come sailing over.

A returned foul ball was worth ten cents and all the kids in town knew it, so the foul ball chase attracted a crowd, sometimes a big one, sometimes, like now, only a smattering of kids.

The challenge was this: most foul balls came straight back from the hitter, or at a slight angle. That meant the best place to stand was directly behind the grandstand, but then you couldn't see the game. Kim and the rest of the chasers had to wait for the distant Crack! of the bat. And there was more.

If the bat "cracked" and the crowd cheered, it probably meant that the hit was a fair ball. If there was a Crack! and no cheering, the odds were that the ball was heading back their way.

Kim put some distance between himself and the rest of the boys. One small kid, probably a farm kid, followed him.

"Get your own spot," Kim said curtly. He suspected the kid was partners with a brother or a friend and his job was to run interference.

Crack! A foul! The ball appeared suddenly over the grandstand and flew off toward the parking lot. Several boys scampered after it, but Kim let it go. It was in the wrong direction and he wasn't even close. Not even in the ball game, so to speak.

The foul bounced right off the hood of a blue Chevy. A few men near it laughed at that, and the boys dashed between the cars to snare the prize.

Kim kept his eyes trained on the stands. CRACK. Another one! Coming his way! He dodged past the small farm boy and spotted one other kid chasing with him, probably the boy's brother, for they looked like big and small versions of the same kid.

Kim and the bigger kid ran under where the ball would hit. There was lots of room. Nobody would be hit or hurt — sometimes he had to yell to warn ladies with babies.

The ball plummeted like a diving hawk. The other kid had his hands out. He was going to catch it!

"No way!" Kim muttered to himself.

He scampered far back from the other kid, and guessed where the bounce would take the ball. Two other boys were charging over. Kim skittered back further. A foul ball always had a big spin on it and it would angle away from home plate most times.

The farm kid held his arms straight out, but he flinched at the last second. The baseball hit the ground and zinged sideways. Kim had the angle right but now he had company — it was a race between him and the other two boys. All three pelted after the bouncing ball like sprinters headed for the tape.

Kim made it just in time and scooped up the ball as it was still rolling. He quickly turned his back to protect it, in case they tried to lunge in and grab it. He had never been in a fight over a foul ball, but if two boys got their hands on the same one there could be a struggle in the dirt, a quick contest of wrestling, rolling and kicking. The strongest kid won and, usually, that wasn't him.

But this one was a clean grab. He trotted back to the grandstand — CRACK, another one — but he let it go.

Kim slowed to a walk as he passed between the bleachers and the backstop wire fence.

The Continentals were winning and the wooden benches were full of smiling faces. There were sunburned kids, babies on blankets, old men in white shirts and suspenders with their sleeves rolled up, and many others.

For as long as Kim could remember, the same man had "announced" the baseball games. He kept his post at a small desk hard against the wire backstop on the third base side. He was the official scorer and he announced the names of the batters into a big microphone on a stand. And dished out a dime for every returned foul ball.

Kim set the baseball on the table and got his ten cents. Two other kids were right behind him. The announcer nodded thanks and kept his attention on the game. He had a very round face and almost impossibly thick glasses in thin wire frames that made his eyeballs look huge and, unmistakably, he was happy, very happy.

I bet Caraway Days are his favourite time of the year too, Kim thought as he trotted back to take up his position.

After two hours, Kim had earned seventy cents, a pretty decent haul. He even got a homer, although that wasn't too hard. Most kids didn't bother chasing home runs, because it was such a long way. The grass beyond the outfield fence was long and thick and sometimes the ball disappeared into it, never to be found, but Kim happened to be the farthest kid down the right field line when one of the Continentals "gave it a ride," as they say. He was able to keep his eye on the ball as it hit and rolled. Then it was just a matter of running it down.

He treated himself to a hot dog and an orange Fanta and watched the Continentals finish their winning game, then he went on a few rides, topping it off with a spin up the big, towering Ferris wheel.

Kim wasn't scared at all. The view from the top was wonderful. He could see the grain elevators at the end of downtown, the entire fairgrounds, and the fluffy clouds drifting off forever.

If there was going to be a storm later, it would start building now, out in the northwest, but there were no black clouds gathering, no blinks of lightning off in the distance.

Kim was jammed into the Ferris wheel chair with two girls and their mother, who he guessed were farm girls from far away, since he had never seen them before.

The girl closest to him had red hair and freckles and squealed like crazy when they went over the top of the circle and swooped down the front. She grabbed Kim's arm and looked right at him as she screamed. Kim giggled along too and hoped he would bump into her later, but he didn't. Caraway Days were like that. You met lots of boys and girls and never saw them again. As for friends, Kim liked to just fall in with whoever happened along, though sometimes news spread of special "attractions."

When he ran down off the exit ramp from the Ferris wheel, and said goodbye to the freckle-faced girl, there was little Rodney, the messenger kid, bouncing from one foot to the other, bursting with news.

"They're at the Crown & Anchor," Rodney announced, "and it's pretty neat!"

There was no explanation of who "they" might be, or just what was "neat," but it certainly didn't matter. If Rodney said the Crown & Anchor was the place to be, that was good enough for Kim!

Suddenly, he had to be there — fast. He ran at top speed through the adults, using a kid's special ability to run full tilt through a crowd and just barely miss everyone in it. He found a thread of a direction and followed it right to the action — the Crown & Anchor wheel.

Crown & Anchor was a game played with a big wheel that was mounted on a stand. The wheel was covered with combinations of crowns, anchors, and the symbols from playing cards: hearts, diamonds, spades, and clubs.

It was a grown-up betting game. Kids were *not* supposed to play. The man running the game yelled, "Place your bets!"

and gave the wheel a spin, which produced a sound exactly like running a stick down a picket fence as a strong piece of leather clicked over the pegs that lined the outside of the wheel.

Click click click click.

"Place your bets!" the man cried as Kim arrived, with Rodney bouncing up behind him. At first Kim could see nothing unusual about the game, nor could he find any other kids there. He gave Rodney an inquisitive look. What's up?

Rodney just turned back to the game as if to say "Wait." The big wheel clattered to a stop.

"Two hearts 'n a diamond!" the man announced loudly. With quick, polished movements, he scooped out the losing bets and paid money onto the spot for hearts and the one for diamonds on the counter in front of him.

The game was crowded and Kim had to press through the arms and elbows of the adults to catch a glimpse of what Rodney said was so interesting. Suddenly, with a quick, polished movement much like the one employed by the grown-up running the game, a kid's hand appeared from under the lip of the counter and snatched two quarters off the diamonds spot.

Bending through the adults, Kim followed the hand down under the counter. Brushcut Bobbie and Lips Lloyd! They were playing the game illegally! Lloyd put his finger to his fat lips.

"Sssssssshhhh!" he said.

Kim scrambled underneath to join them, the nastiness of their last encounter instantly forgotten. It was Caraway Days!

Huddled there, with their backs to the game, they were looking at the knobby knees and fat ankles of countless adults who were crowded close to the betting action. They were perfectly hidden.

"You guys can't do this!" Kim hissed.

"Why not?" Lloyd whispered.

"You're gonna get caught!"

"We are not," Bobbie said flatly, and it seemed to be true. "You wanna bet or not?"

Kim noticed that the underside of the counter had been marked, in pencil, with symbols that corresponded to the ones on the top side where the bets were placed. Hearts, diamonds, crowns, anchors, and so on.

Should he?

"Okay, you do it," he whispered to Bobbie and handed him ten cents.

"You wanna believe I'm doing it," Bobbie said. "Me'n Lloyd are the only two good at this."

"You need at least a quarter," Lloyd said with a little snicker. Kim quickly handed one over. "Anchors," he said.

Bobbie expertly placed the bet, which included two quarters of his own. They huddled silently underneath the counter as the action proceeded above them.

"Place your bets!" they heard the man say. The big wheel was in motion a second later and the whole booth rocked as it turned. Click click click click click . . .

"Three spades!" the man called.

Darn! Kim scowled at Bobbie, who just shrugged. They didn't have to do anything when they lost.

"Maybe my luck has gone bad," Kim said. Bobbie jingled his pocket and withdrew a handful of quarters to show Kim. "Mine hasn't," he grinned.

Lloyd had a serious look on his face.

"Okay," he said as if counting something in his head, "Crowns are overdue. Everything on Crowns."

In a flash, they had placed six quarters on Crowns. The sound of the wheel spinning filled their ears and they waited tensely. Click click click . . .

"Three Crowns!" the man yelled.

With silent shouts, they celebrated as Bobbie reached up and quickly snatched their winnings. Two of the quarters had been Kim's — he had won a buck and a half!

"Okay, okay, okay," he breathed excitedly. "I'm done."

Bobbie paid him out in a flash and Kim wiggled out from under the counter, crawling on hands and knees through the adults' legs until he popped into the open on the midway. Rodney was there.

"Neat, huh?"

"Yeah. Neat."

Kim collected himself and counted his winnings. He moved around to the edge of the booth and could see Bobbie and Lloyd under there going strong, cackling softly to themselves as they played each spin of the big wheel.

Kim watched for several turns and then noticed something curious. He watched the man very carefully as he ran the game, yelling "Place your bets!" and spinning the wheel. The booth was crowded with worked-up adults, and it was noisy, but the man was used to it and smoothly handled all the action. Kim could see Bobbie's deft hand at work, and

Lloyd's. As he watched a few spins, he also realized that the man running the game could see those kids' hands come up from under the counter too!

Kim waited for him to do something about it — angrily run around and send Bobbie and Lloyd packing — but after several spins he realized nothing of the sort was going to happen.

The man knew exactly what was going on! And he didn't say a thing! It was Caraway Days!

Kim stepped away and lightly made his way through the gyrating, grinding rides of the midway. Rodney was beside him.

"Goin' to the grandstand," Kim announced for no particular reason.

"Dennis is there," Rodney reported, and vanished into the crowd.

There was no sign of Dennis, however, when Kim arrived at the grandstand. He bought a hamburger and another orange Fanta and hung around for a few minutes, wondering if Rodney was mistaken, but after thinking about it, he realized Dennis had most likely gone to one of their favourite hiding places.

The grandstand was walled in, like a house. There was a side door that led into a storage area. Kim slipped in there, then climbed up the crisscrossed beams until he was on top of the booth where the food was made. The surface was sloped beneath the rising rows of seats and there, crouched by himself, was Dennis.

It was a tarred surface, which was sticky, and there was a lot of broken glass and small bits of gravel. Kim crab-walked over to Dennis, who was also drinking a pop, and joined him to watch the game, which was visible through the slats of the seats.

Dennis said nothing, nor Kim, for they were right underneath the fans and, if they kept quiet, nobody would know they were there. It was a funny way to see people, from behind, with their bums and backs and legs facing them. Sometimes kids snuck up behind an old man and yelled "Boo!" Or tickled a lady's ankles with a serviette. That made them jump!

But Kim and Dennis just squatted there and quietly sucked on the straws in their pops. Kim took a moment to look around, however, since this was where change fell when people dropped it. All the kids knew this, of course, so the area was thoroughly scoured many times a day and, no surprise, there wasn't any money in sight.

CRACK! A foul ball sailed back over the grandstand. Kim chewed down the last of his burger. Dennis finished his pop, quite loudly, sucking out the last drops from the bottom of the bottle, and through the slats Kim could see a few people turning around, as they realized for the first time there was someone *under* there.

The boys smiled. "I'm gonna see the horse races. Wanna come?" Dennis said in his gravelly way. Kim shook his head. He had just arrived and wanted to stay for awhile.

"Going to the grandstand show?" Kim asked.

"Maybe."

"See ya," Kim said as Dennis left, taking his pop bottle with him. He would get two cents for taking it back.

Kim stretched out and enjoyed the view. He could see everything, but no one could see him. He figured it was about how a dog felt in its doghouse. Safe and warm.

He thought he might take a bike ride around the entire fairgrounds later. The grandstand show was at least four hours away and, oddly, it did not take place at the grandstand, but inside the arena, which was bigger and, of course, safe from rain.

Kim licked his fingers and drank the rest of his pop. He wedged the pop bottle next to a piece of wood so it wouldn't roll down the sloping roof and he would know where it was when he wanted to return it for the two cents.

The tar roof gave off a hot, sticky, black smell and there was smoke from the burgers cooking beneath him, which wafted up to meet it. The sunshine streaked through the slats. Kim stretched out flat, safe and warm, and thought that, yes, for the first time in weeks he was happy and contented. Caraway Days were doing it again . . .

Huh! he said to himself . . . *What happened?*

He propped up on his elbow and, for a second, did not know where he was.

Then it hit him. He had fallen asleep! Inside the grandstand. On the tar roof!

He sat up straight — too fast — and then decided not to move. He felt dizzy.

What time was it? His watch told him. A quarter to eight! He had been asleep for three hours!

Kim could see that the baseball games were over and the bleachers were deserted. The sun was going down and the lights on the rides were lit up. The midway was a twirling, musical playground of noise and coloured lights.

Suddenly, he wanted to get out of the grandstand right away. He scurried toward the way out, then slowed down. There was a big, rusty nail sticking out somewhere, he remembered. A kid had stood up into it once and poked a hole in his back. It bled red and dark and ugly, and the kid had to go to the hospital to get a needle.

Kim crawled slowly, keeping low. He missed the nail, wherever it was, and carefully descended through the crisscrossed beams to the side door and out onto open ground. His bike was there. Everything around him was shut down, the ball games and the hamburger stand, but a crowd of people was going into the arena. The grandstand show! It was starting!

Kim knew he should have gone home for supper. His mom was probably looking for him, and she would be very angry that he had not gone home to eat.

Kim joined the line of people streaming into the arena. The ticket booth was right there, but he told the lady he was only going inside to look for his mom. "All right, go ahead," she replied and Kim could tell she thought it was a fib to avoid paying admission, but it wasn't at all. He knew he'd better find her.

Suddenly, like a gopher popping out of its hole, little Rodney appeared out of nowhere.

"Your mom's looking for you," he said.

"I know!" Kim replied, but he declined to add that he'd fallen asleep in the grandstand, which sounded pretty embarrassing when he thought about it. "Where?"

Rodney motioned with his head and Kim fell in behind him. In an instant, they were winnowing through the rows of seats inside the darkened arena. The grandstand show was held where the ice usually was, and it was packed with spectators. On the wooden stage, a Scottish man in a kilt and uniform played an accordion, sang, and danced a jig. The crowd found him very funny, but Kim paid no attention. He kept his eyes on Rodney's tiny back and followed him right up to the front row.

Rodney skipped down the row and turned around right where Kim's mom was sitting to make sure Kim saw her. Then he vanished.

His mom was sitting with some lady friends, laughing and clapping along with the Scottish song. Kim edged up to her slowly. He was going to get heck!

"Well Kim, there you are," his mom said over the music.

"I missed supper," Kim said.

His mom nodded. "Did you get anything to eat?" she said.

Kim nodded back.

"You can stay and watch the fireworks, then go home, all right?" his mom continued.

Kim nodded and backed away. The Scotsman was dancing on one foot now. The crowd clapped along. Kim blinked. He was still waking up, really. And he was very surprised that his mom was not angry with him, but it was Caraway Days and kids could get away with almost anything!

Kim ducked down to floor level to stay out of the way and rested a second to wake up completely. Slowly, he became aware of a presence behind him in the dark, someone familiar, and when he turned around to take a look, he realized that he was sitting just over from Mr. White!

He hadn't seen him since before the awful day when the rampaging kids wrecked the Haunted House. What should he do? Did Mr. White notice him?

In a flash, Kim saw that he did. Kim smiled tightly and waved a little, just to be friendly, because he really didn't how Mr. White would respond.

The friendly, smiling farmer reached over and mussed his hair. "How are ya, Kim? Enjoying the Fair?"

"Yeah! Lots," was all Kim could think to say. He didn't like having his hair messed up like that, but this time was different, special, for in a second he understood that Mr. White wasn't mad at him for his role in the riot. Maybe he didn't even know Kim was The Kid Who Threw the Rock . . . No, Kim corrected himself, he had to know that. His mom would have told him and, besides, everyone knew it. Mr. White, however, had shown by that little gesture that he forgave Kim for whatever had gone on.

Caraway Days were doing it again and this was the best proof he could ever have!

Kim slipped away from the performance and breezed out the door.

It was night, cool and refreshing. The midway rides lifted and dropped like some sort of complicated, connected lit-up insect and, from amongst them, he spotted a group of his friends walking toward him. Bobbie, Lloyd, Dennis, Tommy, even little Rodney.

"How much did you make on the Crown & Anchor?" Kim asked Bobbie.

"Nuthin'," Bobbie replied. "I was up five bucks and I lost it all." He shrugged. "Easy come, easy go."

"When are the fireworks?" Dennis asked.

A brilliant white light rising into the sky beyond the baseball diamond answered his question. POOM! went the first firework. It was a small one, to signal that the main show was ready to go. Pop! Pop! Pop! went another one.

The boys ran to the fence around the ball diamond, stopped there, and looked out into the dark. They could see shapes moving beyond the outfield fence — the firemen who ran the show, setting off the explosives a safe distance away.

"Let's get closer!" Lloyd urged, and in a flash they were all running down the third baseline fence. Kim joined the crowd eagerly, because he loved fireworks, though he instantly thought of the mob at the Haunted House.

It can't happen here, he told himself and hoped it was true.

They arrived at another fence, a temporary one, the kind that could be rolled up. It was called a snow fence, but Kim usually saw them used in summer.

Bobbie grabbed the slats with both hands and smoothly vaulted it without a word. The rest of the boys quickly followed, though Tom needed help.

"Come on!" Dennis called.

Kim was right behind him. "That's far enough!" he hissed. He certainly didn't want to get caught. He hauled Lloyd down into the grass and that did the trick. Bobbie stopped and so did Dennis. Tom and Rodney huddled around too.

They giggled a bit and crawled ahead through the grass, arriving at a pile of railway ties stacked out in the middle of nowhere. They hunched behind them.

Kim peeked out. The firemen, who wore their full uniforms of fire suits and helmets, were not very far away. Way back past the baseball field and the grandstand, people were pouring out of the arena and milling around. They could hear car doors open and shut.

The railway ties smelled stinky and gooey, sort of like the tar roof. Kim could see Dennis peering around the other corner. Suddenly, he snapped back to rejoin the group.

"That's the fireman we dunked!" he whispered to Kim, and collapsed into a convulsion of cackling.

"Ssssssh!" Kim hissed back, but he was laughing. What if the fireman found them? Would he be extra angry?

"I knew you guys would sink us," Lloyd said, snickering with an accusation as always.

Kim didn't answer. It would just lead to an argument and they needed silence. After a long minute, the sounds of the firemen diminished.

"We lost 'em," Bobbie said and fell back, relaxed.

Suddenly, just behind the railway ties, three rockets launched and seared straight up, blazing white fire!

All the boys ducked as low as they could, then lay flat on their backs.

BOOM!! POW!! POP!! The fireworks went off right over their heads!

Glittering burning bits of golden sparkling spiders floated down all around them, then went dark just before they reached the grass.

"That's why the firemen left!" Tommy yelled. "The fireworks are right here!"

Only ten feet from them, a rocket erupted with a sound like the whistling of a giant. "THHHEE-EEEEWW!!"

They were right next to the launch site!

PACK!! PACK!! POW!! BOOM!!

More glittering spiders. And exploding spiny sea creatures. And popcorn machinegun bursts. Burning flares floating downward. More whistling like a giant.

Against the black sky, the smoke from the explosions was lit up. It took the same shape as the bursts of light, and slowly drifted sideways.

Four more rockets exploded skyward just behind them!

BOOM-BOOM-PACK-PACK!!

More fireworks went up and there was a burst of several large bombs of pure brilliant white light. Then the biggest beach ball explosion of them all. It blew out into a shining blue globe of spines. Then the ends of the spines exploded too. Kim felt like he could reach out, unharmed, and touch the last ones that streaked, then floated, to earth.

The light scratched a hole in the night sky. Then it was gone.

The boys huddled together and looked up for more. But that was it.

Back among the cars, headlights came on and the sound of horns honking "Thanks" reached them.

Kim fell back into the cool grass and looked straight up. White fireworks smoke still hung in the air.

They were the best fireworks Kim had ever seen.

Maybe the best he would ever see.

It was the perfect end to a perfect day.

Caraway Days had done it again.

"DEAR KIM . . . "

Kim went back to the Fair the next day and had just as much fun, though he didn't get as close to the fireworks this time. The Continentals made it to the final game in the baseball tournament, though true to form they lost by four runs to the faraway town of Wesley.

Kim had not been aware of it, but in the midst of all the celebrations, the rides, the parade, the baseball games, the horse races and other attractions, someone had tried to say hello to him and failed. He only understood a week later when a letter arrived in the mail, addressed to him.

Receiving an actual letter was a rare event for Kim, one confined almost exclusively to the time before his birthday or just before Christmas, when cousins and aunts sent along cards with best wishes, just as he had dutifully done for them, at his mother's prompting.

But when Kim did a chore by riding his bike to the Post Office to get the mail, there it was, a letter addressed to him in careful, precise handwriting, jammed in among all the other mail his family received.

Kim was immediately glad he had volunteered for the job that day. This was before now and some things were different. In Caraway there was no mail delivery, so everyone had to journey to the Post Office each day and use a key to open up their own mailbox.

By performing the small chore, Kim got first crack at the mail and he wouldn't have to offer an explanation for the personal letter, for he was sure his mom and dad and Matt would be nosey about it. Especially since the letter was from a girl.

He sat outside on the Post Office steps and tore open the envelope.

Dear Kim, it began. The handwriting was suddenly much squigglier.

> *Did you see me in the Caraway Days parade? I*
> *waved, but you didn't wave back. Perhaps your*
> *attention was elsewhere. I was part of the Woods and*
> *Meadow Riding Club that was grouped just ahead of*
> *the decorated bikes. I saw you leave the parade and*
> *hoped to find you later, but was not successful. Did*
> *you enjoy the Fair? I did, although I was only in*
> *town for the morning of the first day. I was obliged to*
> *return to the farm.*
>
> *Kim, I received news of the awful events at the old*
> *pioneer house on the White property. I have also*
> *heard that several people feel much of the blame for*
> *starting the upset falls on you. I don't think it's fair!*
> *I have an idea of what might have happened, Kim.*
> *It's perhaps too long to describe here. Come out to the*
> *farm one day and I'll fill you in.*
> *Sincerely,*
> *Beverly Alcomdale*

(a.k.a. "Beverly Banana")

Kim burst out laughing when he read the last part. He didn't know what "a.k.a." meant, but the girl who had written him the letter had a "description nickname" too. She was Beverly Banana, because she was famous for wearing long yellow scarves all the time. Calling herself that meant she knew of her nickname and was making fun of herself to boot. It was all pretty funny, Kim felt, and pretty grown-up of her too.

Thinking back carefully, Kim remembered that he *had* seen Beverly Banana in the parade, in the section of horses in front of the bikes. Did she wave when he scooted by? He couldn't remember, but Beverly was easily spotted from a distance with her ever-present yellow scarf flying off in the breeze. It was her trademark. In the winter it was wool, in the summer something lighter, perhaps even silk, but it was always bright yellow.

"Well, Beverly Banana," Kim said out loud, "you and me gotta have a talk."

He stood up and dusted off his bum.

"Mind you, it would sure help if I knew where you lived."

A Map, the Hard Way

"How many?"

"Three honeybees and a bumbler. How about you?"

"One honeybee and two bumblers."

Kim held up his bee-catching jar and stared through the bits of grass and clumps of leaves to inspect his haul. He was the one with the three honeybees and one bumblebee and, as he held his glass peanut butter jar up to the sun, he could put his face right next to the insects as they crawled and buzzed frantically in temporary captivity. He could study them — they didn't know he was there.

Dennis made a quick scooping move over a clover bloom, opening and closing the lid of his bee jar in a smooth, snatching motion. He stood up and grinned triumphantly.

"*Three* bumblers," he announced.

They were spending an afternoon catching bees in one of Mr. White's fields. It was getting late in the summer for bee-catching, since the dandelion blooms had long since turned to fluff and blown away. There was still plenty of nectar in the clover, however, and a few hours spent working through the buzzing fields could yield a collection of six, eight, or even ten bees.

There were two ways to catch a bee.

The easiest was to open the jar real wide and cut off the entire top of the dandelion or clover bloom and take the flower and the bee with it. Often the bee just kept crawling over the bloom, not even aware it had been caught. There was a drawback to this method, however, since it meant opening the jar completely. If there were already lots of bees inside, it was easy for them to escape.

The second way was harder, because it required the bee-catcher to whisk the bee right off the top of the flower by just catching it with the rim of the barely-opened lid and flicking it into the jar.

The math of bee-catching was unavoidable: once there were several bees in the jar, it was necessary to use the second, more dangerous way in order to hang onto the bees already caught. It made bee-catching a sort of "dare game," with the stakes rising as more and more bees were captured.

"Got one — nope!" Dennis exclaimed as a honeybee narrowly escaped him. He was about to pounce just when the bee moved. He couldn't risk opening his pickle jar too wide to snatch it.

Kim took a deep breath and blew it out. His mind was elsewhere and that was not the way to go about catching bees. A tiny lapse in concentration could lead to disaster. He stood up straight and took a break.

"Why the heck would she say she had something to tell me and not just put it in the letter?" he asked again.

"Well, she said it was too complicated."

"Then why wouldn't she at least draw me a map so I could find her place?"

"I dunno," Dennis said. "She must think you already know."

Kim sighed. That was probably true. He knew Beverly from school, of course, and thought she was a really nice girl, polite and funny and quite pretty, but she was a farm kid and, around Caraway, there was a firm dividing line between farm kids and town kids.

In so many ways, they didn't understand each other. Some of the "townies" looked down their noses at the farm kids, because they thought they were stupid and dirty. There were farm kids who came to school with holes in their pants and dirt wedged under each fingernail. They looked like they were neighbours of Barefoot or something.

On the other hand, there were also farm kids — and Beverly was one of these — who breezed into school off the bus as if they were world travellers merely visiting an interesting stopover. All the girls remarked that Beverly wore very nice clothes, and often really flashy cowgirl boots, and her long tawny hair was always perfectly brushed and arranged with combs and clips.

To top it all off: the ever-present, blazing yellow scarf. She wore it with distinct style. Beverly was also relentlessly cheerful and had that farm kid talent for taking most any setback in stride, shrugging it off, and moving on to the next challenge. Kim had noticed that about a lot of farm kids.

"Got ya!" Dennis yelled as he snapped another catch. "Bumbler. I've got four bumblers."

Kim smiled and gave his friend a ribbing: "Yeah yeah, they're easy and you know it . . . "

Dennis made a face back, but he was not disagreeing. Bumblers were easy compared to honeybees, because they were big, fuzzy and slow. Rile a bumblebee and it would fly around you in angry circles, coming close and going ZZZZZZZZZZZZZZ in a low tone before flying away, but it was not likely to sting. You almost had to step on one to make it sting.

Honeybees were another matter altogether.

"Hey, there's Tommy," Dennis observed as they both noticed a kid approaching by himself through the clover.

Tom walked zig-zaggy through the clumps of clover plants and flowers, observing each one to see if it hosted bees at that moment. He was badly sunburned and squinted ahead through his glasses. His tummy jiggled and stuck out under his shirt.

But there was unmistakably a hint of a swagger in his step, because for all of his failings at athletics and physical activities generally, Tummy Tom was a heck of a bee catcher. He could freeze into a pose of perfect stillness while a bee flitted from bloom to bloom in front of him, then loom in with his eyes widening behind his glasses and, wham, catch that bee in an instant.

Tom could even, apparently, withstand bee stings better than others, because on the rare days when he got "nailed," he would clench his fists and shiver all over and go, "Rrrrrrr!!" and that was it.

He carried a jar that was half again as big as the ones Dennis and Kim used and it was like a little jungle of plant leaves, flowers and buzzing bumblers and honeybees.

"How's it going, you guys?" Tom asked, pretty as you please.

"Okay," Kim said, then added the obvious. "You've got a lot."

Tom shrugged as if to say, "Wait 'til I *really* get going."

"Hey Tom, do you know what 'AKA' means?" Dennis said out of nowhere.

"Huh?"

"AKA."

"Never heard of it."

"Well, actually, it's 'a.k.a.'," Kim added. "Separate letters."

"Oh," Tom said, looking up at the sun and squinting. "Oh, yeah. It's short for 'also known as'. Why?"

"Just wondered," Dennis said. Kim had shown him the letter from Beverly and now they had solved at least one mystery in it. Kim grinned to himself again, because it meant for certain that Beverly knew she was Beverly Banana and had made a joke about it.

Kim and Dennis exchanged a glance. Should they tell Tom about the rest of the letter? Kim shook his head at Dennis ever so slightly. He wanted to try another approach.

"School in a couple weeks," he said casually.

"Yeah, school," Tom echoed. "I'm glad actually. Summer's boring."

"No, it's not," Dennis protested. "School's boring." He looked at Kim. What was up?

"Wonder who we'll get?" he mused. He meant which teacher.

"If I get Mrs. Granby, I'm gonna barf," Tom blurted out.

"Why?"

"She displays favouritism toward the girls," Tom declared, sounding like he'd read that in a book. "I was in a map project with Sandra Stedman and Alice Shewchuk and Beverly Alcomdale last year and Mrs. Granby gave them *everything*. Bradley Rooks was in there and he wasn't too bad — well, he can be bad — and once she grabbed him by the ear and hauled him out of his desk right over the armrest. By his *ear*."

"Be nice to tell some of those girls that, wouldn't it?" Kim said as angrily as he could manage. "Just find Beverly Banana at her farmhouse and tell her exactly that."

"Well, good luck," Tom retorted. "It's miles away and it's not a farm, it's a ranch. Didn't you see her in the parade on that horse about a mile high?"

Kim could tell from Tommy's tone that he didn't take too well to Beverly Banana, but that didn't matter.

"Like, *where*, exactly?"

"I dunno, over there a ways." Tom pointed to the southwest. "Quite a ways. I had to visit there for this project once with my mom."

"And which road did you take?"

"I dunno," Tom said defensively. "Who wants to know?"

"I do."

"Why?"

"Oh, just tell him!" Dennis exploded. "What difference does it make?"

Kim gave Dennis a look — *"He'll tease me,"* it said — but he realized he wasn't going to trick Tommy into telling him, so he dug in his pocket for Beverly's letter and showed it to Tom.

Tommy smirked a little when he read it, then said, "What the heck could Beverly Banana possibly know about that?"

"That's why I wanna talk to her," Kim said tensely, leaving off the words he wanted to add: *"you idiot."*

"Look, it's important," Dennis growled.

"She should've just told you," Tom said. "She must want a visit or something. I think she likes you."

"So?"

"You probably like her too."

"I do not."

"Well, I sure don't, so why should I tell you where she lives?" Tom replied.

"Just do it," Dennis said in a threatening voice and he pushed his bee jar into Tommy's protruding tummy.

"Make me," Tom retorted, but he was cowed by the look in Dennis's eye. "It's too far, anyway," he added. "Gotta be four miles."

"That's only too far for you," Kim said bluntly. "You're too fat to bike-ride that far, that's all." He was fed up and didn't mind tossing out a few insults. Tom blushed.

"All right," he said, retrenching, "you catch the next bee before me and I'll tell you."

A contest! In one of the very few things where Tom had an advantage! Kim sighed. He could see he had no choice.

"Look, he said it was that way and it was four miles, why don't we just ride our bikes down there and try to find it?" Dennis said to Kim.

"Yeah, I think he's just pretending he knows where it is, anyway," Kim said back to Dennis.

"And I think you're chicken to try to out-bee-catch me," Tommy shot back, "because you know you're gonna lose!"

The three boys suddenly fell silent, for the accusations were getting out of hand. Calling someone chicken was pretty serious, even if Tom had done it after Kim had more or less called him a liar, and before that, fat. Kim decided he would probably have to find another way to locate Beverly's farm, or ranch if that's what it was, because it would be difficult to beat Tom at this game. He was pretty good at snagging bees.

"It's harder for me because my jar's already full," Tom added in a quieter voice. He was trying to make it sound even.

"Okay," Kim replied evenly. "Next bee."

"I'll say go," Dennis put in. He pointed to an open area near them, away from the clover. "You both stand over there."

Dennis passed near Kim as they set up the contest. "Got any tricks up your sleeve, tricky guy? Now's the time."

Kim shook his head blankly. Dennis hadn't said that for a long time. It sounded old-fashioned, actually, as if the expression were a pair of shoes he'd outgrown.

Kim inspected his bee jar as he prepared to take on Tom in this stupid race. Thankfully, the three honeybees and one bumbler were quieter now, since they had become exhausted buzzing around the jar looking for a way out. Several nail holes in the metal lid allowed them air.

He glanced over at Tom's jar. Although it was bigger, there were probably ten honeybees and half a dozen bumblers in there.

"So is it a rule that if any bees escape, you lose?" Kim asked.

"Sure," Tom answered defiantly. He held up his jar and shook it once, hard. All the bees fell down to the bottom, away from the lid.

Dennis held up his hand, got their attention, and dropped it. The race was on! Kim and Tom scurried back into the clover patch and bent over the flowers looking for bees.

Concentrate, Kim told himself. *Don't look at him.*

Suddenly there were bees everywhere — but nowhere near him, it seemed. When Kim leapt in their direction, they flitted out of reach or zoomed past his ears and away. He pounced through the clover in fits and starts, looking for a likely catch, and out of the corner of his eye he could detect the large, round form of Tom doing the same.

Kim scurried ahead and finally located a bee that was too busy at work on a flower to fly away at his approach. It was orange-striped, hairy, and already laden with a large haul of pollen that bulged in the sacks on its hind legs. A perfect candidate.

"Darn!" Tom exclaimed off to his right, followed by the sound of his bee jar lid slamming shut after an unsuccessful snag. Kim knew he had only seconds to get one.

Now the bee started to flower-hop, floating to a new one, stopping for a few seconds, then floating off again. Kim found himself imitating the movement, floating up and down to follow the bee's progress.

Closer . . . closer . . .

Kim struck. He shook the jar to knock the other bees to the bottom, then opened the lid just a bit — he was going to use the second method and just scoop that bee quickly inside — and swept the lid along the top of the clover bloom.

He missed.

Well, not quite.

ZZZVVVZZZZZZVVVVTTTTTT!!

He peeked around the jar. The bee was half in, half out, trapped there and, boy, was it mad!

"Get it?" Dennis asked hopefully as he trotted over for a look. Kim froze and allowed Dennis to move around him so he could see the problem.

"Ahh-ahhhh!" his friend yelled and shrank back ten feet in an instant. "Don't let it go!"

Of course not! But how could he get it into the jar? Kim's hand was only a few inches from the wildly buzzing bee. What should he do?

"That doesn't count!" Tom yelled over to them, then returned to his own search.

"Shut up, Tom," Kim hissed.

"Kill it!" Dennis yelled. "Squish it!"

"Okay, okay," Kim replied. It was the only thing to do. He pressed the lid against the bee and it buzzed louder and LOUDER but it was still alive.

ZZZZZVVVZZZVVTTT!!

If I can just turn the lid a tiny tiny bit I can squish it, Kim said to himself.

ZZZZZZVVVVVZZZZVVVVTTTTTTT!!

Slowly, slowly, he twisted the lid, pressing with all his strength to increase his slim hold on the bee and crush it —

No! It was loose!

"OWWWWW!" Kim screamed. The bee stung him on the shoulder!

He dropped his jar and all the other bees were free!

The sting felt like a nail hammered into his skin!

"Ahh-ahhhh!" Dennis wailed and he ran back some more.

Kim skipped away from his jar, now open on the ground, but the bees in the small, sun-filled prison were dopey and slow.

But the sting! AHHHHH!

PURE PAIN.

He hadn't been stung for a couple of years and he had forgotten what it was like. *PAIN PAIN PAIN.*

Kim staggered out of the clover field into the open area. He looked over at his shoulder — the bee was still there! It was stuck! It was pulling itself off its stinger, pulling its insides right out and still buzzing!

Kim flicked the main part of the bee away, like he was shooting a marble. The stinger was still jabbed into his arm, with a string of bee guts tied to it. He tried to flick the stinger away too, but that only made it pulse and shoot more poison into him.

More whacks of the hammer on the nail. *PAIN!*

Kim bent over and squeezed tears from his eyes.

"Here, let me . . . " Dennis said. He pinched the stinger between his thumbnail and his fingernail and yanked it out. Kim staggered in circles.

"Ow . . . ow . . . ow . . . "

From back in the field, he was vaguely aware of seeing Tom stand up, smiling. "Got one!" he announced. "I win!"

Kim had lost. And got stung. He no longer cared about losing, or anything! It just hurt too much.

He and Dennis ran away from the bee field, abandoning their peanut butter and pickle jars, and Kim had the strong feeling that he was leaving his friendship with Tommy there too, for he thought Tom had been a real jerk for not telling him the directions he needed.

The two boys scrambled away from the bee field and they didn't look back.

By that evening, the sting no longer hurt, though the spot where the bee nailed him remained a raised, red welt.

His mom made him an ice compact for it and he kept it pressed to the sting for hours. She also surprised him later when she found him down in the basement, huddled on the couch next to the lamp, reading a book.

"Tommy dropped this for you," she said, handing him a piece of paper. "It appears to be a map."

Kim inspected the paper. It was, indeed, a map. The directions to Beverly's place.

There was a scrawled message too, from Tom:

"I guess you earned this. Hurts, huh?"

BEVERLY BANANA AND CARAWAY KIM

The plan was that Dennis would accompany Kim on the bike journey to Beverly Banana's ranch, but at the last minute he had to go shopping with his mom.

So, with Tom's map in his pocket, Kim set out alone from Caraway. First, he took the road that headed straight south from the west end of town by the fairgrounds, which he followed for the first two miles. This was to prove the most challenging part of the trip, since it was a main road and regularly traversed by many cars and big trucks that tossed off clods of mud and — much more dangerous — bouncing stones. Although it was a main road, it was gravel, not pavement.

Kim kept well to the right and, on a few occasions, did the smart thing by riding into the ditch when two vehicles crossed next to him, churning up a storm of dust, dirt and gravel. It was best to get well out of the way. He became quite filthy and laughed to himself that Beverly, the farm kid, was going to be presented with a dirty town kid.

After reaching the turnoff, it was a mile west, then another two miles south before he came upon the stretch of road, indicated on the map, that ought to run past Beverly's farm.

Along the way, he could hear the telephone wires singing in the wind beside him, buzzing and humming as though they were live things. Beverly hadn't suggested a phone call and Kim had not even considered such a thing either.

This was before now and some things were different. In the countryside, telephones were weird. Some farms, Kim knew from what he gleaned at school, didn't even have phones. Others were served by "party lines," which was a rather strange way to describe phone lines that were anything but a party.

They were a big snooperoo, as far as Kim could tell, because he had heard from farm kids that several families shared the same line. Each farm family had a different ring on their phone to indicate if the call was for them, but *anybody* on the shared line could pick up the phone and listen in. Weird!

As Kim pedaled along he imagined that the telephone lines hummed and sang so much because there were so many people talking and yakking on them at the same time.

"Who's that? Who is that? Watch out!"

What could Beverly possibly tell him about that?

Kim had wondered how he would tell exactly which farm, or ranch, was Beverly's, but as he approached it, there was absolutely no question it was hers. There was a freshly-painted, white wooden fence along about half a mile of field leading up to the main gate, and then at the entrance there was a large sign made of sticks over top of the entranceway that read "Alcomdale Acres."

That had to be it. Kim slowed to a crawl and debated whether to pedal up the long, straight gravel driveway.

"Mmmm . . . gonna look around," he said out loud. It was pretty imposing and it didn't feel right to just ride in. Besides, he happened to know that Beverly had at least two older sisters and two older brothers and, for the life of him, he didn't know what he might say to them to explain his arrival.

Kim cycled right past the main gate. The ranch continued for farther than he could see, with the regular pattern of the white wooden fence carrying on over hill and dale and out of sight. The ranch didn't have grain fields of barley or wheat, but rather big rolling green pastures of short grass, perfect for horses to run in and munch down their breakfast, dinner, and supper.

And there were plenty of horses. Close to him, and farther off in the distance, pairs and small herds of gleaming brown and black steeds could be seen prancing and trotting about. Kim had not realized anyone could have so many horses. What did they do with them all?

Suddenly one of the horses in the distance turned to him, galloped in his direction, and seemed to grow a top as it came nearer. A rider!

As casually as he could manage, Kim stopped his bike, dismounted, and leaned against it on the edge of the road. The horse, an immense black and brown animal that ate up the field in huge strides, was soon near him. There was a girl aboard — was it Beverly? — no, she just looked like Beverly. She reined in the snorting horse at the fence across from Kim.

"Hey there," she said, "I'm Carol. What can I do for you?"

She really did look like an older version of Beverly, for her hair was of the same long golden sheen, and she had that same "Say hi to everyone" approach to people.

"Are you Beverly's sister?" Kim guessed.

"Yes!"

"I'm a friend of hers from school," Kim said. "Just, oh, out for a bike ride," he added, as if a four-mile bike trip was not at all out of the ordinary. Actually, it wasn't. He went for all-day bike rides with Dennis and Bobbie quite frequently, and many were into the countryside.

"I see," Carol said, smiling as if she had just heard some kind of private joke, "Is she expecting you?"

"Probably," Kim said with as much confidence as he could muster. "We, uh, we were talking at the Fair and she mentioned I should come out here some day." He couldn't possibly say, "She sent me a letter."

"Hmmm. I was with her at the Fair. Didn't see you. But that's neither here nor there. Who should I say is calling?"

"Kim."

"She'll know who that is?"

"Kim from Caraway."

"Okay. I'll find her. Stay here Caraway Kim and she'll be right over, I'd say."

Carol winked and smiled, then spurred her horse and clicked her tongue to make it run, and she was off at a gallop.

Kim watched her rip through the grass like a cowgirl in a Western movie and felt himself wondering why he didn't go to farms more often, especially if they were ranches.

It was actually quite some time before Kim saw another horse approaching across the grassy field. He used the interval to eat the peanut butter sandwich he'd brought, and drink his jar of milk.

Where's the yellow scarf? was all he could think of as Beverly thundered down upon him aboard the same gigantic horse he'd seen in the parade. She waved as soon as she crested the last rise and brought the horse in like a boat zooming in to shore, pulling it up sideways at the last second and spraying out what would have been water, but was of course dust.

"He-eyy, Sadie Sadie Sadie . . . " Beverly said in a sing-song voice as she patted the horse on the flank and popped off in one smooth bounce. She suddenly appeared tiny compared to the huge animal.

"Hi, Kim, so good of you to visit!"

"Hi, Beverly. I got your letter," Kim said bashfully. He set his bike down in the ditch and crossed over to meet her, feeling just a little thankful there was a fence between them. He had no idea what to expect from Beverly on her home territory, for he realized in an instant that the girl he knew at school was far away from home then and probably putting on a bit of a show.

Beverly swept her arm back toward the ranch. "We're loading hay and straw into the barn today. Going to take till nightfall but then we'll have it all in for winter. Yep."

"That's quite a horse," was all Kim could think to say. "It's yours, right?"

"She's all mine, that's for sure," Beverly smiled. "Sadie's quite a lady."

Kim smiled and looked up at the enormous, rippling stack of muscles that made up Sadie the Lady. She ripped a mouthful of grass out of the earth and loudly mashed it around in her teeth. Her eyes were huge, dark, and bottomless.

Beverly crossed her arms on the top of the fence and rested her chin there, looking at Kim.

"Pretty tough spot about the White place, hey?"

"Yeah," Kim shifted uncomfortably. "It's done me no good at all," he said, realizing he sounded like a cowboy all of a sudden.

"I never believed it, Kim, I never did," Beverly stated. "People talk a lot of bull, if you ask me, pardon my French."

"I guess."

"Neither do I see why you should be blamed for something you didn't start, 'far as I can see, and didn't progress, even if you *had* started it."

"Yep." Kim cleared his throat. "You mentioned in your letter you had an idea about what went on . . . ?"

"Well," Beverly stood up straight now and gripped the fence with her hands, rocking back and forth as she looked at Kim, "everyone says you were this left-handed kid who tossed the first rock and set off the big rampage . . . "

Kim nodded, though his stomach sank at Beverly's mention of "everyone." It must have spread over the whole countryside!

" . . . but I've heard tell there were a lot of boys there that day who weren't usually around town," she continued.

"That's right," Kim confirmed. "But it was hot and dusty and nobody knows for sure who was there."

"Neither do I, Kim," Beverly said, leaning close to the rail, "but I do know this, and perhaps you haven't thought of it:

that incident occurred on a Tuesday and that tells me something."

"What?"

"Tuesday is Auction Day, Kim. Did you ever think of that?"

"Uh, no. What's it mean?"

"It means, on a Tuesday, that Caraway is suddenly filled up with farm kids with nothing to do. Okay, they go to the auction, but unless you're buying a horse or have stock on the block, there's a whole day to occupy and most of those kids have four-five hours on their hands. I figure some of 'em range around looking for trouble. Boys, mostly."

Beverly's voice dropped low, as if she were telling a ghost story.

"Why, some of those boys might meander along down the White property and start something. You know boys. No offence, but you know what I mean."

"Yeah, I do," Kim agreed. For an instant, he thought of sharing his "boys are like a balloon" theory with Beverly, but decided against it. Besides, she seemed to know it already in her own way.

"Do you know who was in town that day, by any chance?" he asked.

"No, I do not."

"Well, who goes to auctions?"

"Lots of kids from far and wide, that's for sure, but if you were to ask around at the Auction Mart, maybe you could get a clue. What do you have to lose, Kim?" Beverly said, concerned, and shaking her head side to side.

"Nothing," Kim agreed. "Worth a try." Beverly was lost in a bad dream of worry and he could see she was out of things to say, but he had a question:

"Why was that old house so important anyway? Do you know?"

Beverly brightened, for she had an answer.

"Oh, it was an original pioneer house and my mother says there was a movement afoot to transport it somewhere safe and make it into a museum."

"Yeah, it should have been a museum," Kim said, and he wasn't just agreeing. He meant it. "It would have been a perfect museum."

"Exactly!" Beverly exclaimed. "We have to save the past so we know where we came from when we go ahead into the future. I'm so glad you agree, Kim! But you know what?"

"What?"

"That's why I think it was farm kids who contributed to its destruction."

"What do you mean?"

"Well, I can see that you understand its worth — the value of old things — but sometimes the people right next to old things don't appreciate them. Farm kids, in this case. That's what my mom says, anyway."

"Yeah, look at the old train station. They say it's going to be torn down."

"Exactly! It's a shame."

Kim nodded. He was very glad he'd found Beverly's place and made the trip to her ranch. She seemed like a whole different girl to him and he knew they'd be good friends from now on.

"Okay, I'll see if I can find any clues, Bev. Thanks."

"Okay, Caraway Kim," she smiled, and he knew she'd been talking all this over with her sister. "Good luck!"

"Hey, where's your scarf, Beverly Banana?" he tossed back, also with a smile.

She climbed up her enormous horse as if she were ascending into a tree house and gave him a big fat wink.

"Oh, that's just for town."

The Auction Mart Lead

"What exactly is going on here?" Dennis asked Kim in frustration.

Kim just shrugged his shoulders. "They're selling the cattle."

"Yeah, I know, but to *who*?"

It was a good question. On the next Tuesday, Kim and Dennis had found their way into the Auction Mart and navigated down a long series of corridors to make it into the selling ring. They climbed up into the wooden bleachers and took a seat.

"Gee . . . it's like we're in a cave or something," Dennis had remarked, because the entire building was dark and spooky, even though the ring where the livestock was sold was brightly lit. The illumination only served to make the dark corners even darker.

"Yeah. It's weird," Kim had agreed, peering around.

Weirder still was the strange auction ritual.

The auctioneer loomed out of an elevated booth across from them. He was a stout man with gray hair that protruded from both sides of his cowboy hat and, like everyone there except Kim and Dennis, he wore a cowboy shirt buttoned right up to the neck and right down to the wrists.

"Twenny-twenny-twenny-come-twennytwo-twennytwo-HO-twennytwo-twenny-two," the auctioneer sang with his roller coaster voice over the microphone system. Animals appeared from chutes at one end of the ring, stayed a few minutes, then vanished out the other side.

Somebody was buying them, but Kim and Dennis could not figure out how it worked. Nobody moved a muscle in the stands.

"Weird," Kim repeated.

The parade of livestock continued: cows, steers, a few enormous blinking bulls, horses that were pranced around by a handler one by one, even a herd of goats. It was hypnotic to watch, at least for a while.

"You see any farm kids?" Dennis whispered to Kim. A quick glance around proved negative.

"This is a flop," Kim finally said in exasperation. "A clever idea, Beverly, but a flop."

"My name is Dennis, pal," his friend said, pretending to be angry. Kim appreciated the attempt at humour, but his conclusion was unchanged. The foray to the Auction Mart was a flop.

"I gotta pee," Dennis announced. He skipped down the bleachers and out into one of the corridors. Kim continued to scrutinize the auction process, but still could not figure out who was buying what.

"SOLD for fortytwohunnerd dollars, lot of four, number six two ni-ine . . . !" cried the auctioneer in his blaring metallic voice.

Soon Dennis returned — excited — and sat down next to Kim, squirming as if he hadn't had a chance to pee at all.

"They're here!" he whispered noisily in Kim's ear.

"Who?"

"Farm kids!"

"Where?"

"In the bathroom. They came in when I was there."

"Did they see you?"

"No, I was in a stall."

"I thought you only had to pee."

"Kim! Who cares? I heard them talking that they're going to go to the show this afternoon. We should go too!"

"Did they say anything about the Haunted House?"

"What do you think?" Dennis retorted sarcastically. "They all just blurted out full confessions about being involved or something? I don't even know if it's the same kids!"

"Then why should we — ?" Kim stopped. Suddenly a group of six farm kids appeared at the edge of the ring near them.

"That's them," Dennis hissed.

The kids also wore jeans, cowboy shirts, and several had big wide cowboy hats. Like all the other cowboys there, they spat a lot.

"Why should we tail them if we don't even know it's the right kids?" Kim said. His manner must have been irritating, since Dennis turned on him and scowled.

"You got any other bright ideas?"

"No."

"You'd make a lousy detective, you know that?"

"Why?"

"You have to check out *leads*. Clues, you know, hints, things that might turn out. This is a lead."

Kim suddenly smiled at how hot and bothered Dennis had become.

"It's the only lead we've had in a week," Kim confirmed. "Good work, Dennis."

Dennis eyeballed the farm kids at the rail. "Let's wait till they leave, so they won't figure out we're headed to the same place."

"Okay."

"Darnit," Dennis added. He squirmed in his seat.

"What?"

"Never mind."

"Let me guess. You hurried out here so fast you didn't finish."

Dennis's grimace told Kim he was right.

"See? I'm not *that* bad a detective."

ELVIS AT THE STRAND

Before going to the show, they needed some money. Tearing back to their neighbourhood on their bikes, they split up and agreed to meet over at Dennis's house in ten minutes. The show was on in half an hour, so they had plenty of time.

Kim barrelled into his house and made straight for his bedroom. He kept the money he received for allowance, and any more he made by collecting pop and beer bottles to return, in a ratty old matchbox that was hidden underneath his bed. The movie cost ten cents, but he usually got popcorn, which cost another ten cents, and a bottle of pop, which added five more, for a total of twenty-five cents.

Twenty-five cents was a fair bit of money. That's how much he got for allowance each week and Kim was used to blowing it all on one wild extravaganza at the "Show Hall," which was what they called the movie theatre. A movie was a couple of hours of flat-out fun and it was worth spending all of your money for a week on it. He did it all the time — and this time was important.

It would be necessary, however, to tell his mom where he was going and that would require some skill. He certainly didn't want to lie, but he didn't want to be interrupted in this mission either. If there was anything to be learned at the Show Hall, he had to be there!

"Mom, I'm going to the show. It's a matinee," he said to his mom breezily as he sailed back up to the kitchen.

"Are you sure?" she said. She didn't mean, "Are you sure it's a matinee?" She meant, "Are you sure you want to spend all your allowance on a movie?"

Kim nodded.

"Well . . . what's on?"

Kim winced. He had to tell the truth.

"I don't know."

"Well if — "

"Dennis asked me," Kim added hastily. It was always better if it was another kid's idea.

"All right then."

Kim was out the door in a flash before she could change her mind. He dashed to his waiting bike — and there was Matt coming up to the house with his mealy-mouthed friend, Greg.

"Hi, Matt," Kim said quickly, with an equally quick smile, before he jumped on his bike and screeched out of there as fast as he could go. Matt said nothing in return, but he watched Kim's departure with more than a touch of curiosity before he and Greg went into the house.

Dennis was waiting by the curb when Kim tore up on his bike.

"Okee-dokey!" Kim yelled as he sped past without slowing down hardly at all. Dennis grinned and gave chase on his bike. When he caught up, Kim yelled across the gap as they raced down the street, "What's on?"

"Elvis."

Kim just nodded back. It's what he expected. In the summer especially, there were two main kinds of movies that came to the Show Hall: Beach Movies, about surfing in California, and Elvis movies. Most of them had been in Caraway many times before and Kim and his friends had seen them all several times. They knew the stories by heart and, in the case of Elvis movies, the words to half the songs.

They rattled their bikes on a short-cut through the school yard and, by tearing down a few alleys and cutting through a deserted lot, were closing in on the Show Hall in less than two minutes. Kim knew perfectly well there was no real hurry, but it was fun to go fast and skid to a stop on the sidewalk outside The Strand, which was the proper name for the movie theatre.

Kim and Dennis propped their bikes against a wall and joined the crowd milling around outside. They both scanned the faces expectantly.

"I don't see them," Kim reported.

"Yeah," Dennis agreed in a disappointed and sort of worried way. "Should we go in anyway?"

"Why don't we wait awhile? I mean, if they don't show up, what are we going to do?"

"I don't know," Dennis replied. "They *said* they were going to the Elvis movie."

"Let's wait," Kim said evenly. There was no reason to get excited. "There's Lloyd."

Their demonstrative and often-troublesome friend was in the middle of the group of kids waiting to go in. Lips Lloyd loved the Show Hall and was at the movies almost every chance he got. It was like a second home to him, it seemed, and it was that way for a lot of the kids from across the tracks. Lloyd was already going through some sort of routine and was getting a few laughs.

"And there's Bobbie," Dennis pointed out, as another of their friends approached. Kim had an idea of what was about to happen and he wanted to act fast before it played out.

"Let's go in," he hastily whispered to Dennis.

"Why? I thought you wanted to wait."

"Naw. Let's go. If they don't show up, what are we going to do, go home? Let's see the movie at least. This way we can get good seats."

It was a pretty lame reason to go in early and Kim knew it, and he also knew that Dennis knew it, but he managed to herd his friend ahead toward the ticket wicket.

An ancient, wrinkled man was perched high on a stool behind the glass of the wicket, which had a hole in it so he could talk, and another hole for exchanging money. This was Henry, the owner of The Strand, who had been on that stool ever since Kim could remember. The place was actually known as Henry's Show Hall and the owner, of course, was Old Henry.

"How old you are?" Henry asked in a gruff, accented voice. He never ever got the order of the words right.

"Eleven," Kim replied and slid forward his ten cents admission. It happened to be the truth in his case, but every kid who came to that wicket said the same thing, unless they were clearly younger and could say "Nine" or "Eight" and be telling the truth. Kids who were thirteen or fourteen came in front of that wicket and said "Eleven." The reason? The price went up for twelve-year-olds, so every kid at the matinee was suddenly, magically eleven!

Kim had seen lumbering teenagers, maybe as old as fifteen, walking nearly on their knees, crawl past Old Henry and mumble "Eleven" — and get in! He had also noticed the same kids, as he passed by The Strand later on a Saturday night when a "restricted" show was on, approaching the wicket standing on their toes and mumbling "Eighteen" when the gruff owner demanded their age — and get in!

The Show Hall was like Caraway Days. A lot of the normal rules were off. Old Henry was prepared to let just about anyone in if they had the money. Lips Lloyd had been the one who pointed this out to Kim, and coming from him it was probably the truth, for Lloyd knew the Show Hall like the back of his hand, and understood the rules and how to break them.

"How old you are?" Old Henry growled at Dennis, who growled "Eleven!" right back so convincingly that there was no further discussion or challenge. Kim looked back at the line-up. Good. They were safely through. He wanted no part of what he suspected might happen next, but he also realized he shouldn't stare and draw attention, so he sauntered into the lobby with Dennis and pretended to study the poster for today's movie, even though he'd seen *Viva Las Vegas* about ten times already.

He glanced back at the line-up. They were doing it! Lloyd and Bobbie were trying to sneak in!

Lloyd must have had several friends in the crowd outside, because his method took a lot of organizing and many accomplices.

Several kids, including a bunch of giggling girls, crowded the narrow entranceway around the wicket. They bunched together tightly in a line and, Kim knew, one of them would soon pick a fight with Old Henry. Sure enough, in a few seconds, one of the tallest girls was yelling, "Look, I'm eleven, you old codge!"

Then, as if on a signal, these kids — they were all from across the tracks — bowed their legs to form a tunnel down at floor level. The mouthy girl kept up the dispute with Old Henry and, in a quick mad scramble, Lloyd and Bobbie crawled down the "tunnel" and into the theatre! Without paying!

"Hey there Kimmie boy, how ya doin?" Lloyd said pretty as you please when he was safely in the lobby and had ambled over to join Kim and Dennis, because he wanted to look as if he'd been there for a long time. He even whistled a little tune.

"Yeah, hi Lloyd," was all Kim could manage to say. What a wiener!

Bobbie was not as sneaky. He just milled around with the others and then joined the popcorn lineup.

Anxiously, Dennis was watching the doorway for the farm kids, but it appeared as if the foray to the Show Hall was going nowhere, except to Las Vegas for the tenth time, of course.

Dennis sighed. "You getting popcorn?" he asked Kim.

They quickly bought their bags of popcorn, and pop, and plunged into the dim theatre as a way of putting distance between themselves and Lloyd and Bobbie.

As they descended the gentle slope of the middle aisle, Kim remembered how Lips Lloyd and Brushcut Bobbie could be pretty unpredictable and even dangerous together, but he didn't think they'd get out of hand here — not any more than usual for the Show Hall, that is — because it was sort of Lloyd's home base. He would protect it in the end, Kim felt.

They settled into their seats.

"Woah!" Dennis cried out as they pitched straight back and almost fell right over. The seats were not bolted properly to the floor — like many of the ones in The Strand — and kids had to be careful where they sat. Kim thought they were in a safe zone, but then again, these things changed from week to week.

Both boys held their popcorn and pop level above them as they swooned backwards, then rebounded upright as the entire row snapped back and propelled them to their feet again.

"Over here!" Kim said firmly and they tried another row, again sitting down with both hands occupied. They swayed way back, but weren't threatened with a crash, so they settled in.

They knew they had a long wait. As Lloyd had pointed out, Old Henry never started the show on time. He waited until every last possible kid was inside and had a chance to purchase popcorn and pop. *Then* he ran the movie.

Slowly, the seats became occupied. Kim and Dennis smirked as they watched several other sections of kids swaying and crashing in the broken rows. There was one entire section of the theatre that had been pretty well destroyed over the years and it was simply left empty for every show.

A projected notice appeared on the screen. It read, "An ad on this screen will increase your sales." It had been there for every movie Kim had ever seen. There were never any ads.

Kim and Dennis passed the wait sipping on their pops and munching their popcorn as the same songs that were played before every show filled the air. Sometimes they glanced around to see who was coming in.

"Hey, there's Matt and that friend of his," Dennis observed. Kim twisted around and confirmed that his brother and Greg had come to the movie. *They must have figured out where I was going,* he said to himself, then aloud to Dennis, "I wonder if they got in for eleven?"

"Probably."

Kim could also see that the flow of kids into the theatre was slowing to a trickle. There were only a few of them visible as shadows way back in the lobby.

"Come on, Henry, run the movie!" a voice shouted from the darkness.

"Yeah, come on! Everybody's here who's gonna be here!" Kim recognized the second voice as Lloyd's.

"Where's the show?" someone else called out.

Kim looked around and laughed. It was useless and they all knew it. He scanned the audience. It was almost entirely kids, except for a few older teenagers who were huddled in the row right at the back. Kim could make out a few boys with arms around the girls next to them. They all slumped way down in their seats.

The rattle of the first pop bottle filled the theatre. When kids finished their pops, they often rolled the bottles down the sloped floor underneath the seats. If they got lucky, they might get a bottle to roll most of the length of the theatre without hitting a seat or someone's feet and its clanky rattle got louder and louder on the cement floor the farther it went. A bottle that made it a really long way drew a cheer from the audience.

Kim and Dennis did that sometimes, but for now they just slumped back and waited for the movie. Would it ever come?

"Show time!" a voice shouted.

"Movie!" another one demanded.

Kim twisted around again and looked upward. When Old Henry appeared in the projection booth, the movie would soon follow. It meant he had given up on any more admissions, though his wife continued to patrol the front door and dispense candy and popcorn. His wife would also make a certain, crucial appearance shortly after the movie began.

Kim peered into the darkness. There he was! The silhouetted form of the old man was visible poking around in the high up cubicle at the back of the theatre.

"Hey — !" Kim said sharply to Dennis, and his friend whirled around too.

"Is that them?"

Kim had spotted a final group of kids entering the theatre — and they wore cowboy hats!

"That's them," Dennis replied.

"How can you tell?"

"Gotta be. The hats."

"Yeah, I know but — "

"Come on, it's gotta be!"

"I hope so," Kim said.

"What are you going to do?" Dennis asked. "Any ideas . . . ?"

"You bet. I'm going to get in behind them and see what they're talking about. Maybe they'll admit something."

Dennis nodded at Kim in the darkness.

"Good idea."

Suddenly a brilliant shaft of light beamed from the projection booth and lit up the screen. The show was on!

"Finally . . . !" someone moaned from behind them.

The audience turned to the screen with rapt attention, because like Kim and Dennis most of them had also seen the movie several times, so the previews were the best chance to see something new. The first one flickered on.

"The Blob!" a voice yelled from behind them, probably Lloyd, for the first preview was about a movie called *The Blob* and, unfortunately, nearly everyone had seen both the movie and the preview for it. It was about this blob of gooey stuff, like Jell-O, that went around eating everyone in a small town.

"Don't look!" Kim giggled to Dennis. "Don't *look.*"

He didn't mean at the preview, he meant at the back of the theatre, because in *The Blob* the nasty, attacking blob flows into a movie theatre at one point and swallows everyone. This part was in the preview and, when it came on, nearly the entire audience always turned around to see if the Blob was oozing into *their* theatre. They just couldn't help it.

On the screen, the Blob oozed into the theatre. Dennis made a show of resisting, then turned around to look and Kim fought an urge to do the same. Kim snickered. Dennis stuck his tongue out at him. They both laughed loudly.

The second preview was also familiar. It was about a space ship that crash lands on a strange, far-off planet and the crew have to fight the aliens that live there.

The first few kids took the opportunity to zoom to the lobby to use the bathroom. There would be many more.

Finally, the previews ended. The screen simply went blank for a minute and they could hear bumping and scuffling noises in the projection booth high behind them, then the whirring of the projector and another shaft of brilliant, powdery blue light dancing over their heads.

Viva Las Vegas — for the tenth time!

The crowd was pretty quiet and orderly for about the first five minutes. They all knew what to expect next. Soon, Old Henry's wife appeared at the top of the aisle with a flashlight, which she shone down many of the rows as she made her way to the front.

She was a stern old lady who always wore long, old-fashioned dresses and her hair tied up in a cruel-looking bun. Most of the kids knew enough to sit up straight, get their feet off the back of the seat ahead of them, or down from overtop of the row in front of them, and sit there quietly chewing their popcorn.

If Mrs. Old Henry's flashlight lit up an offender, the old lady barked a command with a thick accent that none of them could decode, but all could understand: *"Get your feet off the chair!"*

She was mean, all right, but she was also predictable. She appeared once in the movie, early, and then left them alone. She went right up beside the big movie screen and looked in behind it, for there was a space there that could hide kids if they were up to no good. And she opened the exit doors at each far corner of the theatre and looked outside — blinding daylight poured in momentarily — before slowly wending her way back up the middle aisle, flicking the flashlight beam left and right.

Then she was gone. And all hell broke loose.

Pop bottles rolled noisily down the slope underneath the seats. Popcorn and other projectiles flew through the air. A kid sneaked up to the front — it was Lloyd! — and dashed over to one of the exit doors, quickly popping it open. Four other kids raced into the theatre and instantly dove into the seats and slouched down out of sight.

That Lloyd! Kim said to himself. *What a cheater!*

Obviously, Lloyd had set it up with his friends earlier. Mrs. Old Henry had checked outside to shoo away any kids waiting there, but the kids knew she would do it, and outsmarted her just as they had many times before. Everyone in the theatre saw it, and a wave of giggles passed over the crowd before they turned their attention to the movie.

In *Viva Las Vegas*, Elvis was a racecar driver who was going to be in a competition in the desert near the city of Las Vegas. There were many obstacles in his way, but naturally Elvis overcame them one by one. And kids started heckling him:

"Look at his hair — he was just in a fight and it's perfect!"

"He just came out of a swimming pool and he's all dried off!"

"How come he never gets dirty?"

"Oh, no — he's gonna sing!"

In his movies, Elvis was always breaking into song and most of the kids hated it. It wasn't so bad if it was kind of an action song, or with dancing or a jazzy band or something, but if

Elvis started into a love song or, worse, actually *kissed* a girl, half the audience headed up the aisle to the bathroom or to get more popcorn and pop.

Kim used one of these mass exits to join the crowd of kids moving up and down the aisle, then slip into the row behind the farm kids.

They had all taken off their cowboy hats and were sitting up considerably straighter than anyone else. As Kim slumped into the seats behind them, it occurred to him that maybe they *hadn't* seen *Viva Las Vegas* ten times.

He sat there for half an hour and learned nothing. They barely talked amongst each other, these farm kids, while at the same time the rest of the theatre exploded in arguments, out-sized laughing at Elvis and his crazy problems, catcalls, dares, bluffs, snickers, guffaws, and a general, endless din of plain old talking in the movie.

At length, Kim returned to his seat beside Dennis.

"Find out anything?"

"Naw."

They both slumped down in their seats and watched the movie in silence. Would they ever learn anything about those farm kids? It didn't look like it.

Kim sighed and just watched for awhile. The mayhem of earlier in the movie had settled down and now quite a few kids were watching Elvis's troubles getting the desert car race going. Kim heard a few little kids crawling around on the floor beneath the seats near him, but he ignored them. He glanced over his shoulder once and realized that Matt and Greg were only four rows behind him to his right. He reminded himself not to fall asleep, like in the grandstand, and sat up straight to prevent it.

The movie was action-packed, so it didn't seem long at all, except for the songs. Before he realized it, Kim was watching Elvis roar through the desert in his racing car while several other drivers spun out into the dust, rolled over in the ditches, or just couldn't keep up.

He glanced back again, because the ending of *Viva Las Vegas* often produced a kind of song-and-dance competition up on the narrow little stage just below the movie screen. If it was going to happen, Lips Lloyd was sure to be a part of it.

And there he was! Charging down the aisle, with several other kids falling in behind. They all raced to the front of the theatre and jumped up on the narrow stage. The movie was almost over and Elvis movies nearly always ended with a song, in this case the title tune, *Viva Las Vegas.*

Elvis was on one side of the screen and the blonde girl in the story, who was a really good dancer, was on the other side, dancing to the song as Elvis belted it out. Silhouetted in front of them were five or six girls and two or three boys — Lloyd was the biggest and brashest — moving along to the dancing and singing along to the song!

"*Viva Las Vegas!*" Elvis sang, matched by Lloyd's own pretty good imitation of him.

"*Viva Las Vegas!*"

The entire audience stood up to cheer and heckle. Some were on Elvis's side and wished the kids would sit down, but others were yelling encouragement to Lloyd and the others to out-do the performers on the screen.

"*Viva Las Vegas!*"

There was so much garbage in the theatre by now that the kids couldn't resist tossing most of at the screen. Lloyd expected it, for it had happened before, and was an expert at using his arms to imitate Elvis and deflect popcorn bags and candy wrappers at the same time.

"*Viva Las Vegas!*" sang all the kids. Kim and Dennis stood and clapped along with the rest of them as projectiles zoomed over their heads toward the stage.

Lloyd suddenly leapt down to floor level and danced up the middle aisle for the big ending.

"*Viva* — yeah! — *VIVA* — *Las* — "

Kim glanced over and saw that the farm kids were on Elvis's side and they'd had enough. A few of them jumped right over two rows of seats to yell "BOOO!" at Lloyd. Others tossed garbage.

Lloyd was unstoppable.

"*Viva* — yeah! — *VIVA* — *LAS* — *VE-GAS!*"

Then Kim turned and saw him. One of the farm kids stood up straight and high and aimed a crunched-up popcorn bag at Lloyd. Everyone saw him. He reared back and threw it — with his left *LEFT* hand.

The bag bounced off Lloyd's forehead and the show was over.

Kim whirled around to find Matt. His brother was right behind him and looking at the farm kid. They traded a glance and a shared thought zapped between them. *That's him!*

The lights came up and the crowd began to shuffle up the aisle. Kim, Dennis, Matt and Greg stood stone-still watching the farm kids file out. They plopped their cowboy hats back on their heads and joined the mass of kids. Kim and the others fell in behind, pressing their way into the crowd to ensure they didn't lose sight of them.

All the kids poured through the lobby and out the front doors. Matt was suddenly agitated and pushed ahead into the clear.

It was like awakening from a dream. The daylight washed over them like a liquid splash and they all had to stop and let their eyes adjust.

"There they go!" Matt called, pointing down the street. He ran over to the farm kids, who numbered five now that Kim could count them, and danced in front of them, forcing them to stop.

"Hey!" Matt said loudly and he pointed straight at the left-handed kid's face. "You were at the Pig Farm that day. On Mr. White's farm. The day the old house was wrecked."

"Was not," the kid replied quietly. He had a straight nose and freckles.

"You were so," Matt asserted. He was bigger than any of the five farm kids and stood his ground, even though they edged around in a half-circle and more or less surrounded him. A crowd of kids from the theatre gathered nearby and Matt's friend Greg angled in behind Matt too, in case there was a fight.

"You didn't have a hat. You must have been one of those kids tossing rocks and mud at first," Matt said loudly.

"Was not," the farm kid repeated. He spat on the ground dangerously close to Matt's running shoe. Kim figured those cowboy kids spat so much they could aim it pretty good.

"You were so," Matt repeated. "You calling me a liar?"

"Yep."

"I'm not a liar. You are. You were *there*."

"So he was there — so what?" said another of the farm kids, knuckling under to Matt's pressure. The left-handed farm kid's nose twitched and he shot a nasty glance at the other kid.

"See?" Matt said.

"See what? That don't prove nuthin'."

"Proves you just lied," Matt crowed as he looked back at Greg.

"Get outa our way. We're leavin'," the farm kid said. He stepped forcefully toward Matt, but Matt caught him by the shirt and shoved him backward two full steps, so hard his friends had to catch him. The farm kids stood still now, because it was clear they were not going to escape easily.

Kim looked around quickly. There were a lot of town kids there, but most were from across the tracks and, like Lloyd, would not be inclined to back up Kim and Matt and Dennis and Greg.

But the farm kids don't know that, Kim reminded himself.

"And I think you're the kid who threw that first rock," Matt continued, speaking right in the farm kid's face. "I saw it, even though it was windy and dusty. It was a left-handed kid — *you* — and I know it 'cause I just saw you do it again, same way, same throw."

The farm kid smiled confidently. "Come on, everyone knows it was this kid from Caraway who threw the rock."

Kim stood perfectly still. He wasn't going to give himself away, that's for sure!

Matt didn't look at him either. "Don't think so. It was *you*."

The farm kid said nothing. He looked back at his friends and set his jaw firmly before saying quite loudly, "We're leaving!"

Matt stepped aside. He had done what he wanted and there was no use getting into a fight now. The farm kids formed a wedge and forced their way past Matt and Greg and a few of Matt's other friends who had gathered around. They all muttered taunts and insults at each other, but none of them was deadly enough to provoke a punch.

The farm kids walked quickly off down Main Street away from the crowd outside The Strand. They were safe now. Nobody was going to chase them.

Dennis, however, couldn't resist joining in on the exchange of barbed words. He stepped out of the crowd and yelled, "Aw, go back to Greely!" That was a pretty big insult, since all the Caraway kids treated Greely like the end of the earth, a loser little place they'd never be caught dead in. The crowd of town kids burst into laughter.

One of the farm kids wheeled around and, walking backward, yelled, "It's Merton, ya dummy!"

FREE!

Kim lay flat on his back and gazed straight up at the black starry night.

What a day it had been!

He ran it all over again in his mind, starting with the visit to the Auction Mart that didn't turn up any clues at first, then Dennis's discovery that the farm kids were going to The Strand for the movie, then the startling climax of *Viva Las Vegas* and the revelation that a certain farm kid had a heck of a left-handed toss, the one that bounced the popcorn bag off of Lloyd's forehead.

And best of all, Matt confronting the farm kid on the street and yelling it out loud and clear for all to hear: *you* threw the rock!

Kim was free! It was an amazing feeling.

Dennis was right beside him and they both stared straight up at the stars. After the startling events outside the Show Hall, Kim and Dennis had returned to Kim's house and celebrated. So many kids had witnessed the exchange with the farm kids, Kim was confident that word would spread quickly all over Caraway and, in a day, he would no longer be The Kid Who Threw the Rock. Little Rodney the messenger kid had been there and that pretty well clinched it. Anything that Rodney knew, everyone would know, and soon.

They rested on a big blanket in Dennis's backyard. It was late, past eleven PM, but it would be some time before they went to bed. Kim was on a sleepover, which was pretty well the perfect way to end such a successful day.

He had been afraid he wouldn't get permission, because he had been up to a lot that day and his mom and dad often countered a request, like the one to go on a sleepover, with, "Haven't you had enough excitement for one day?" and wouldn't allow any further activities. Apparently, they felt too much excitement was bad for kids and it was only during, say, Caraway Days that they allowed it.

There was a much nastier question parents reserved for kids who were really stepping out of line, one that Kim tried to avoid at all costs: *Who do you think you are, anyway?* It was terrible when parents said that. It made Kim feel about two inches tall.

Fortunately, he hadn't heard either of these nasty questions, because his lucky, successful, freedom day continued when his parents remembered they had been invited to a grown-up barbecue where Kim and Matt would be kind of out of place anyway.

So the sleepover was on! Kim was Dennis's guest and Matt was visiting Dennis's older brother, Randy. It all worked out and they all had a plan for a secret mission well after midnight too. It was great!

"That was pretty funny when you told that kid to go back to Greely," Kim said.

Dennis laughed. "Yeah, where is Merton anyway?"

"You know, down past Bledsoe and Church Hill. Sort of west-southwest," Kim replied, employing his flair for directions. "They came a long way into town and Beverly Banana was right, the only reason they'd be here was for the auction."

"Yeah."

"That was great how Matt told him off — !"

"Yeah."

"Amazing. Finally, I'm off the hook," Kim pronounced.

"Yeah, pretty well."

Kim propped up on his elbow and looked over at Dennis.

"What do you mean 'pretty well'? He accused that kid in front of half the town of being the one who threw the rock!"

"Well, I just heard him tell my brother now he's not so sure."

"*What?* Where is he?"

"In the basement."

Kim dashed into the basement of the house and found Matt and Randy playing a game of pool. This particular basement was very popular in the neighborhood on account of that pool table.

"Dennis says you're saying you're not sure now about that kid being the one who threw that rock!" Kim blurted to his brother, quite aware he was barely making sense.

"Just a sec," Matt said as he bent behind the cue ball to line up a shot.

"No just a sec!" Kim screamed.

"Just a sec," Matt hissed. He shot and missed, then glared at Kim. "Look what you did."

"You're always blaming me!" Kim yelled. "For the rock! For this!" Furious, he dashed around the pool table and grabbed the white cue ball so the game had to stop.

"Hey — !" Randy said.

"Put it back," Matt warned. "In the same spot."

"I will. Tell me what you're saying now."

"All I said was maybe I made a mistake — "

"Like, *again?*" Kim snapped, very sarcastically. He couldn't help it.

" — maybe I made a mistake and that kid was right after all."

"And who did you tell?"

"Nobody."

"Who?"

"Nobody. Just Dennis and Randy maybe, here, tonight."

Kim set the cue ball back in its original spot, but kept his hand on it. He had Matt's complete attention.

"Why don't you figure out what the hell you saw, and what you mean, and who did what, and *stick to it?*"

Kim was surprised at himself for swearing, but the situation called for it.

"And if you can't figure it out for sure, why don't you just *shut up?*"

Randy suddenly burst out laughing at Kim's attack. It was quite something for a little brother to talk like that to an older brother. Kim thought Matt might thump him out right there, but Matt sort of laughed too, and shrugged.

"Okay."

Kim released the cue ball and stepped back from the table. He was so mad he was muttering to himself. Finally, he stomped toward the door.

"Hey, Kim," Randy said after him.

"Yeah?"

"You're gonna get a chance to settle with that kid anyway, you know."

"What do you mean?"

"Didn't you see the schedule for your baseball tournament on the Labour Day Weekend?"

"No."

"That kid's from Merton, right?"

"Yeah . . . ?"

"Well, Merton's in the tournament. My dad has the draw." Randy and Dennis's dad helped with a lot of the baseball games and tournaments.

"Oh," Kim said emptily. "But how do you know that kid is playing?"

"Well," Randy reasoned, as he lined up a shot, "it's a small town and they probably use a lot of farm kids. And he's left-handed. Heck, he's probably one of the pitchers."

"Yeah. You're probably right."

Kim slowly returned to the backyard and flattened himself beside Dennis. Above them, there was a wild, blue-white display of the Northern Lights, dancing and shimmering high in the black sky, and Dennis was watching it carefully.

"Did you know we're gonna play Merton in our tournament coming up?" Kim asked.

"We are?"

"Yeah. Your brother saw the draw. Merton's in it."

"Gee . . . I wonder how old that kid is."

"Well, at the movie he'd be eleven," Kim cracked, surprised he could make a joke in the midst of all of this.

"Yeah," Dennis agreed, "and you know, he actually looked about eleven too."

"So we'll be playing him."

"I guess so. He'll pitch."

"Yeah."

They both lay back flat and stared straight up, mulling over the consequences of their discovery. Kim suddenly felt quite ill.

"Aw, don't worry about it," Dennis reassured him. "It's just a baseball game."

"Yeah."

"The way we've been playing, we'll lose out early anyway."

"Probably."

"Hey — shooting star!"

It was a big one too, slashing across half the sky in a bright white streak, then gone.

They lay there in silence for quite awhile after that. Kim felt that his big, perfect day had turned bad on him and he wished he were home in his own bed and fast asleep.

There was, however, a plan for later and they both knew it.

As the clock rolled past midnight, they heard Matt and Randy coming up from downstairs and into the backyard. There were no lights, except for the distant bluey glow of a streetlight halfway down the block.

"You guys coming?" Randy asked.

"Sure," Dennis replied. "Kim?"

"Yeah, sure."

Kim didn't feel like going along now, but it was quite an honour to be asked along on a crabapple raid, especially by two older kids asking their younger brothers. Kim remarked to himself that this would not normally happen. *Must be 'cause it's dark*, he said to himself sarcastically.

Soon they were in position a few alleyways away, crouching behind the fence of the target backyard. There, hanging heavy in the darkness, was the crabapple tree, perfectly centred in the middle of the grass.

The four boys jumped the fence soundlessly and scurried forward through the garden.

"Hey, peas," Dennis murmured. He stopped to help himself, shelling several on the spot and downing them with a gulp.

"Do they have a dog?" Kim hissed ahead to Randy.

"No. That's why we're here."

The house was completely darkened. Kim didn't know who lived here, just that they had no kids. Crawling ahead like raccoons, they made it to the base of the tree and Kim was quietly elected to be the one to go up into the high branches and flick the crabs down to the others.

It was easy, for the tree branches were drooping with crabapples. Kim found his footing on a sturdy limb, then just pinched the crabs free and let them fall to the waiting trio below. He did it without question, because it was his job. In ten minutes, they had all they could carry.

Kim dropped to the ground, filled his pockets, and joined the other three at the fence.

"There's a light!" Dennis growled and they all saw the kitchen light come on in the house. Half their haul was lost in the scramble to get over the fence and down the alley, but they made it easily and heard nothing from the house. Kim turned around and saw the light go off again, so he knew they were clean away.

The alliance of older brothers and younger ones dissolved the second they made it back to Dennis's house. Randy and Matt vanished downstairs and Kim and Dennis contented themselves with tumbling their crabs onto the blanket and staying in the backyard.

"Hmmm, let's see," Dennis said as he bit into a crabapple. Instantly, he spit the piece out. "Yuk."

Kim tried one and he certainly agreed, but in the end it didn't stop each of them from eating several of the hard little apples. What was the point of raiding crabs if you didn't eat them?

"Hey, why don't we sleep out here?" Dennis suggested.

"Can we?"

"Sure, why not? I'll get some more blankets."

"Okay."

Kim looked up and saw that the Northern Lights were going strong, so it seemed like a good idea. It was late August, so the mosquitoes were pretty well gone and it was a warm, kind night. Why not?

He went through the last of his crabs, just biting into each one once, then tossing the remainder into the garden. They really weren't very good at all.

Dennis brought out the blankets and they settled back to watch the show in the sky. Kim didn't remember how long they remained awake, but the Northern Lights were fabulous, dancing and spangling above them in waves of blue and green rays that somehow reminded him of a fireplace curtain.

He did remember, however, waking up much later, when the dim shape of the curved moon had risen above the eastern horizon and the sky was empty of Northern Lights.

His stomach had prodded him awake, because it was swollen and hard as a brick and he felt awful! It was the crabapples!

He was glad it was only a few quick steps to the garden, where no one would notice, and only a few more moments of complete, helpless sickness before he threw up, twice, and then felt much, much better.

The Draw

"See? Merton."

Dennis put his finger under the line of the baseball tournament schedule where the town's name was listed.

"Right. Have we ever played them before?" Kim asked.

"No."

"Then why are we playing them now?" Kim pushed the schedule, known as "the draw," across Dennis's kitchen table. He didn't want to look at it and didn't want to think about it, either.

"My dad says they were invited because some of the other towns around didn't have teams this year. Remember? There used to be a team from Newberg, but I guess they didn't have enough kids this year the right age."

"Yeah, and Jeffers Corners used to come some years too," Kim agreed. "Not this year."

He grabbed the draw back and looked it over. There were eight teams entered in the Caraway Labour Day Invitational Baseball Tournament for their age group. Six of them were from their regular league, where Kim and Dennis's team had finished a disappointing third in league play, since they had started strongly in the spring before their "big fade" in mid-summer.

Then there were the other two teams added in to make up a field of eight, but of all of them, only two names on that sheet of paper stood out for Kim: Caraway and Merton.

"Aw, don't worry about Merton," Dennis advised breezily, for he could see where Kim's attention strayed. "What are the chances we'll face them? Not great, I'd say."

"Yeah, you're right," Kim agreed, for Caraway was perched right on top of the draw and Merton was way down at the bottom. They wouldn't play each other early in the tournament and, perhaps, not at all.

"It's straight knock-out," Dennis stressed. "We'd have to win two games, and so would they, before we'd play them."

"In the final," Kim pointed out.

"Yeah, in the final, but we'd have to beat Roxbury and the winner of Canton and Poplar Creek and how likely is that?"

"Not very," Kim agreed.

"Not the way we've been going," Dennis laughed. "We'll be out of it by Saturday afternoon."

Kim sighed. It's certainly what he hoped would happen. Merton was too far away, and too little was known about it in Caraway, for him to have gained any more information about their team or the farm kid, the leftie, who he was sure had been at the Pig Farm that day.

But he accepted the blunt reasoning about southpaws and baseball that Dennis's brother Randy had offered earlier: if that kid was on the team, and he most likely was, he'd be a pitcher. Kim dreaded the thought of going to bat against him. It was even possible he would be pitching against that kid himself. Kim was one of three pitchers his team normally used, and the only leftie. It might be southpaw versus southpaw. It almost made him consider not trying very hard against Roxbury or the winner of Canton-Poplar Creek, if they got that far, but Kim knew that was not in the cards. Everyone on his team wanted to win, and so did he, no matter what.

"Wanna go bike-ride?" Kim offered to Dennis, who quickly shook his head no.

"Naw. Watch TV."

Alone, Kim cycled off down the wide streets of his neighbourhood and quickly reached the edge of Mr. White's field. He charged off the road without fear of hitting a rut or a mudhole, because at the end of summer the ground was hard-packed and smooth. The barley in the field had been swathed into long, thick rows and each space between the rows was its own little road where the stubble pricked and stickled at Kim's bike tires as he zoomed through.

He pedalled hard, harder, and raced up and down the gentle rises of the field until he was closing in on the Bush. He veered wide to the right, so he could keep riding through the field and avoid the trees. In half a minute, he was rounding the Bush and closing in on the pigs' feeding troughs and the Haunted House.

A twinge of regret passed through him and he coasted to a stop well back of the troughs and the pigs' mudhole, the trees, and the wrecked old pioneer house. Even though he was quite certain he was winning the war of words over the destruction of the house — almost every day little Rodney reported to him what kids were saying and it was mostly good — he still wished the rampage had never happened. How could a place of such fun turn into a place of so much trouble?

"Boys are like a balloon . . . " Kim murmured to himself. When you blow a balloon up, it gets bigger and bigger, stretching itself out. Another puff and another, and the balloon expands and expands, and its skin becomes thinner and thinner. It is huge and tender and delicate — stretched to the limit. And if someone pricks it with a pin — KAPOW! It explodes!

Boys are like a balloon, Kim thought. *When their energies are expanded as big and wide as they can go, when they're stretched to the limit, it just takes one more jab and those boys blow up just like a balloon.*

All it took was one kid to throw a rock and that mob of boys blew up.

He rode his bike further toward the Haunted House and the road that ran past the Bush, heading again for the spot where Matt was standing when the first rock was thrown.

"Who's that? Who is that? Watch out!"

Matt would never, ever realize he had muttered those words when he was knocked out, Kim knew, and never know how far he had been carried in the woods at cub camp, and never hear about loopy old Barefoot and the pulley, or the letter that Beverly Banana had been so thoughtful to write, or the trail of events that led them all to see the farm kid toss the popcorn bag at Lloyd at the end of *Viva Las Vegas.*

Kim laughed out loud. He felt a sudden surge of strength from everything he knew that Matt didn't. *It's funny how those things work,* he thought.

He was thankful, too. At least Matt had realized what he was looking at in The Strand. At least he'd gone out and confronted the farm kid, because Kim certainly wasn't going to take on five farm kids by himself on the sidewalk, no matter how many friends he had around. At least Matt had spoken the truth out loud in front of everybody.

Sadly, the old Haunted House wasn't looking any better than before. Kim suddenly knew it would probably burn down some day, or perhaps Mr. White would just use one of his big farm machines to demolish it. It would never be the way it was before.

He pedalled a little further and saw that the sign was still there, but it was now difficult to read the words "Police Investigation. Do not enter premises" and "No boys at the farm for now. Thanks."

The sign had been all scrawled over with other writing and part of it had been torn off and thrown away, and it was leaning precariously over to one side.

Kim sighed. Boys had been there again wrecking things, that was clear, and with a bitter laugh he decided he had better get out of there before he was blamed for that too.

THE PITCHING DUEL

CRASH! The pitch hit Kim right in the head!

He dropped to the ground, hard, and rolled out of the batter's box. The impact of the ball rattled his batting helmet so terribly, with such a horrible crashing sound, he was certain he was badly hurt.

"Time!" he heard his coach, Mr. Reilly, yell from the third base line, instantly echoed by "Time!" from the umpire behind the plate.

Kim rolled over and up on his knees and tore the helmet off his head. He needed to separate the rattling, scary banging noises inside the helmet from the pain in his own head — and he quickly realized he wasn't really hurt. Even before Mr. Reilly reached him, he knew it.

"Kim — you all right?" Mr. Reilly asked, leaning in and staring directly into Kim's eyes.

"Yeah, yeah, yeah," Kim responded breathlessly. The worst of it was the horrible bashing noise the batting helmet made. His ears hurt more than his head where the ball hit. The helmet had done its job — but it made a lot of noise doing it!

"Take your base," said the umpire, pointing down to first.

"You want to stay in?" Mr. Reilly asked him. "You okay?"

"*Yes*," Kim said through clenched teeth. There was absolutely no way he was leaving the game now. *No way.* He walked very slowly toward first base. Suddenly he was dizzy, but he was not going to leave the game. He just wanted to buy a little time to feel better.

Kim detoured to the dugout to get a drink of water, knowing the umpire would let him take as much time as he needed, then continued his very deliberate walk toward first base. He fixed the helmet back on his head.

You jerk — you're gonna pay for that, he cursed to himself as he touched the bag and turned to face the pitcher.

It was the farm kid from Merton. The kid they'd seen at the movie and Matt had confronted on the sidewalk. The real Kid Who Threw the Rock. Now he was throwing baseballs.

His name, Kim had found out, was Travis Trent and, as everyone predicted, he was a pitcher for the Merton Marauders. A southpaw, like Kim.

"Batter!" the ump called and Bobbie, up next for Caraway, shuffled toward the plate. The ump pointed to the pitcher and barked, "Play it!"

The nightmare Kim feared had come to pass. His team from Caraway, with Dennis, Bobbie, Alan, and Lloyd on it, along with a batch of other boys, had pulled it together after their disastrous tailspin late in the year and somehow beaten both Roxbury and Canton, the winner of Canton-Poplar Creek.

Incredibly, they were in the final game and their opposition was none other than the Marauders from far-off Merton, who had cleaned out Greely twelve-two, then gotten by Pemberton eight-six. They were a good team and their best pitcher, by far, was the leftie farm kid, Travis Trent. He had pitched only an inning against Greely, then come in after three to hold Pemberton to two runs over the last four innings.

Travis Trent was fast and he was accurate. It meant that tossing a beanball pretty well had to be deliberate. The pitch had flown off his hand like a runaway missile and homed in straight for Kim's head. He could have ducked out of the way if he had been trying to avoid it from the get-go, but he was trying to *hit* it and that meant stepping into the swing, toward the pitcher and the pitch. By the time he realized the ball was zooming in straight for his head, all he could do was make sure he didn't take it on the cheek. He had time to turn, a bit, but not to turn and duck.

Kim took a small leadoff and bent over with his hands on his knees. He was facing directly at Travis Trent, because as a leftie, the pitcher faced first base when he was in the "stretch," the pitching position used when there were baserunners.

Kim hoped his look said, *"Watch yourself next time, buddy boy,"* because the southpaw on the mound must have realized he had crossed a line by beaning the other pitcher — the only player on the opposing team who would be in a position to toss one at *him* when he was at bat.

The other pitcher was Kim, and he couldn't wait to make Travis Trent squirm.

"All right boys, let's get one now, let's get one!" Mr. Reilly called from his spot by third base. It was three-three in the bottom of the third, with one out. Kim looked across for the signal. Mr. Reilly went through a complicated sequence of moves, like a man searching for a lost set of keys all over his body, and ended up with the sign that meant "steal."

Instantly, Kim realized his mistake. He should have waited for the sign before taking any leadoff, because now he had to step out a few feet farther to have a chance to steal, and by doing that, he would pretty well tip off the pitcher that he was going to go.

Stupid, he scolded himself, but there was no choice now. He ventured out two more steps — pickoff! Travis Trent fired the ball over to the first baseman, who was glued to the base and waiting for it. Kim dove flat for the bag — he couldn't reach it! — but the ball zinged on a hop past the first baseman's glove!

Kim didn't have to steal. He got a free ride down to second courtesy of Travis Trent's wild toss. He made the turn around second and bluffed going for third just to draw the throw. It came over to third base hard and accurate, so Kim skittered back to the bag. He spit casually, in the direction of the mound, for good measure.

Nice try, idiot, he said to himself as he looked scornfully at the opposing pitcher.

Travis Trent ignored Kim on second, as he should, and quickly dealt two pitches in to Bobbie, a ball and a strike. He threw again — and Bobbie cracked a single up the middle!

Kim raced around third and cruised home, beating the throw easily. They were up four-three in the championship game!

The Caraway team — they didn't have a name, they were just "Caraway" — were hopeful for a big inning to get a nice lead on Merton and most of the players in the dugout didn't sit down to watch, but paced up and down along the wire fence, hanging on to it, yelling through it, and cheering on every pitch.

Lloyd was up next, but he struck out looking and the next batter popped up to shallow right field. Bobbie was stranded at first and the inning was over.

Caraway hustled back onto the field. Sometimes the kids were lazy or, if they were losing badly, had no spirit and the entire team walked out to their positions. Not this time. Everybody ran, except the pitcher, since he didn't have far to go and was supposed to save his energy.

Kim ambled out, took up the ball, and threw his warm-ups in to Dennis, the catcher. He had studied the line-up card and knew that his rival was due up fourth. Kim's job, of course, was to prevent that many batters from coming to the plate, but a one-two-three inning was unlikely. He hadn't had one yet.

Mr. Reilly had picked him to pitch for only one reason: there were five left-handed hitters in the Merton lineup and it was harder for them to hit a left-handed pitcher. The ball came in on the same side as they were standing, and it was harder to see. Kim knew all about it, for he hit left-handed and that's another reason Travis Trent was able to bean him. The ball was hard to see coming in from a leftie.

Kim had pitched two innings against Roxbury and two more against Canton. He was good, but no better than Alan or their other chuckers.

"All right, Kim, you'll start," Mr. Reilly had said, pointing to him before the game and Kim knew that "start" meant exactly and only that. He would start, but only finish if he could hold them off. It was okay. Kim understood the logic completely. He certainly didn't want to be on the mound if he wasn't doing his job.

"Batter! Play!" the umpire ordered and Dennis settled into position behind the plate.

"Come Kim now, come buddy, come to me now!" Dennis hollered through his catcher's mask. "No hitter here, nuthin' here!"

It was the catcher's job to *yell* and Dennis was great at it. He was already filthy after the Canton game earlier in the day and when he pounded his glove a storm of dust erupted into the air.

"Come now, come now Kim-mie!"

They struck out the first guy, then Kim walked one, and the third batter singled to right. There were runners on first and third and only one out. Darn!

Travis Trent sauntered up to the plate and Dennis stood up.

"Time!"

"Time!" echoed the umpire.

Dennis trotted out to Kim and they huddled together.

"You want to put him on?" Dennis breathed, holding his catcher's mitt up over his mouth for complete privacy.

"No."

"Look, if you want to pop him one, this is the time to do it. It'll be bases loaded, one out. We can try for a double play."

"I don't want to pop him," Kim breathed in response to Dennis's suggestion to throw one hard at the batter, just as the farm kid had done to Kim. "I want to strike him out."

"Well, put one up his nose at least," Dennis replied. He meant throw one in high and tight, but not trying to hit him.

"Sure," Kim said. "Be ready for the guy on first."

Dennis nodded and trotted back to the plate.

Runners on first and third with one out was a tough spot for the catcher. Usually, the guy at first would try to steal second, knowing it was awfully tough for the other team to risk throwing him out, because the toss to second gave the runner on third a head start to go home and score a run. And it was a one-run game.

Dennis, however, had a pretty good arm and Merton knew it. He had already pegged out two guys trying to steal.

Kim threw over to first a couple of times to keep the runner close, then knew he had to deal with the hitter. Travis Trent also hit left, so their confrontation was identical both ways. A southpaw pitcher throwing to a batter hitting left.

Dennis flashed through the signals, wriggling his right hand as if he was making shadow shapes on a wall. He did it all with his hand well hidden by his legs and catcher's glove, so only Kim could see.

Kim shook his head at each suggestion until he came to "change-up."

He figured the runner on first would expect a fastball, to cut down the chances of a successful steal, and so would the batter. Dennis wasn't sure, so he flashed it twice. Kim nodded both times.

He reared back and delivered. The key to a good change-up was a little bit of show, to make it look as if the ball was *really* coming, really screaming in there. Kim let his head flop back a bit and gasped out loud — "Uh!" — and floated the ball right down the middle.

The farm kid swung for the fence and missed by a mile. Strike one!

Better yet, the runner at first base had decided to stay put for at least one pitch. When he realized he'd been tricked, he kicked at the dirt.

As if communicating by telepathy, Kim and Dennis knew exactly what they wanted to do next. It was like that between a pitcher and a catcher after awhile. They started to understand each other's patterns and were often locked into a sequence of pitches they both could anticipate perfectly.

"Fastball," the sign said. "Up and in." Kim nodded. He drilled the baseball as hard as he could, aiming for a spot about an inch off of Travis Trent's nose. It pretty well went there too — and Travis had to snap his head back at the last second to avoid getting clipped in the face. He had nerves of steel, though, for he only moved as much as he had to and not an inch more.

Dennis caught the high pitch and stepped ahead quickly. He rifled it to the shortstop, Alan, who checked the runner at first, forcing him to stay where he was, then drilled it back to Dennis, who was now well ahead of home plate. They were doing everything they could to protect that one-run lead.

But on the next pitch, Travis Trent hit a line-drive into centre field and the score was tied. It was Kim's turn to kick the dirt. *Darn!* It was the second single the Merton leftie had hit off him and Kim's hope of striking him out would have to wait.

Caraway got the ball in quickly, however, and the lead runner had to stop at second, which was good. If he'd made it to third, it would be first-and-third with one out again, and another tight spot for Kim. This way he could hope for a double play.

He got it. The next batter swung on a tight, inside fastball and bounced a grounder hard to Bobbie at third base. He made a clean toss to second, and really fast too, giving them ample time to get the batter at first. Double play! Three out! Score tied at four.

The Caraway team hustled off and prepared to bat. Now it was Travis Trent's turn to saunter out to the pitcher's mound and take his time warming up. Kim sat on the bench to rest. It was not likely he'd be up this inning, unless they staged a big rally. So he sat still to gather his strength to pitch the next inning.

Zing! Travis tossed a warm-up fastball way over the head of the catcher.

"Look what he's doing," Lloyd said fearfully.

"Yeah," Kim agreed. "Pretending he's wild in the warm-up, so when he hits the next batter it'll look like he has no control."

"Yeah," said Lloyd. "It's gonna cost him. Sooner or later, it's gonna cost him."

"Already did," Kim pointed out. "He hit me and I came around and scored."

"Maybe he's just doing it to keep us off balance," Lloyd offered.

"It's working," Dennis said as he joined them. "The littler kids are shaking in their shoes."

"I don't think he'll throw at any more hitters," Kim said. "It'll cost him the game and he won't do that."

"Yeah, probably," Lloyd agreed.

It was true, however, what Dennis said about some of the younger Caraway players. They were clearly scared to go up and face the Merton southpaw now that he'd nailed Kim in the head — he had grazed Alan on the leg earlier too — and they stood about six inches further away from the plate than normal. It made them easy prey for a strikeout pitch on the outside corner.

In only a few minutes, two of them struck out looking and Kim tried to prepare mentally for the next inning. It was hard to concentrate on the hitters, however. His attention kept straying to the pitching mound, where Travis Trent stood tall. *He must know*, Kim said to himself. *He must know everything.*

He scanned the grandstand and the field. They were playing on the main diamond, usually occupied by the Continentals. The bases were not at regulation men's distance, however, and the pitching rubber was in closer, though it was still on the mound a little bit and gave the chucker a real pitching mound view of the plate. They would play seven innings, not the usual nine.

The seats were filling up as the championship game moved toward its conclusion. He didn't recognize most of the people, but he could see that Tommy was wedged into a lower row to watch his friends play. And he had noticed Matt and Dennis's brother, Randy, milling around earlier.

It would have been real easy for Travis Trent to discover exactly who Kim was in relation to the time earlier in the week when he'd been pushed around on the sidewalk outside the

Show Hall. *He's that kid's little brother,* Travis Trent would have learned. *He's the one everyone said threw the rock that day out at the Pig Farm . . .*

All of that, of course, had changed the moment Matt accused Travis on the sidewalk. Suspicion had fallen on him and it stayed there, like the stain that had been on Kim. The farm kid knew all that and, by clocking Kim in the head with a beanball, he was getting even.

"Strike three!" the umpire bellowed and the inning was over. Travis Trent had struck out the side! He was getting even in other ways too. After four complete innings, it was tied four-four.

Kim and the rest of the Caraway team took to the field again. The warm-up felt fine, but Kim was soon in trouble with the hitters. He just couldn't get the ball to go where he wanted it and before he knew it, he had walked the bases full. The exact opposite of what the Merton southpaw had just done! He knew what was coming.

"Time, please," Mr. Reilly said from the dugout as he began to walk out to the mound, his eyes fixed on the dirt of the infield. Dennis slogged out too, clunking in the dust in his heavy catcher's equipment.

"Good job, Kim," Mr. Reilly said and he patted Kim on the back. He held out his other hand and Kim gave him the ball. He didn't have to add, "But we'll try a pitching change," because when he took the ball, that's what it meant and everyone knew it.

Kim had lost the pitching duel with Travis Trent.

Mr. Reilly pointed to Alan, who came in from shortstop to the mound to take over.

"Get 'em, Alan!" Kim said, to sound encouraging and sort of apologetic at the same time. Kim had left Alan with a heck of a tough situation — bases loaded, none out, game tied — but it was better to go with a fresh arm than allow Kim to blow the game right then and there by walking in runs.

"Kim, first base," Mr. Reilly said. It was an expected move, one they'd gone through many times before. As a southpaw, Kim was valuable at first too, because his left-handed throw made for a natural toss to the other bases. Mr. Reilly pointed to other players to complete the change: Lloyd departed from first base and trotted to centre field, and the player there moved in to shortstop.

Alan was at least as good a chucker as Kim, though as a right-hander he was at a disadvantage against the Merton line-up. He struck out the first hitter, but then had to face a left-handed batter, one who would more easily see his pitches coming in.

"Come on, Alan! Let's go buddy!" Lloyd yelled from centre field.

"No hitter here, buddy! Come now, come to me!" Dennis chattered from behind his mask.

Even Bobbie at third joined in with a chant of "Two, two!" reminding everyone they wanted to try for a double play to end the inning.

The count went to one-and-one. Kim and all the other infielders tensed and bent real low, hoping to get a chance at a ground ball. If they couldn't pull off a double play, at least they wanted to get the ball home and prevent a run from scoring.

SMASH! The batter corked a solid line drive into the gap in right-centre! Kim kicked at the dirt and watched the ball sail between the outfielders. It was a double at least! One run scored, two, then three, and the hitter rounded second but was stopped from going to third by a good relay to get the ball in. It was seven-four for Merton and all those runners had gotten on base because of Kim!

"Come on, guys, shut 'em down! Get 'em out now, let's get 'em out!" Mr. Reilly yelled from the dugout.

The Caraway team set up again, desperate to limit the damage and not fall too far behind, but Alan was forced to pitch around the next hitter, a real slugger, and ended up walking him. Merton had runners at first and second with only one out.

However, it meant the double play possibility was back on and, sure enough, Alan got the next hitter to hit a hard line drive straight back to the mound. He snagged it, then flicked the ball over to Kim at first and they doubled off the runner. They were out of the inning, but now losing by *three* runs.

Kim sagged on the bench, deeply upset. If they lost, it would be his fault. He'd be the losing pitcher, since those three runs were "charged" to him. He'd put them on base, even though Alan gave up the double that drove them in.

"Let's get it back, guys," Mr. Reilly yelled. Belatedly, Kim realized he was up third, so he started preparing to bat.

Alan started the inning at the plate and cracked a solid single to get on base. Then Dennis struck out swinging and it was Kim's turn. Four pitches later he was out on a called strike three. It was close, but he had to admit the ball had caught the low-outside corner and it was a strike. It was entirely futile to argue with the ump anyway! Travis Trent had coolly and cleanly whiffed him, underlining without words just which left-hander on the field was the best.

Two out, with a runner on first. It was an obvious steal situation and everyone, on and off the field, knew it. Alan was a great baserunner, however, and he played the cat-and-mouse game with Travis Trent perfectly. He stole second by quite a good margin, easily beating the throw. Bobbie was up, with two outs, and Lloyd was on deck.

"Oh no . . . !" Lloyd wailed, because he could see what was coming. Sure enough, Merton chose to walk Bobbie with two out and pitch to Lloyd, because they felt Lloyd was an easier out and, by putting Bobbie on first, they restored the "force" to every base in the infield.

"Come on, Lloyd, base-hit him!" Kim screamed from his seat on the bench. "You can do it! Come on!"

The cheers from the grandstand rose in volume too, and the entire Caraway bench was on its feet cheering Lloyd on. They even kept it up when Travis Trent blew two fastballs right by him for strikes, though in the pit of their stomachs, they all felt Lloyd would surely strike out.

Lloyd fooled them all. Perhaps he was helped by a bit of cockiness on Travis Trent's part, who must have decided he could strike Lloyd out on three pitches, because he dished up a real fat fastball down the middle — and Lloyd singled to left!

Alan came around to score and cut the lead to two, seven-five for Merton!

"Attaboy, Lloyd!" they all screamed. It was a great piece of hitting. And it showed that the Marauders' pitcher could be confronted and beaten. Now there were two out, with Bobbie at second and Lloyd at first. They were into the bottom of the Caraway line-up, however, and Mr. Reilly must have felt a hit was unlikely, because he signaled for a double-steal. It would put a runner on third in case a pitch eluded the catcher and they could score on the passed ball.

It was a tricky thing to pull off, a double-steal, because it meant that both baserunners had to go at the same time. It was difficult to steal third under any circumstances. The double-steal relied on a bit of confusion in the mind of the opposing catcher as to where to throw the ball. Instead, the Merton catcher kept his cool and when his bench yelled "Going!" he calmly fired the ball to third and Bobbie was out by a mile.

It was Merton seven and Caraway five after five complete innings.

Kim didn't say a thing to Alan during their time on the bench, so Alan must have taken it upon himself to deal out a little justice to Travis Trent, who was up second for Merton.

Alan put a fastball right in his ribs and the Merton pitcher hit the dirt like a sack of potatoes! He got up cursing and clutching his side. His coaches called for "time" and it appeared as if the tough farm kid was really hurt. But he wasn't about to leave the game any more than Kim earlier. He trotted down to first base and took a leadoff.

Kim didn't look at him. He didn't want to get involved in any taunts or teases back and forth. Travis Trent said nothing as well. It was all business.

Kim felt pretty sure he'd try to steal anyway, and he wouldn't have to put up with him for long, and perhaps that's what the farm kid intended, but he waited one pitch too long. Maybe his ribs hurt too much to make the steal attempt right away.

Dennis must have sensed it too, because when Travis wandered out too far after the pitch came to the plate, Dennis lunged one step toward first and *drilled* the ball down the line.

Kim snatched the perfect throw and swept his glove down to the bag as fast as he could.

"He's out!" yelled the base ump. They got him!

Kim danced out of Travis's way as the farm kid, who had dived back to the base, picked himself up out of the dirt. Kim snapped the ball over to second to go around the horn and kept his distance from the Merton player. However, as Travis dusted himself off he turned to Kim, so no one else could hear, and hissed, "Watch yourself next time, batter."

It was as good as saying, "I'm gonna put another one in your ear," but Kim just spat over near his shoes and sneered, "Yeah, yeah . . . "

Merton didn't score in the top of the sixth and, miraculously, the bottom of the order for Caraway squeezed a run out of two Merton errors in the bottom of the inning. At the end of six complete, it was seven-six Merton.

The Marauders got another one, though, in the top of the seventh by converting a leadoff triple. Dennis couldn't hold onto one of Alan's low-outside teasers and the runner trotted home on the passed ball. Suddenly it was eight-six Merton and, after Caraway got the other opposition hitters out, Kim and his friends were down to their last chance.

The mood on the bench was subdued. They needed two to tie it and force extra innings. Three to win.

"Let's go boys, let's go, let's get some baserunners," Mr. Reilly chanted among the players as they prepared to hit. "Top of the order, boys, top of the order, lookin' good," he added as he trotted over to his coaching spot at third base.

Alan was up first, then Dennis, followed by Kim, and Bobbie and Lloyd if they got that far. They needed a hit!

The first three hitters huddled together and watched the Merton pitcher warm up.

"He's gotta be gettin' tired," Dennis growled as he licked a rim of foam off the edge of his dirt-lined mouth.

"He's their ace," Alan said. "I think they'll stick with him, no matter what."

"Let's get *on*," Kim said tensely, though it was hardly clear whether he was speaking to the other two, or himself.

"Batter!" the ump called and Alan stepped purposefully to the plate. A gust of wind whirled through the fairgrounds and spun a cone of dust around the infield. As Kim selected his bat, he glanced to the northwest, but could see no storm clouds building. There was a hint of a chill in that breeze, though, and it was certain that summer was almost over and baseball would come to an end. In two days, school would start!

Kim's attention was drawn back to the game by a great bunt laid down by Alan! He pushed it beautifully up the third base line and beat it out. They had a runner!

"Yeah yeah yeah!" the Caraway players screamed as they pounded at the wire cage on the front of the dugout. "Careful Alan, don't get picked off!"

"Take two, guys, take two!" the Merton catcher yelled in reply. "Two now, let's shut 'em down!"

Dennis dug in and looked at a strike and a ball. Kim studied the Merton pitcher to see if there was any sign at all of fatigue. Any let-up, any flailing of the arms or legs, any indication he didn't have the same energy he had an hour before.

Travis Trent blew a fastball right past Dennis, who swung through it.

Guess not, Kim said to himself and it made sense. Farm kids, of all kids, were the least likely to flag over the course of a ball game. They worked so much, doing so many chores, they were almost unnaturally strong compared to town kids. Travis Trent wasn't big, not by any stretch, but he seemed to have loads of power in his lanky frame and he was as dangerous as ever.

He threw over to first to keep Alan close, then teased Dennis with an outside change-up. Two and two.

Kim found himself guessing what the next pitch would be. All batters did that and, as a pitcher, he was well aware of it. *What's the next pitch? Curveball? High, low, inside, outside? Heater? What?*

Dennis must have guessed correctly, because he snapped a single up the middle! Alan beat it out to third base and they had runners on the corners with none out!

The cheers for Dennis rang in Kim's ears as he took a deep breath in and out and walked up to the plate.

"Come on, Kim, come on, come on, come on!" his bench screamed. Mr. Reilly clapped his hands together and pointed to the outfield, which meant *"Just hit it!"* There was no steal on, no fancy play. Just hit it!

Kim dug in and stared out to the mound. Travis would have to pitch from the "stretch," so he wasn't looking at the hitter all the time, but glancing at first base where Dennis had a lead, then glancing back at home.

Kim couldn't help but ask himself whether Travis would get even — again — and sail a fastball at his head or into his ribs. There had been a lot of hit batters in this game and one more would not surprise anyone.

He wouldn't take the chance, Kim concluded. *I'm the winning run.*

Even so, the first pitch was high and tight, right at the same place Kim had put it when he zipped the ball past Travis's nose.

Ball one.

The next pitch fooled Kim completely. It was an inside curveball that started coming toward his ribs, then ducked into the strike zone. He didn't have a chance on that one and had to let it sail over the plate.

"Stee-rike!" the ump called and he gripped his right hand in the air as if he were catching a bug.

Low outside, Kim guessed to himself about the next pitch. That's where he would put it, if he were pitching. Sure enough, the fastball came in hard and low and Kim was very tempted to go for it — but it seemed to miss by an inch or two. And suddenly Dennis was stealing second!

The catcher grabbed the ball and flung it down to second base, but they didn't get Dennis. Safe!

Alan wandered way off third and the shortstop, who had the ball, threw it back to home plate, right on the money. Alan bluffed a bit, but there was no throw and he wasn't going to tempt fate by trying to steal home. They needed at least two runs, not just one. It wasn't worth risking an out.

They needed a hit!

"Come on, Kimmie, let's go now, pay attention buddy!" Mr. Reilly called, quite harshly, and Kim realized he must have missed a sign — the signal that Dennis would steal — so he stepped back to regroup. It hadn't cost them, but still, you should never miss a sign.

"Two and one!" the ump barked to ensure everyone knew the count.

"Time, please," Kim said, for in an instant he realized what he must do.

"Time," the ump echoed.

He could see his coach looking down from third with his entire face turned into a question mark. What was up?

Kim knew it was time to stick his neck out, way out. Time to take a big chance.

He trotted quickly over to the dugout, where Caraway's bats were lined up against the fence. Normally, Kim preferred a light bat. He wasn't really strong in the hands, certainly not like a farm kid, and with a light bat he could swing in time to hit most any pitch.

He set down the one he'd taken to the plate and scanned the row for another one. There it was, down at the end, where it had rested the entire game without any of the Caraway kids touching it. This bat was bigger, fatter, and heavier than the rest. A real slugger — if you could swing it in time.

This was before now and metal bats hadn't been invented yet. They were all wood, and even the grain of the wood on this slugger was tighter and darker than the other bats. It was a solid, thick piece of lumber. Like swinging a fence post, as the saying went.

Kim picked it up and suddenly noticed someone right there at the screen. Tommy!

"That pitcher — that's the kid who threw the rock!" Tom whispered, as if he were a cartoon kid with a light bulb on over his head.

"*I know*," Kim growled back. That Tom! What a genius for bad timing!

Kim stood up and hefted the bat and just then he also noticed a flash of yellow up in the stands. *Well, I guess everyone's here*, he said to himself as he walked back to the plate and tried to re-concentrate on his hitting.

The umpire was plainly annoyed at the delay, but most umps would give time — once, anyway — when a player asked for it. Kim prayed he had made the right choice. He dug in and the catcher muttered something about how a new bat wouldn't make any difference.

Travis Trent bent over to get the sign. None out, runners on second and third, and a two-run lead.

Maybe they'll walk me to put the force back on, Kim said to himself, but he didn't really believe it. He was the winning run, after all, and you just don't put the winning run on base. They'd try to strike him out, or get a ground ball and hold the runners, then toss him out at first.

Kim's job, at the very least, was to drive the ball to the outfield, so Alan would have a chance to tag up at third after the catch and get home. Dennis might make it over to third and then it would be a one-run game, with one out, and a runner on third.

That's the very least he had to accomplish.

But Kim had bigger plans and that's why he traded bats. He was pretty sure on a two and one count Travis Trent would throw a fastball down the middle. It was a "hitter's count" and Kim was prepared to take a chance with the heavy bat.

He was going to swing for the fence.

He got ready. Swinging a bat this heavy meant he had to start bringing it around a split second sooner than normal, and commit to the swing sooner than normal too. Otherwise, he'd be late and miss for sure. But if he got wood on it . . .

Kim also knew if he swung like crazy and missed, he'd look stupid and wild and might even fall over, but it would still only be strike two. He could go back and get his other bat.

All of that flashed through his mind as Travis Trent prepared to throw. He started his wind-up . . . Kim stepped into the swing and gripped the heavy bat as hard as he could. Here it comes!

The ball flew straight for his head! Kim gasped and his swing was instantly destroyed. He cringed and pulled back from the plate, even as the bat went through the strike zone, and suddenly the ball curved down away from his head and across the plate!

"Strike two!" the ump yelled. It was a curveball for a strike! Kim had guessed wrong — completely wrong!

And now he was really in trouble. It was two and two and he didn't have his usual light bat to swing quickly at whatever came next. Kim glanced at the ump and considered asking for time, but he could tell — *he could just tell* — it was useless. He wouldn't get time. He was caught up there with a gigantic, unwieldy bat and now he would strike out!

And probably cost Caraway the game, because Merton could walk the bases full, pitch to Lloyd, get a double play, and win!

Stupid, Kim cursed at himself, *stupid, stupid, stupid.*

His only hope now was to choke up, a lot, and hope he could transform the big slugger into a swingable bat. He did it and braced himself for the throw, and humiliation.

Travis Trent wound up and tossed it hard, right at the knees. Kim followed the pitch in, bending low to track it, and at the last moment blurted "Nope!" hoping to influence the ump. If he was wrong, he was out.

The catcher grabbed the ball and shifted his glove back up a few inches into the strike zone, trying for the strike.

"Bah!" the ump yelled. It was a ball. The umpire stood up straight and held up his fist, which meant the count was now three and two. "Full!" he boomed.

Kim stepped out of the batter's box and went into the guessing game again. It was like gambling with cards. It was impossible not to anticipate the pitch.

Fastball, he told himself. *This one's gotta be a fastball right down the pipe.*

He gripped the bat at full length again. It was remarkably heavy and, as before, he would have to swing early. If he missed, he would really miss!

But Kim didn't care. He was backed into a corner and willing to take a chance. What choice did he have?

No choice, he said to himself. *Just hit it.*

"Contact, Kim, just make contact!" Mr. Reilly called from third base. He could hear his bench yelling too, and a few people in the crowd, balanced by the distracting chatter from the Merton infield — *"Batta batta batta, no hitter here!"* — and out of this din and the dust stirred up by the rushing wind, he saw Travis Trent's front foot kick high in the air and his pitching arm drop way back behind him.

Here it comes!

Kim swung for all he was worth.

He braced his legs and exerted his arms as much as he could to keep the fence post of a bat from dropping too low as it came around. It was an all-out, swing-from-the-heels attempt to hit it deep and if he missed, he'd miss by a mile and strike out *very* convincingly!

Travis Trent's left arm snapped like a striking snake and out of the jumble and haze the baseball appeared — coming right down the middle, belt-high and a little inside.

Right where Kim liked it. He dropped his back shoulder to convert the swing into a long-ball attempt and drew a bead on the oncoming rocket of a pitch.

CRACK!

He got it — he got it all!

Where did it go? Kim couldn't find it at first, but he saw Travis Trent spin around violently and look out to right field. Panic streaked his face.

Kim ran hard for first base. *Where was it?* He was rounding first when he finally spied the ball way out over the right fielder, who was running flat out after it.

"Go, go, go, go, go!" his bench screamed. Kim pumped his arms and headed for second. Alan scored easily and Dennis was beating it around third and in. Tie game!

Kim hurtled across second base, heading for third, and took a look to right-centre field. It would be his last glimpse, because now he had to turn his back on the ball and watch for Mr. Reilly's decision.

The ball landed and bounced toward the fence. Because they played on the men's field, the fence was way too far for any kid to hit the ball over and home runs were not accomplished at a lazy trot. Kim had to keep digging as hard as he could and, in that last glimpse, he saw the right fielder reach the ball and instantly hurl it back toward the infield.

Sucking wind and dust, Kim sprinted toward third and saw Mr. Reilly right in his line of sight wind-milling one arm like a crazy man and yelling, *"Home home home!"*

Kim dashed around third base and dug for home plate. There was no time to look back and it would be a mistake to do it. He concentrated on the catcher, whose movements would tell him when the ball was coming.

Kim churned his dead legs as fast as he could, then saw a little white projectile appear out of the corner of his eye. The ball! It bounced once — right up into the catcher's glove! He was still three steps away!

In a flash, baseball became football and Kim and the catcher prepared to collide.

With nothing to lose, Kim accelerated and barged straight ahead. The catcher ducked to take the hit low.

They crashed together — suddenly Kim was flying through the air, way up and over the catcher's shoulder. Kim spun around in mid-air and in the midst of it, he could see the ball roll away in the dust.

Dropped it!

The force of the collision flattened the catcher just in front of the plate, which was clear for a landing. Kim led with his arm and felt a violent snap! in his right wrist when he hit the plate and he knew instantly it was broken.

A lightning bolt of pain jolted up his arm and through it he heard the umpire yell *"Safe!"* and suddenly the entire Caraway bench raced toward him screaming, *"We win, we win!"*

Mr. Reilly ran in too just as Kim struggled to his feet and cried out, "I broke my arm!"

He held it out away from him so they wouldn't hug him there.

"We win, we win!" his teammates shrieked. They danced around him deliriously and Kim could see Merton leaving the field, defeated. Travis Trent walked off quickly, staring at his shoes.

Behind the screen, the trophy for winning the tournament championship had appeared out of nowhere. You didn't get a trophy just for showing up — you had to win — and this year Caraway would put their name on that big shiny emblem of victory!

Kim laughed along with Dennis, Lloyd, Alan and Bobbie. Tummy Tom pressed himself against the wire screen and his entire body shook with glee. Up high, he could see Beverly Banana whirling her yellow scarf in the breeze and letting out a real cowgirl yell. Even Matt and Randy were clapping their hands — what a finish!

Kim laughed and he cried, too, for his broken wrist throbbed horribly. He held it out, separate from himself like a dead tree branch, and could see that it was actually bent, inside under the skin. He blinked and almost fell over from the pain.

Kim looked out at the ball diamond. It was empty, but they had won and, for certain, he would no longer be The Kid Who Threw the Rock.

He would be The Kid Who Hit the Home Run and Broke his Wrist!

Caraway Kim . . . Southpaw!

And, Kim thought as he blinked back his tears, *that is the very best part of all.*

ACKNOWLEDGEMENTS

This book travelled a path of many years. Along the way, no one believed in it more or worked harder to get it into the right hands than my agent, Penny Noble.

No group helped more with the content than the boys who read it in manuscript, especially Nicolas Liakas and my son Carson Mangaard. Other sharp-eyed readers were Gabriel Davis, Owen St. John-Saaltink, Tiernan Shuttleworth, Greg Wright, Noah Klar, Arun Aggarwal-Schifellite, Andrew Chalmers, Louis Progosh, Henry Preston, and Daniel Bergman.

Others slogged through an earlier version. Josie Massarella was uniquely enthusiastic as she read it with her son, Felix Werth. Cheryl Hawkes and Bill Cameron guided their son, Nick, through it, as did Sybil Goldstein with her boy, Jacob Fromer, and Annie McClelland with her son, Riley Weyman. Jake Sherman, Max Davis, and Daniel Glassman tackled it all by themselves.

The cascade of praise I wish to shower on teachers everywhere falls on the shoulders of Donna Midanik and Carol Tait at Toronto's Ossington Old Orchard Public School (known to all as OOOPS!). Along with Linda Baker, Marcel Gauthier, librarian Joyce Cram, assistant Teresa Wisniowski, and principals Agnes Adams and Susan Tirimacco, they infused my son's early education with everything it should be.

I wish also to salute the diligence, rigour, and good humour of my editor, R.P. MacIntyre, whose acumen elevated the quality of these pages. Any errors or excesses that remain are my own.

Writers? I've known a few. Their excellence and perseverance showed me it could be done: Hugh Dempsey, Fred Stenson,

Theresa Tova, Ken McGoogan, Michael Helm, Amy Friedman, Arthur Kent, Nicola Furlong, Tom King, Bill Cameron, the late L.R. (Bunny) Wright, and my writing instructors at the University of Alberta, Rudy Wiebe and Greg Hollingshead.

Helpful friends and colleagues? These are only a few of the many: Beno John, Lucinda Chodan, Lindsay Brown, Anne Klar, Aaron Davis and Candida Girling, Martin Waxman, Al Young, Bonita Siegel, Julia Bennett, Annette Mangaard, Nancy Wright, Sandra Bishop and Tom Pendlebury, Brian Bergman, Marc Glassman and Judy Wolfe.

Fiction produces its own realities. My mom and dad, and my brothers Ted and David, are nowhere found in this book, though the stories, incidents, legends and lore related here would not exist without them.

Like so many denizens of "Caraway", they're not here though they echo through every line.

abook4boys.com